forbidden *love*

USA TODAY BESTSELLING AUTHOR

LEA COLL

ABOUT THE BOOK

INESCAPABLE LOVE

After being the rebound one too many times, I accepted love wasn't for me...

Once, I'd been a hopeless romantic. But getting tossed aside time and time again made me jaded. Happily ever after wasn't for me. Instead, I focused on being my niece's favorite uncle. It was enough.

Until Natalie and her daughter.

Recently divorced, she's determined to open a bed and breakfast and hires me to renovate it. I should be focused on the job, but instead I'm distracted by the undeniable attraction between us.

When a late-night water leak brings me face-to-face with Natalie wearing nothing but barely-there wet lingerie, I can't ignore my desires any longer. She and her daughter remind me of the family I'd always wanted but had given up on.

Is this relationship the real thing I've always dreamed of, or am I once again a rebound?

GET THE FREE NOVELLA

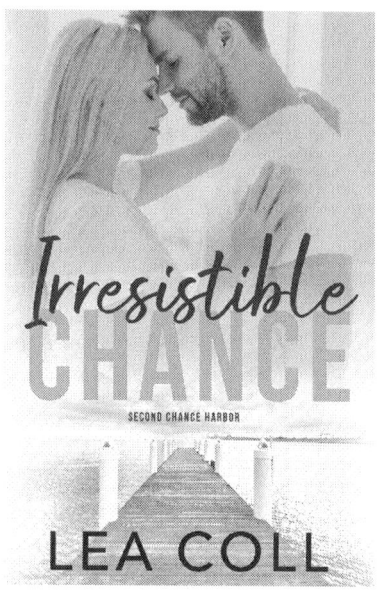

To sign up for my newsletter, and get the free novella, *Irresistible Chance,* visit https://landing.mailerlite.com/webforms/landing/v5z3m1.

CHAPTER 1

NATALIE

*M*oving back to my hometown as a single mother to renovate an older Victorian house into a B&B was the biggest risk I'd ever taken. After my ex-husband, Carter, left me for another woman, my daughter's well-being rested solely on me.

After leaving South Carolina to move to Colorado, I didn't have a husband or an extended family to fall back on anymore. It was just me. I had no idea if this was a good move or the worst decision I'd ever made.

Since we'd moved into the owner's suite of the soon-to-be B&B, I'd had a difficult time sleeping. I woke up in the middle of the night several times, worrying about the timing of the renovation, the cost, and when I'd be able to start taking reservations.

Tonight, I couldn't fall asleep at all. Giving up on sleep at ten, I went to the bathroom I shared with my daughter to splash cold water on my face. Feeling restless, I grabbed a blanket and a book, quietly opening and closing the door that separated our space from the rest of the house.

I listened for any sign that my daughter, Delaney, had heard me. When I determined all was quiet, I tiptoed to the couch that had appeared at some point.

My suite was a one-bedroom with a kitchen, eating area, living room, and one bathroom. There was a tiny sitting room off my bedroom that Delaney slept in, and she accessed it by walking through my bedroom. Sometimes, it felt like the walls were closing in on me.

During the day, the main areas of the B&B were a construction zone, loud and filled with activity. But tonight, it was quiet.

I removed the tarp covering the couch and settled onto the overstuffed cushions. I hoped I'd feel better once the renovation was completed. Or maybe it would only worsen when I had guests to worry about too.

I read for a few minutes before heading into the kitchen to grab a glass of water. I turned on the faucet, but it sputtered and then sprayed me with shockingly cold water. Momentarily stunned, I could only stand there while water spewed at me from seemingly every direction.

Finally, I regained my senses and attempted to slide the handle into the off position, but nothing happened. The water kept spraying me. I shrieked in frustration and took several steps back from the spray, wiping water from my face.

Boots sounded on the stairs and then Mac appeared. In worn jeans, a Fletcher & Sons branded T-shirt, and work boots, he flew past me. "We need to get this under control before it ruins the floors."

He didn't seem to mind that he was now soaked too. The shirt clung to his well-defined pecs, sending me into a fantasy where the water was warm, and Mac was interested in me.

I was worried about getting him naked, and he was concerned about my floors. I needed to get my priorities straight. How long would this disaster set me back? I couldn't afford any more delays. I'd prepared for renovations but not major setbacks. I was naïve. Just like my ex-husband said.

He threw open the cabinet doors under the sink and twisted something. The water slowed until it was a trickle and then finally stopped.

"Did the water turn off?" Mac asked from under the sink.

"It's off." I hurried to my suite to grab towels. Armed with them, I put them on the floor to mop up the excess water. My hands were shaking, and my heart thundered under my rib cage.

Mac stood, watching my motions to clean it up, and ran a hand through his hair. "Fuck."

"Are you going to just stand there and swear, or are you going to help me clean it up?" I didn't know what it was about this man, but whenever we were around each other, we were like oil and water. My usual sunny disposition dissipated, and I was short with him. He was just as irritated with me.

He moved to me, snatched a towel, and threw it over a large puddle. "What are you doing out here, anyway?"

"I wanted a minute to myself. What are you doing here?"

Usually, the crew was done by four or five, and it was quiet in the evenings. I wasn't sure why I didn't just tell him I enjoyed the solitude. His attitude was usually so surly that I didn't want to confide in him.

He used his foot to move the towel over the wet spot. "I was working on the tile in the upstairs bathroom."

We worked side by side to mop up the puddles. "Do you usually work late?"

His jaw tightened, and he said, "I just wanted to get it done."

With most of the water cleaned up, I threw my towel onto the pile and stretched my arms over my head, leaning to one side, then the other. "I appreciate you working so hard."

When he didn't answer, I glanced over at him to find him tracking my movements. His gaze was locked on my breasts.

That's when I remembered I was wearing a silky top with sleep shorts. It felt decadent against my skin, and I loved the way it made me feel beautiful. But I was soaked. My pajamas were probably see-through at this point. I just hadn't anticipated Mac seeing me in them. I lowered my arms and wrapped them around my body. "I didn't know anyone would be here."

"You shouldn't be either. You could step on a nail."

"Is that the reason, or is it that I was out here at the same time as you? Because someone put that couch in the living room." Sometimes, I thought my mere presence set him off. That nothing I did or didn't do made a difference.

He threw his hand in my general direction. "I don't need my guys seeing that when they're working."

My hands instinctively went to my hips. "No one was supposed to be here. *You're* not supposed to be here. This is my time." When Delaney was asleep, I could breathe and stress about all the reasons why I was crazy for doing this.

"It's safe to assume someone could be here at any time," he said gruffly, gathering up the towels with shaky movements and tossing them into the laundry room off the kitchen.

My nipples were hard, aching points. Did some part of me get off on a man who growled at me? If so, it was a betrayal. Because my brain definitely hated Mac in my space.

Mac crossed the room toward me with purpose. Goose bumps raced over my skin. "It's dangerous to walk around like that."

"Like what?" I snapped, my gaze narrowing as he stepped into my space.

He drew a dry towel over my shoulders, gathering it around me in an effort to cover me. Then his hand grazed my nipple, and we both froze. The warmth of his hand seared the damp fabric, piercing my skin.

I swayed on my feet. My core ached.

He snatched his hand away and took a step back. Then two. "You should dry off."

"What are you going to do about this?" I gestured at the

floors so that his attention would be anywhere but on my nipples.

"I'll turn on some fans to dry the floors. Hopefully, they don't warp."

"Were they wet long enough for that to happen?" I asked, chewing my lip.

"I don't know. But I'm going to take every precaution. We can't afford any more setbacks."

Was that for professional reasons or that he couldn't stand being around me? I couldn't get a read on him.

Initially, I bought the house and attempted to direct renovations from South Carolina. When there was an issue with the floors, everyone at Fletcher & Sons thought it would be best if I lived closer. Mac had been on board with diverting the crew to the owner's suite to get that ready for me and Delaney. His determination to create a space for us as soon as possible had been sweet, but I hadn't seen any other evidence that there was a heart underneath his gruff words.

I clutched the towel to my chest, my skin prickling for a different reason. I shivered and couldn't seem to stop.

"You need to get dry," Mac said.

"In a minute." But it was hard to talk. Every part of my body was trembling, my teeth chattering.

Mac stepped into my space, this time pulling me into his warm, very hard body. He wrapped those steel arms around me, and I breathed in his masculine scent mixed with sawdust. His warmth was too enticing. I melted into his body as he held me tighter.

I rested my cheek against the soft material of his shirt and the hard pec underneath. He was all man. I'd seen the way he worked around the B&B every day, but being this close to him, touching him, was a whole other thing. The heat unraveled around me, seeping into my skin, and the shivers slowed.

He used the towel to rub my skin dry and squeeze the water

out of my hair. I felt warm all over now. His gaze was appraising, his touch gentle. My cheeks flushed as he took me in.

He stepped back, regret on his face. "You should change into warmer pajamas and get into bed. You'll feel better."

I wasn't sure I'd ever felt better than I had in his arms. Definitely better than I'd felt in Carter's arms. Mac had never appeared to be interested in me before. Was it the unexpected display of skin, my body's reaction to the cold, or something else? Was he short to mask his attraction? Had he pushed me away because he was attracted to me? I wasn't sure what to think.

Finally, he said, "I'll take care of this."

I swallowed, suddenly unable to have a coherent thought. Confused by my revelation, I stepped back from him, the damp towel loose around my shoulders. Tightening my fingers around it, I felt exposed and vulnerable when I hadn't shared anything with him.

"Thank you," was all I could manage before I turned on my heel and hurried toward the door that separated my space from the construction zone. Closing the door softly behind me, I was very aware that Delaney might have heard us. I listened carefully for a noise, and hearing none, I leaned against the door that separated me from Mac.

Was he attracted to me? Warmth spread through my body, my nipples tingled, and my pussy clenched. What would have happened if he'd kissed me? If his hand would have lingered on my nipple or even cupped my breast? I knew I wouldn't have said no.

I hadn't felt an attraction to anyone in a long time. Far longer than I cared to admit. Carter cheated on me and moved to Texas to be with his new girlfriend, leaving me living in a town where I wasn't from, with his parents who weren't mine.

I'd felt so alone when his parents sided with him. They'd said he needed time to explore what he wanted. That had made zero sense to me because he'd married me. We had a child together. He didn't have the luxury to explore his attraction to another woman, who'd also left her husband and kids. It was selfish. And every time I stood up to them, our relationship fractured even more.

Feeling more alone than I ever had, I reconnected with my best friend from childhood, Kylie Wilde. She was the one who'd convinced me to come back home, even though I'd never planned to return.

It was her idea for me to buy this B&B so I could work with my daughter. She took pictures of the house and sent them to me. She said I needed space and time away from Carter's family.

I closed my eyes, feeling the solid door against my back. What would happen if I went back in there and asked for what I wanted? Something told me Mac wouldn't say no. He seemed like a man who knew what to do with his hands, who'd never leave me aching for more. He knew how to satisfy a woman, and there was a desire in his eyes. He wanted me.

Could I have something physical with a man and keep it separate from my daughter? It didn't seem feasible, but I wanted someone to relieve this ache in my core, and I knew Mac was the man to do it.

Kylie would tell me to go for it, but then she'd always been a little wild, as her last name suggested. Her whole family was. That's what happened when you had four older brothers.

I'd always been more cautious, and now I had Delaney to think about. Her father left so abruptly that her entire world and safety net was ripped from under her. I was the one who kept things stable for her. I couldn't act on a whim. It would make me no better than Carter.

I left South Carolina because there was nothing left for us. I was worried my in-laws were saying things to Delaney that they shouldn't. I wanted to protect her from what was going on. She didn't know the details, and my mother-in-law thought it was her duty to feed it to her.

I started a bath in the incredible tub Mac had installed in my suite. When I protested the cost, he'd said I'd need a good one if I was going to be managing the B&B on my own. He told me not to worry about the expense, saying some ridiculous thing about it being a good advertisement for his business, but no one would see it but me. I'd sing its praises to anyone who asked, but it wasn't the same as putting a tub into a guest bathroom.

I wasn't sure what to make of the couch, the tub, or the way he'd worked so hard to get the apartment ready for me.

I slipped off my damp pajamas and stepped into the steaming water. I hoped this would relax me, but I couldn't stop thinking about how aroused I'd been from Mac holding me. I sank into the water, resting my head on the lip of the tub. I reached for my tiny vibrator, the one I used because it was so small and quiet, and turned it on. I pressed the tip where I needed it the most, and a moan slipped out before I could cover my mouth.

I was so ready to combust, and it was all because of Mac. I imagined what would have happened had one of us made a move to kiss each other. Dream Mac said he wanted to make me feel good, and I was all for that.

I licked my lips as the vibrator did its job to take me over the edge. It wasn't the same as Mac touching me, but I'd take my pleasure where I could get it.

Hooking up with the contractor who was renovating my B&B was a bad idea. Ever since his brother, Sam, formed a side company that created outdoor spaces, Mac had taken over as the foreman. I'd see him every day, and I didn't want things to be awkward—or any more than they already had been.

But the irrational part of my brain pointed out that we were alone. Delaney was sleeping; we could give in to our baser instincts. But every time my naughty side got on board with that idea, I remembered the look on Carter's face when he told me via video that he was leaving me for his girlfriend.

I wouldn't be that selfish. I had a child to think about and a business to get off the ground. I didn't have time for built contractors who had a way with tools. I'd just need to take care of my own needs.

CHAPTER 2

MAC

*N*atalie's see-through silky camisole left nothing to the imagination. She was all delicious curves, perky breasts, and hard nipples. I couldn't get the vision of her pebbled nipples out of my head.

She was either cold or just as aroused as I was. I was doing a fairly good job of resisting the pull until she shivered. I couldn't resist my instincts anymore. I pulled her into my arms with the sole desire to get her warm, which had the added bonus of feeling her soft body against mine.

I was hard as a rock when she snuggled deeper into my embrace. I had to hold my lower half away from her so she didn't realize where my head was at.

When her tremors subsided, I had to let her go. I was seconds away from tipping her chin up and taking her mouth. I wanted her with an intensity I wasn't used to.

No one had ever aroused me so quickly. But then again, I didn't run into half-naked women who were soaking wet. It was an image I wouldn't get out of my head anytime soon. I had a feeling I'd be jerking off to it in the near future.

I imagined her taking a bath in that gorgeous tub I'd

installed in her suite. It was the same one my brother's fiancée, Alice, wanted for their new house. Since Natalie was living on her own with a daughter, and opening a business, she deserved something special.

I had no idea where Delaney's father was. Natalie hadn't even told Alice, and they'd become fast friends since Alice opened a shop in the front room of the house.

I shouldn't care why Natalie moved here—if she was running from something or looking for something in particular. I gave up on the idea of a committed relationship a long time ago. I'd been burned enough to know it wasn't meant for me.

Seeing my youngest brother fall for Alice didn't even have me questioning my vow to never get serious with another woman again. But a part of me knew that if she'd given me a sign that she was interested in more, I would have taken it. But she deserved more than a quickie when her daughter was asleep next door.

Natalie was a woman who deserved a man who'd take care of her and support her in her business but stand aside so she could blossom on her own. She didn't need a guy who only wanted something physical and was incapable of commitment, even when the voice in my head said I used to want a relationship. That was then, and this was now. Everything had changed. I was smarter. I couldn't go down that road again.

Natalie Anderson wasn't the woman for me, no matter how many times I would run into her half-naked and soaking wet.

I ran a hand through my hair, knowing that was a lie. Nothing like that could happen again because there was zero chance I'd be able to resist her a second time. I was so screwed.

Next door, the water turned on. I imagined Natalie stepping into the steaming water. With blonde hair and those long legs, Natalie was a vision that would haunt me forever.

I gripped the kitchen counter, knowing I wouldn't get any more work done tonight. Not when I wanted to walk through the door separating us, and into that tub with her. I was hard as nails, and I couldn't do anything about it. I couldn't take what I wanted from Natalie. It was a bad idea.

I needed to go home and escape Natalie's scent and my overactive imagination. It would be a long time before I'd get the sight of her body out of my head. Determined to get some distance between me and whatever she was doing in that tub, I gathered my things.

I paused when I heard a moan; my heartbeat accelerated.

I grabbed my keys and rushed out of the house, not caring if tools were sitting out or if a light was left on. I needed to get out of there and away from the alluring woman who was quickly getting under my skin.

The cool night air instantly cleared my head. The engine of my truck roared to life, and I pulled away.

No more late nights. No more accidental run-ins with the B&B's owner. I should have insisted that her living in South Carolina was best for everyone, even if it wasn't. If I'd known how she would affect me, I never would have suggested renovating the owner's suite.

It was infinitely harder working with her so close by. I found myself wondering what she was doing or if she'd show up unexpectedly.

I needed to talk to someone about this pesky attraction. Tyler, my middle brother, wouldn't have good advice. He'd tell me to fuck her hard against the wall and that her kid was an excuse to have a no-strings relationship. Actually, that plan sounded good right now, so I drove to Sam's. He was the voice of reason since he had a kid and was in a relationship with his former nanny, Alice. He'd tell me what to do.

I parked in Sam's driveway, then got out and headed up the sidewalk before knocking on the door. I hoped that Maggie wasn't sick or that they weren't going at it. I needed to sort these crazy thoughts in my head.

"What are you doing here?" Sam opened the door, stepping back so I could enter.

Walking through the doorway, I asked, "It's not a bad time, is it?"

"It's a little too late to ask that, isn't it?" Alice said, sidling up next to Sam. He placed an arm around her and kissed her temple. I'd never get used to seeing Sam so smitten with a woman. He'd sworn off women after he'd gotten Felicia pregnant, and she decided it was best that she move across the country for a job. But he was invested in his little girl, Maggie, and now, Alice. I'd never seen him happier.

"I need to talk to you," I said to Sam, hoping Alice would get the hint. I was here for brotherly advice. I didn't want to hear a woman's opinion.

Alice smiled softly. "I'll go read in bed."

I wanted to say she didn't need to leave, but I really wanted to talk to Sam in private.

"Want to sit outside?" Sam had built an amazing outdoor space for his house and recently convinced us to expand the company to offer outdoor living spaces. So far, it had been a popular add-on to our new builds and renovations.

"Sure." I followed him through the house.

He grabbed two beers from the outdoor fridge and handed one to me. Outside, we sat on Adirondack chairs, facing the view of the mountains.

After we were quiet for a few seconds, Sam asked, "What's going on?"

"I was working late at Natalie's." I sucked in a breath when I realized I'd referred to it as her place and not the B&B, which was what we'd called it since day one of the project.

Sam settled back into the cushions. "Doing what?"

"I was finishing up the tile in one of the upstairs bathrooms." I didn't want to admit I'd felt bad that the mistake with the floors had pushed back the time line. I knew money was tight for Natalie, and I wanted to help her in any way I could. I just hadn't realized the reason until now. I was attracted to her. "Natalie used the kitchen faucet, but water spewed everywhere."

"You turn it off and figure out what the problem was?" Sam asked, as if it wasn't the single most defining moment of my life. The vision of her body was embedded in my brain.

I shifted in the chair, not wanting to admit my focus was on something else. "The issue seemed to be isolated to the kitchen faucet. I turned off the water to that sink. I figured I'd look at it tomorrow."

Sam tipped back the bottle and took a long drag. When he lowered it, he set it on the thick arm of the chair and asked, "So, what's the problem?"

I shifted again, not sure how to explain it. Maybe I shouldn't have come. "It was—"

"Was Natalie upset?" Sam interrupted.

I shook my head. "What? No. It's not that. She didn't even mention it."

"You're telling me water flooded her new kitchen and she didn't care?" Sam was paying attention now.

"I mean, there were other things going on that were more pressing." Like the outline of her nipples and the silhouette of her body under that silky material.

"What other things could possibly be more pressing than a flooded kitchen? When something happens, you two go at it like —I don't know what." Sam shook his head.

When he said *go at it like—* I groaned, finishing that sentence in my head. "She was wearing silk pajamas when she got soaked."

There was a pause when Sam's eyes widened, then he shook his head and chuckled. "Now I get it. Were you too busy helping her dry off?"

"Something like that." I waved a hand at him, very uncomfortable with how easy he was taking my confession. I'd expected him to lecture me on not getting involved with a client.

"Was it see-through?" Sam asked carefully.

"Possibly."

Sam laughed again, shaking his head. "Something similar happened between Alice and me one night. She dropped a glass, and she was wet. I could see everything. That's when it all started for us."

I dropped my head into my hands. "That's what I'm worried about."

"You like her." It wasn't a question.

I ran a hand through my hair. I wanted to fuck her. Was that the same thing? "I don't know about that."

"Does she feel the same?"

I picked at the label on the bottle. "I mean, you can't just ask a woman that. Maybe some, but not her."

"What did you do?"

My skin heated all over again when I thought about Natalie in my arms. "I helped her dry off, and she went to her apartment. It sounded like she took a bath."

Sam's lips twitched. "Okay, creeper."

He was enjoying this entirely too much. "It wasn't like that. I was still in the kitchen, trying to sort things out in my head, when the water started running."

Sam smirked. "And you imagined her naked in the tub?"

"Trust me, she didn't leave much to the imagination in that wet lingerie."

Sam chuckled, and when he sobered, he said, "I'm a little confused. Why are you here? You don't need my permission to fuck her. Just don't let it get messy or interfere with the business."

I sighed. "That's the thing... I don't think it's fair to her. She's a single mom—"

He nodded as understanding passed over his face. "You're here to get my advice as a single parent."

"Yeah." I wanted him to tell me not to pursue it. I was a little worried this was something more than just physical. When I held her, something akin to tenderness flowed through me.

"I'll be honest. It's a tricky situation. None of us know her past. But if you're up-front with her, I think it will be okay. Just don't mess with her if you think she wants more."

"I have no idea what she wants." Sam was right. I didn't know Natalie, what she was thinking, or what she wanted.

"Sounds like you two need to have a conversation. But don't let whatever happens between you two mess up the business side of things."

That was a good reminder that I should keep my dick in my pants. Women weren't worth sacrificing my livelihood or the company's. "I think I'll take a step back. Keep it professional."

Sam considered me carefully before he finally asked, "Are you sure that's what you want to do?"

"It's the right thing." I didn't let women lead me around anymore. I had to be practical in this situation. Standing, I stretched my back, then threw out the empty beer bottle in the garbage. "Maybe when the B&B is done."

Sam stood to join me, patting my shoulder. "Just don't let something good pass you by."

Bitterness flooded my mouth. I'd never experienced anything good from a relationship. I'd been prepared to propose to my college girlfriend when she told me she was moving across the country for a job. She didn't ask me to join her. A few years later, I dated Ivy, a single mom, thinking she was perfect for me. I fell hard and fast. When she went back to her ex, I was crushed. Relationships weren't for me.

I'd wanted what everyone did, someone to love and a family, but it just wasn't in the cards for me. Ever since, I kept relationships casual so I wouldn't get hurt. Everything with Natalie already felt too intense. I didn't want to get more tangled up in her.

"Thanks for the talk," I said to Sam as I made my way through his house to the front door.

"I don't feel like I helped you." There was regret in his tone.

"It was good advice. Otherwise, I would have taken what I wanted without a thought to the consequences."

"But that's not you," Sam said solemnly as he opened the front door.

I knew what Sam was trying to say. Underneath everything, I was still the same hopeless romantic. But he was wrong. I had to resist Natalie. I didn't have a choice.

I thanked him again as I got into my truck and headed to my house. I'd built it recently when I concluded a wife wasn't in my future. I didn't need to wait to build the perfect house with someone else. I didn't have anyone to build that future with. I was alone.

Unfortunately, the large house on three acres near my parents' place was cold and empty. I unlocked the door, but no one greeted me. And no one ever had. Maybe I needed to get a dog.

I'd resisted before because I worked long hours, but maybe it was time. It would give me an excuse to cut out of work early and get home. No more late nights at the B&B. I didn't need any more temptation.

CHAPTER 3

NATALIE

I wondered if Mac heard me take a bath with my vibrator the other night because he'd avoided me ever since. He was polite, even ma'am-ing me, which had me gritting my teeth. I wasn't that old. Sure, I was a mom, but it made me feel ancient. Was that how he thought of me after he saw me in wet lingerie?

Maybe our encounter freaked him out. Either he wasn't interested in me, and I'd imagined the heat in his eyes, or he wanted nothing to do with a single mother. When Carter broke things off, I figured that might be the case with some guys.

Not that I was interested in anything serious. I was supposed to be focused on my daughter and the B&B, not on its hot contractor.

Instead, I worked at the front counter, pretending not to notice how his ass looked when he bent over, or the way his biceps bulged when he lifted something over his head. He was sexy. I noticed he worked alongside his crew, not afraid to do the heavy lifting or get his hands dirty. It was admirable. Since he was the foreman, I was sure he could have gone about things differently and taken a more hands-off approach.

I was lost in thought while watching him hang drywall in the foyer when someone said, "Good afternoon."

I blinked at Sam, Mac's youngest brother and single dad of an adorable four-year-old named Maggie. He smiled wide, his gaze going from me to Mac.

"What are you doing here?" Mac asked, setting the board on the ground and wiping his hands on a cloth that hung out of his back pocket before he joined us.

"Just wanted to check on your progress," Sam said, his lips tipped up.

"Since when are you the foreman?" Mac asked.

Earlier on, these two worked together. But I rarely saw Sam around anymore. He was busy with the new branch of his business. But I remembered how they bantered like brothers, teasing each other and joking around. As an only child, I'd found it amusing and heartwarming. I knew they had a third brother, and I wondered how his mother had managed to raise them without losing her mind.

"I'm still a part of this company." Sam turned to me and smiled warmly. "I was curious how things were going."

There was a glint in his eyes that made me think he knew something. My gaze darted to Mac, who shifted on his feet. Had he told him? If so, that would be interesting. It would mean he thought it meant more than an awkward encounter with a woman he wasn't interested in.

Instead, Mac quipped, "I got the pipe fixed in the kitchen, *Dad*."

Sam punched him in the shoulder, hard enough for Mac to grunt. "Don't *Dad* me."

Mac grabbed the spot. "Hey. Don't hit me."

Sam shook his head. "What are you going to do? Tell Dad?"

Mac pulled out his phone and held it up. "Nope. I'm going to tell Mom."

"You wouldn't," Sam grumbled.

I couldn't resist smiling at their antics. This was the kind of tight-knit family I'd wanted growing up. They reminded me a little of my best friend Kylie's older brothers.

"Stop messing around and show me what's what." Sam walked with Mac to the kitchen, but I stayed behind.

I didn't understand all the ins and outs of the renovation. I had a picture in my mind of what the B&B should look like. At the end of the day, I tried to pay attention to Mac's updates, but most of them went over my head. Or I was too busy admiring the confident way he explained everything. The two things I paid the most attention to were an increase in the budget and an extension to the time line. Those two things impacted me greatly.

I needed the B&B open soon to welcome clients. Anytime would be good since Telluride was a year-round tourist destination, but spring was more realistic for our time line.

I wandered to the front room, eager to have female interaction. I was surrounded by men with tools during the day and a nine-year-old in the evenings. I didn't get out much.

Alice was carefully hanging new mosaics on the floating shelves in her shop.

"It looks amazing in here." I'd ordered mosaics for every room in the B&B, and these looked beautiful in the windows with the light streaming through.

Alice smiled at me over her shoulder before slowly stepping down. "I'm working on some new designs for Telluride. People don't appreciate my crabs like they do in Annapolis."

"It's a wintery theme here for sure," I agreed.

A store in Annapolis ordered a ton of crabs in every color combination. It was a thing there, apparently. "Sam's here."

Alice smiled. "I saw. I think he wanted to talk to Mac."

"He doesn't usually come over to my side." If he visited, it was only to see Alice. Occasionally, he brought in Maggie to visit. If Delaney was home, the girls played together. Delaney adored little kids.

"Mac came over the other night after the issue with the faucet in the kitchen," Alice said carefully, keeping her gaze on my face.

I couldn't stop the flush to my skin. "Oh?"

Alice moved closer, leaning a hip against the table in the center of the room. "Is there anything going on between you two?"

I shook my head hard. "Definitely not."

"What happened with the faucet?"

I wrung my hands as I looked to see if the guys had returned. "I didn't know anyone was here. Some nights I hang out in the B&B's living area for some privacy. I was getting a glass of water when the water started shooting from the faucet, going every-where. I was wearing pajamas—the silky kind."

Alice's head tipped to the side. "But Mac was here."

"He was tiling the upstairs bathroom. I had no idea." I remembered the initial shock when I heard his footsteps, then relief because he knew what to do to stop the water.

Alice's eyes narrowed. "Something happened."

I sighed, needing to talk to someone about it. "We argued like usual. Then I started shivering, and he helped me dry off."

Alice's eyes widened. "Is that code for *warmed you up?*"

My face heated as I remembered the feel of his arms around me and my pebbled nipples flush against his hard body. "I thought he might have felt something, but I was wrong. He hasn't said anything about it since."

Alice's frowned. "I don't think you're right about that. He came over to talk to Sam. I think he wanted advice."

"What did Sam say?" I felt like I was in middle school all over again, wanting to know if the boy I crushed on told someone else he liked me.

"He wanted to talk to Sam alone." She was quiet for a few

seconds as she gathered the supplies to set at each chair. "Whatever happened between you two was something."

"It shouldn't matter because I just got divorced. I don't have the time or the energy to deal with a relationship or even the potential of one." I wasn't ready to date, but my hopeful heart wanted a love that lasted a lifetime and more kids. I needed to focus on what I had—Delaney and the B&B.

Alice gave me a sharp look. "Just because one man cheated on you doesn't mean you should avoid men forever."

"I have no desire to go through that again." I shuddered at the thought of meeting someone, going through the motions of dating, and then a relationship. Trusting someone enough to marry them? That sounded impossible.

Alice squeezed my hand. "Keep an open mind. Don't close yourself off like I did."

Alice had done some things in her past that she wasn't proud of. She moved here and became a bit of a recluse for a few years before taking the job as the nanny for Sam's daughter. They weren't able to resist each other for long, and now they were engaged. "Just because it worked out for you doesn't mean it will for me. Besides, you swore off men for three years. Don't you think I need a similar break?"

"It sounds like a long time when you say it out loud. But it's different because you're older and you have a child. Besides, Mac's a good guy. He'd never cheat on anyone."

I sighed, feeling the weight of responsibility on my shoulders. "It is different. I have someone to shield and protect. I won't let Delaney be hurt like that again."

"Any new guy won't be her father, so it won't be the same," Alice persisted stubbornly.

"Maybe not, but I don't know." I felt conflicted. I was attracted to Mac. Our late-night interlude solidified that. But should I act on it?

Alice pulled out a chair and sat. "We should go out—just us girls."

The thought of getting dressed up and going to a bar didn't appeal to me. "I don't know. I have Delaney."

"You need to find a babysitter so we can have some girl time. Have you been out since the divorce?"

"Not at all. I suppose I could ask Kylie." She was my childhood friend, and her family owned the Wilde Ski Resort on the top of the mountain, just outside of town.

Alice tapped her fingers on the table. "Don't you want to have Kylie come with us, though?"

"Probably." Kylie was a lot of fun when we used to go out.

Sam appeared in the doorway. "What are you two talking about?"

Mac stood next to him.

Alice waved a hand in my direction. "I'm trying to get Natalie to go out."

Sam smiled. "That's a great idea."

"But I don't have a sitter for Delaney." It was a good excuse. I didn't even know many people in town anymore besides Kylie.

"I'm sure my mom would love to watch her. She watches Maggie all the time," Sam offered.

Mac glared at him like Sam was overstepping.

"I couldn't ask her to watch Delaney. She doesn't even know me." Especially when it was clear Mac was not happy about the suggestion.

"Mom loves kids. Trust me." Sam exchanged a look with Mac. "She'd be all for it."

"I'm too tired at the end of the night to do anything but take a bath and collapse," I said.

Mac's eyes darkened.

Was he remembering the night the faucet spewed water everywhere? Was he thinking of me in that see-through lingerie, or had he heard me in the bathtub?

"You can't be a mom twenty-four seven. I mean, you can, but you deserve a break every now and then. My mom gave me the same speech when I insisted on being the only one who could watch Maggie," Sam said, and I could tell he'd thought a lot about it.

I softened at his honesty. He'd felt a kinship with me because we were both single parents. It had nothing to do with Mac. I bet they hadn't discussed what happened, other than how to fix yet another problem with the renovation. That's why Sam was here today. "Sure. Why not?"

It wouldn't hurt to ask his mom if she would be willing to babysit. And I needed someone to help out here and there. Not just for a girls' night but if something came up.

Alice clapped her hands. "I'm so happy that worked out."

"No one has asked her yet," Mac said.

"Oh, she'll say yes," Alice said with a smile. "No worries about that."

"You think she'd come here, or would I take Delaney to her?" I asked, working out the details in my head.

"She'd do whatever makes you comfortable. I'll give her a heads-up that you're going to call, and I'll send you her contact information." Sam pulled out his phone to do just that.

"I should get back to work," Mac said abruptly before he walked away.

"What's gotten into him?" Sam asked, but his gaze was on me.

"I'm sure it's all the delays. I think he's ready to be done with this project."

Sam burst into a guffaw; his head flew back and everything.

I frowned, looking from Sam's amused expression to Alice's content one. "What? Did I miss something?"

"I think we have to disagree on that." Then he held his hand out to Alice. "Want to go to lunch?"

She placed her hand in his. "I'd love to."

24

I watched them walk out—his arm around her shoulder and her tucked into his side—and felt more alone than ever. I couldn't remember a time that Carter had held me like that. Not even at the beginning of our relationship. I just got out of a divorce. I shouldn't be interested in anyone, but I hadn't been touched in so long that I couldn't even remember what it felt like.

The demise of our marriage happened slowly over time. I was busy with Delaney, and Carter was obsessed with work. We drifted apart. We had sex less often; intimate interactions were few and far between until we were reduced to roommates sleeping in the same room.

I realized too late that we never talked about anything important. I thought we'd have time to work on it, but Carter had other ideas. He'd said it was my fault for being too involved with Delaney. But he was absent between working and traveling. The thing was, when it was over, I felt betrayed, but I didn't particularly miss him. I just hated that he'd left Delaney.

I didn't think he even realized the level of abandonment she'd have to deal with for the rest of her life because her father was impulsive and put his own needs ahead of hers.

I made my way up the stairs, checking empty rooms until I found Mac in one of the bathrooms. No one else was there, so I asked, "Do you mind if I ask your mother to babysit?"

Mac looked at me briefly before turning back to his work. "Why would I care?"

"I don't know, but you seem to." I was hesitant to get involved if Mac truly had an issue with it.

He picked up tiles and placed them on the floor of the shower, using the spacers in between each one. "It's none of my business who my mother babysits."

"I don't want to intrude if it makes you uncomfortable." The last thing I wanted to do was create problems with my contractor. I was friends with Alice, and by extension, Sam, but if Mac wanted me to stay away from their mother, I would.

Mac turned slightly toward me and raised a brow. "Does it make *you* uncomfortable?"

I thought about it for a few seconds but couldn't come up with any reason why it would be an issue for me if Mac's mother babysat Delaney at the house. "No."

Mac nodded and returned his attention to his work. "Then you have your answer."

"It would be nice to go out. I haven't done anything since I moved here." I literally stayed in the house all day, had groceries delivered, and ordered takeout.

"Why not?" He shifted slightly so he could see me.

"I'm busy between the renovation and Delaney. I grew up here, but other than Kylie, I haven't reconnected with anyone yet."

"You don't have family here?"

Shaking my head, I said, "My parents moved shortly after I graduated from high school." I never told them how much it hurt that they sold the family home so nonchalantly, throwing out any of my childhood mementos because there wasn't room where they were going. They hadn't even discussed it with me. The part that hurt the most was that I didn't have a home to return to after the divorce.

"You're friends with Kylie Wilde?"

I laughed at his question. "If you can believe it. We've been friends since kindergarten. She was the wild one, and I was the reserved one."

"You don't say." He considered me a moment before continuing, "I don't remember you hanging around the lodge."

He was referring to the Wilde Ski Resort, which Kylie's family owned. "We were younger than you, but you're right. I wasn't as adventurous as Kylie. I didn't ski or snowboard."

"Hmm. You grew up in Telluride and don't know how to ski?"

"I was always too afraid to try it, and my parents never pushed."

"You should have one of the Wildes take you out."

Remembering what they were like as kids—no-holds-barred, skiing at night, lucky they never ran into a tree—I shuddered at the idea. "No, thanks."

I felt Mac soften toward me. If all it took was a little small talk, then it was worth it.

"You should do something for yourself. Call my mom. She'll be ecstatic. She loves helping people, and she loves kids even more."

Throughout our discussion, he listened intently when I talked. It hadn't been like that with Carter. I hadn't confided in him because I wasn't sure he cared what I was doing. I should have known that wasn't a good sign for our relationship.

"Thanks for listening." Since the divorce, I'd learned to feel grateful for every little thing in my life—help from friends or babysitting from someone's mom.

He smiled ruefully. "I've been told I'm good at it."

"It's a great skill to have." And I loved that I'd put him a little at ease. Hopefully, I'd put space between our unfortunate run-in in the kitchen the other night.

Clearly, he wasn't interested, and I didn't need the distraction.

"What do you think you'll do?"

I hadn't thought about going out with girlfriends in so long I wasn't even sure what they did. "Maybe dinner or a wine bar. I'll leave it up to Alice."

"I'm sure you'll have fun."

"Just thinking about dressing up for a night out sounds amazing."

Mac stood, and the room suddenly shrunk. I was attracted to

Mac. He moved with confidence when he was working, and he exuded responsibility. He was the oldest brother, and his father gave him a lot of responsibility in the company. And he'd listened to me. Hanging out with him was dangerous. I was only going to like him more, and I couldn't do anything about it.

Even if we managed to be friends, a part of me would always wonder what he'd be like in bed. Those confident hands roaming my body, finding the spots that made me hum and cry out. Suddenly, I was hot all over, and I wondered if he knew what I was thinking.

Mac stood in front of me. "You deserve some time away."

I swallowed hard, wondering what he was doing.

"Excuse me. I just need to find the other box of tiles."

"Oh, sorry." I moved out of his way, feeling flustered and out of sorts. Mac made me forget everything, including my good sense and the reasons I couldn't make a move on him. But I couldn't forget that it was one-sided. There was a slim chance he was interested in me. I was a single mom who'd just come out of a divorce. I'd moved to a town where I didn't know most people, and I was trying to renovate a house into a B&B. I was in over my head. I didn't have time for distractions.

I spun on my heel, determined to disappear before Mac returned. Thinking about what was in my closet, I wasn't even sure I had an acceptable outfit for a night out. Maybe I needed Kylie's advice. I texted her on the way down the hall, asking for her help.

She immediately said yes, with about ten emojis. I smiled at her predictable response. It reminded me that I needed to focus on what mattered: my business, my daughter, and bonding with old and new friends. I needed to make Telluride my home again.

CHAPTER 4

MAC

I'd left the bathroom in search of a box of tiles I didn't need because I wanted distance between me and Natalie. The more we talked, the more I was intrigued by her.

The fact that she was friends with Kylie Wilde was a little mind-blowing. I had a sense that something important had been under my nose this whole time. Which was ridiculous because I didn't remember her hanging around back then. But when we hung out with the Wilde brothers, we went skiing, snowboarding, and four-wheeling. If it wasn't fast, we weren't doing it. And they never wanted their little sister along for the ride, much less her friends.

When we were older, Kylie was off-limits. There's no way one of us would have gone after their little sister or her friends. Not when she had four protective brothers.

Pursuing Kylie wasn't worth the trouble. Not that I was ever interested. She was a little too wild for my taste. I liked to have fun, but I was more cautious. My brothers liked to say I was boring. That I was born an old man, but I was just responsible. I was no different from other eldest siblings.

By the time I returned to the bathroom with the box of tiles,

Natalie was gone. I shouldn't have felt a sense of loss. I'd been the one to leave, but we'd connected through tidbits about her life she'd shared, and I wanted more.

I wanted to know why she'd moved home when her parents didn't live here anymore. Why was she divorced? Where was Delaney's dad? If I had a daughter, I'd be all in like Sam. Having a family was the one thing I'd wanted most when I'd gone away to college. My parents had been the best example of a loving relationship, and I wanted something similar.

I hadn't lied when I said I didn't care if my mom babysat. If it made Natalie's life easier, I was all for it. Ever since she mentioned needing a safe place to stay, my mind had been spinning with the whys and hows of her story, but I didn't want to push for it because I was afraid it would only draw me in more.

I knew my mom would fall in love with Natalie and Delaney. That's just how she was, and she'd always wanted a daughter. I suspected having Alice in the family was fulfilling that particular desire, but I was positive she'd want to adopt Natalie when she realized her parents were gone and she had no family here.

I could help Natalie with the renovation and give her access to my family, but I didn't need to get to know her. Talking to her today made me feel all these things for her, about her, and it wasn't smart.

No matter how much I wanted a committed relationship, marriage, and even kids, it never worked out. I couldn't forget that.

* * *

I SPENT the rest of the week in the bathrooms, finishing the tile. I could take a step back and merely supervise, but that wasn't my style. I liked to work and keep my hands busy. Carefully cutting and placing tiles kept me occupied so I wouldn't go looking for Natalie and ask her all the questions swirling in my brain.

One night, after everyone on my team had said good-bye and left, the house was quiet. Natalie didn't let Delaney walk through the house when the bus dropped her off, so I never knew when she returned home. Usually, they stayed in their suite for the rest of the evening.

I relaxed, thinking I had the night to myself. It was quiet, and I could get a lot of work done. Maybe even shave some time off this renovation. Not because I was eager to move on to another project, but because I knew Natalie was stressed about the time line.

She needed to get the B&B open and accepting reservations to get money coming in. I never had to start a business since my dad had done the hard work with that, but I'd heard him talk about it enough to know that starting a new business was risky and difficult.

I couldn't imagine doing it as a single mom.

"Natalie said I'd find you here."

"Mom." I startled, seeing her in the doorway. "What are you doing here?"

"I'm babysitting Delaney so Natalie can go out with the girls."

I bristled at that characterization. I didn't think of Natalie as a girl when I saw her nipples through that wet silk. I'd wanted to lick and suck every inch of her skin.

I stood, stretching out my stiff muscles before washing my hands in the sink. I leaned over to kiss my mom on the cheek, not wanting to transfer tile dust to her clean clothes.

"Natalie said you work late," Mom said in a disapproving tone as I took the plastic bags she was carrying.

"Not as late as I had been." Before I ran into an almost-naked B&B owner who got my blood pumping. "I'd love to finish the tile in here this weekend."

"You work too hard. Your dad never meant for this to be your life."

"What are you talking about? We love the business, and we want it to succeed." Dad always said no one worked as hard as a business owner.

"I know, but he wanted you to have a life. Especially you. I always thought you'd be the first one to get married and give me grandbabies."

My jaw tightened. "You know why that didn't work out."

"But that doesn't mean you give up. The right woman is out there for you."

"I'm busy. My life is full." It was when I thought about work and my family. They took up every nook and cranny of my life. My brothers would stop by, and my parents loved having us over for family dinners, and the responsibilities only increased with the addition of Maggie and then Alice. We were a big, tight family, and I loved it.

Mom patted my cheek. "I want more for you."

"Don't worry about me." Guilt unfurled in my chest. I hated disappointing my mother.

"That's what mothers do." Mom turned and headed down the steps. I followed her, not wanting her to get hurt if someone left a tool or box of supplies in the way.

When she reached the door to the owner's suite, she knocked. Before I could leave, Delaney appeared. "Hi," she said shyly.

Natalie kept her daughter away from the renovations and my team, so I didn't know her at all.

"Hello, dear. I'm this one's mother. You can call me Miranda."

Natalie appeared behind her, and I almost swallowed my tongue. She wore some black, slinky halter top over jeans that looked like they'd been painted on her and stilettos. She looked sexy as fuck.

"Come on in," Natalie said, and when she turned, it revealed a bare expanse of tan skin.

I couldn't seem to stop myself from following them into the space, mainly because I couldn't look away from the bare skin on display.

The space had been transformed with framed photographs, soft-looking throws, and blush-colored pillows. It was homey. The perfect space for a single mother and her daughter.

"I was just telling Mac he worked too hard," Mom said to Natalie.

Natalie's cheeks flushed pink. "You don't need to babysit for me. I'm sure you have other things to do on a Friday night."

Now I felt like a loser. "I'll call Sam or Tyler."

Mom frowned. "I doubt Sam is leaving Maggie or Alice for a guys' night, and Tyler's probably out already. He has a million friends."

Everything she said was true, but she didn't have to point out that I didn't have a lot of options. "I can call a friend."

Unfortunately, most of my friends were married with kids or had one on the way. Friends had definitely fallen away over the last five years, as they moved away or started their own families. And I always thought I'd be in the same position.

"Humph," Mom said.

"You can hang out with us. I got out a few games," Delaney said, her eyes hopeful.

How could I say no to that?

"I'm sure you have other things to do," Natalie said, and suddenly I wanted to stay. Especially if it bothered her.

Mom smiled. "That's a great idea. You two play a game while I get started on the cookies."

"You're making cookies?" I asked hopefully.

"Yes, that's what good babysitters do." Mom patted my cheek again before I dropped her plastic bags of supplies onto the kitchen counter.

I wondered if Mom had manipulated me into being in Natalie's space, and now it was too late to escape.

"You're sticking around?" Natalie asked, her expression dubious.

"I have work to do," I said, but when Delaney's expression fell, I added, "but I have time for a game."

"Really?" Delaney asked hopefully.

There was no way I could disappoint this little girl. I decided to tease her. "You'll have to help me with the tile because I'll be behind."

"You'll do no such thing. You leave that girl alone," Mom chided from across the room.

Natalie moved into my space and lowered her voice. "You don't have to."

"I know." Looking down, I saw the tops of the globes of her breasts, and it made me remember what her nipples looked like the other night. I wanted another glimpse. I wanted to touch her hip and slide my hand under the slinky top to see if the skin underneath was as soft as it looked.

Natalie's phone buzzed, and I saw Kylie's name flash across the screen when she lifted it. "I have to get going."

"Don't worry. We have everything covered here, and if we have any problems, we'll call," Mom said cheerfully.

Natalie tucked her phone into her back pocket, drawing my attention to her perfect ass. I wanted to cup it while I lifted her in my arms. How would her long legs feel around my waist when I rocked in her heat?

"Bedtime is eight thirty. No exceptions," Natalie said to Delaney.

I tipped my head back to stare at the ceiling. Even her stern mom voice was hot.

"Yeah, yeah," Delaney said.

I returned my attention to their exchange in time to see Natalie hug and kiss Delaney. I was drawn to the bare skin of her back again. That's when I realized there was zero chance she was wearing a bra.

Were her nipples hard under that shirt? My fingers itched to touch her. I was having inappropriate thoughts in front of Natalie's daughter and my mother. I was clearly not cut out for family life. This was why I was still single. It had nothing to do with shutting myself out of the possibilities over the last few years.

"Are you going to be okay?" Natalie asked Mom, but her gaze was on me.

Mom waved her off. "We've got it handled. You don't have to worry about a thing."

"Where are you heading?" I asked Natalie, my heart suddenly in my throat, wondering who'd approach her in that outfit.

"Kylie said there's a club at the resort now," Natalie said hesitantly, as if clubbing wasn't her scene.

"You're going to a club?" I asked, unable to disguise my surprise.

"Well, yeah," Natalie said, her hand on her hip. She'd done the same thing the night she'd been soaked and in nothing but that ivory lingerie.

"Are you sure that's a good idea?"

"Of course, it's a good idea," Mom said as she bustled past us and opened the door to the private entrance of the suite. "Now go. We're fine here."

Natalie gathered her purse and keys.

"I'll walk you out." Before Natalie could protest, I touched her elbow and guided her through the door. I couldn't be sure, but I thought Mom chuckled.

"You don't need to do this," Natalie said.

When she stumbled over the pavers on those thin spikes, I said, "I think I do."

Her lips pressed into a thin line. "You don't have to stay and play a game with Delaney. She's a big girl."

"I said I would. I don't make promises I don't keep." That was something I never backed down from, especially since I'd been let down so many times by women.

Natalie turned as we reached her SUV. "It's just, she's been disappointed enough the last year with her father leaving and never showing up for his visitation."

"Where did her father go? I thought you lived in South Carolina?" I frowned; she made it sound like he was gone.

Something passed over her face. "He moved in with his girlfriend in Texas."

"Are you serious?" Every thought of her in this outfit and what it would be like to peel her out of it vanished.

Natalie looked away from me. "He said he's in love. I guess he can't be bothered to worry about the daughter he left behind."

"Jesus. I'm sorry." I reached out to tuck a strand of silky hair behind her ear, and her breath hitched.

Her gaze met mine. "We don't need him. We're fine."

"I'm glad you have your friends and now my family."

Natalie shook her head. "Your mom's just helping out."

"I'm pretty sure she just adopted you, so there's that."

An adorable crease appeared between her eyebrows. "What are you talking about?"

"Before you know it, you'll be invited to family dinners."

Natalie looked away. "I don't want to intrude."

"You won't be." She'd fit easily into my family. She was strong enough to take my brothers' antics and sweet enough to bond with my mother and Alice. She was the perfect combination of sweet and sexy. She was exactly my type. "I'm sorry about your ex. He sounds like an asshole."

She chuckled, and her whole body relaxed. "He is."

"I wouldn't waste any time worrying about him. We've got you." I opened the driver's-side door for her.

"Thanks," Natalie said. "Don't feel like you have to stick around long. I know you have work to do."

"I have a game to play." There was zero chance I was letting that little girl down. If I made a promise, I was sticking with it.

Natalie settled into the seat, and before I could ask if she planned on drinking or taking a car service home, she'd said, "Thanks," and closed the door. As the engine rumbled to life, I stepped back, watching as she backed up and drove off.

I pulled out my phone and texted Alice.

Mac: Take care of Natalie.

Alice: Don't worry. I'll watch out for her.

Mac: Call me if any of you need a ride home.

Alice: Will do.

Alice had Sam looking out for her, but who was looking out for Natalie? It didn't sit right with me that she drove herself.

I went back inside, where Delaney already had several boxes of games on the table. "Which one do you want to play?"

Delaney's eyes lit up as she described what she liked about each one.

When she looked at me expectantly, I said, "Pick your favorite."

I didn't care what we played as long as she was happy. Now I knew why I'd steered clear of Natalie's daughter. She was sweet, and I could easily get attached to her.

She explained the complicated rules of some exploding card game, and we played, stopping occasionally to check the rules, while Mom baked cookies. When the dough was ready, Delaney put down her cards and helped Mom scoop the dough into balls on the parchment paper.

I stood at the counter, wondering if it was time for me to leave. "I should probably clean up the bathroom."

"You aren't doing any more work tonight?"

Between Natalie's outfit and playing with Delaney, my motivation was gone. "I don't think so."

"Wait for the cookies to be done. You know you want one," Delaney said as Mom put the tray into the oven.

"I guess I could stick around."

Delaney smiled at me. "Besides, we haven't finished our game."

We played several rounds with me pulling an exploding card and then Delaney picking one. It was nothing like how my brothers and I played. We cheated, hid cards, and made up rules, and it inevitably ended up with us wrestling around on the ground and fighting. It got so bad when we were little that Mom hid the cards and games and told us to play outside.

That was worse because we would have sword fights with wooden sticks and made whips with string we found in the garage. We climbed trees way too high for our parents' comfort, and, despite their warnings, no one ever fell and broke a limb. We were resourceful and not afraid of getting hurt. We probably aged our parents by ten years.

The suite smelled like fresh-baked cookies, reminding me of my parents' house. My mom was always baking for us. It was like her way of saying she loved us, and it wasn't different here with Delaney.

When the cookies were cooling, I grabbed one, burning my hand, and threw it into my mouth. "Whew, that was hot."

"You could never wait for them to cool," Mom said with a smile as she poured two glasses of milk and slid them across the counter toward us.

"Cookies and milk. The best combination."

Delaney nodded as she chewed her first cookie. "You always bake when you babysit?"

"I only babysit for Maggie, but now I have you."

"Oh?" Delaney asked, and I was sure she was wondering what made her special.

Mom smiled. "You're a joy. I'm happy to watch you anytime."

"Really?" Delaney asked, her gaze flitting from me to Mom. Was she insecure because her father left her? Did she think it was her fault or that she wasn't worthy of his attention? I hated that for her.

Maggie's mom had done something similar. She'd moved to Maryland for a job and never returned. She rarely visited. I was sure there would be some residual abandonment issues, but we worked hard to make Maggie feel wanted and loved. She had Sam and now Alice, my family, and Alice's family.

"You're fun," I said to her. "My brothers wouldn't have handled losing as well as you did."

"It's a little crazy when the boys get together. You'll see," Mom said as she wiped the flour from the counter.

It warmed me that Mom had already included Delaney in future family gatherings and that she still called us "boys." "You know we're grown men now, right?"

Mom finished spooning out another tray of cookies and put them into the oven. When the oven door was shut, she set the timer and waved a hand at me. "You'll always be my boys."

"I'd love a little brother or sister," Delaney said, popping another cookie into her mouth.

"Be careful what you ask for. My brothers are—"

Mom shook the wooden spoon at me. "Don't you dare finish that sentence."

"Mean. That's all I was going to say." If she were older, I might have said the devil or evil. "I know how to talk around kids."

Mom gave me a look that said she didn't believe me.

"I control my language around Maggie," I insisted, although I wasn't so sure about that.

Mom shook the wooden spoon at me. "That's not what I hear."

"Is Sam telling on me again?" I whined.

Delaney giggled. "You sound like a kid."

"That's what I've been telling them since they supposedly became adults and moved out. They're overgrown children."

Delaney laughed so hard she almost fell off her stool.

"It's not that funny," I said seriously when she sobered.

"I can't wait to meet your brothers."

"Tyler, the middle one, is a troublemaker, and Sam is the youngest, the immature one." Although that wasn't really true anymore. He had to grow up when Felicia left him with Maggie.

"Oh, he is not," Mom said, placing the cooled cookies into a container. "He's a perfectly sweet boy."

"Tyler has classic middle-child syndrome that you desperately tried to make up for, and Sam was babied."

"Oh, I did not. You three were always jealous of each other. I suppose that's typical with siblings, brothers especially. There wasn't anything they didn't compete to do. Who can spit the farthest, run the fastest…"

It wasn't a good idea to mention our peeing contests. She'd have a fit if she knew about those.

Tyler was a bit more charming than the rest of us. He was skilled at avoiding my parents' radar, frequently getting away with pranks and tricks. My mom used to say that the oldest and youngest were the most demanding, so she needed to give Tyler special attention, which did not go over well. We made Tyler's life hell for it. But I couldn't tell Delaney that.

I helped Mom box up the rest of the cookies. She reserved a smaller box for me and left the large one in the kitchen.

"I'm going to clean up. Thanks for playing with me, Delaney. I had fun."

"Will you play with me again?" Delaney asked with such expectation in her voice I couldn't say no.

I winked at her. "Of course. You can't go down with a loss on your record."

"It's time for you to get ready for bed, missy," Mom said.

"Good night, Mac."

"Night, Delaney," I said before I left their suite and headed upstairs to clean the mess I'd made. That little girl was slowly raveling her way around my heart.

To take my mind off it, I wondered if Mom would consider baking for the B&B. It would give her something to do with her free time. She could socialize with the guests and stay active. She'd even have time to travel with Dad like she wanted. It was an idea I should probably discuss with Natalie first. I didn't know what her plans were for operating the B&B. It might be good for both of them.

CHAPTER 5

NATALIE

I hadn't been out with friends in forever. I was so preoccupied with Delaney in South Carolina that I hadn't made many friends outside of playdates. Nerves fluttered in my belly as I pulled up to the lodge. I hadn't been here since I was a kid. We loved to play hide-and-seek in the lodge, and we begged her parents to let us sleep in one of the guest rooms. When they allowed it, it was the ultimate sleepover.

My phone buzzed with an incoming text from Alice.

Alice: I'm sorry to cancel. Maggie just barfed.

Natalie: No worries. We can meet up another time. I hope Maggie feels better soon!

Alice: I feel bad because Mac asked me to keep an eye on you.

Warmth spread through my chest that Mac was worried about me.

Natalie: Tell Mac I can take care of myself.

Alice: I know, right? Have fun!

I sent a thumbs-up emoji, and I stepped out of my SUV. I'd invited Alice, hoping that she and Kylie would become friends too. I hadn't seen Kylie since I'd been back because I'd been so busy with the renovation.

"I can't believe you're here!" Kylie approached with her arms raised. She hugged me tightly. "I missed you so much. I never thought you'd come back."

"It's a little weird when my parents don't live here anymore." Could you still call it your hometown when your parents lived in Arizona?

"It will always be your home."

"As kids, I felt like I spent more time here at the resort than I ever did at my parents'."

Kylie draped her arm over my shoulder as we walked toward the entrance. "We had the best time. When you weren't around, I had to hope my brothers would let me play with them."

I knew that rarely worked out unless Kylie figured out where they were and snuck out. There was one occasion when she'd gotten hurt, and her parents found out about it. That put an end to her adventures with her brothers.

"Alice couldn't make it. Maggie's sick."

Kylie's expression morphed into sympathy. "Ugh. Poor thing."

"It's the worst when your kids are sick," I said, suddenly feeling old compared to Kylie, who'd been living a different life-style than me for the past nine years. Wanting to change the subject, I asked, "Are all of your brothers still in town?"

"All but one. Killian's still falling down mountains in search of fame."

"You mean he's a professional snowboarder," her brother Xander said.

Kylie rolled her eyes before hugging him. "Whatever that even means."

With an arm still wrapped around his sister, Xander asked, "And who is this?"

"This is my friend, Natalie Anderson. She just moved back to town with her daughter."

Xander wore a red Wilde Resort ski jacket that made him easily visible on the slopes. He held his hand out to me. "I don't remember all of Kylie's friends' names."

Shaking his hand, I said, "I don't remember you wanting to hang out with your little sister back then."

Xander shuddered. "Definitely not. Barbies and bows were not my thing."

Kylie smacked him in the chest. "They weren't my thing either. Which you'd have known if you'd bothered to spend any time with me."

Xander shook his head. "I had three brothers. I was hardly going to hang out with my little sister."

Kylie moved out of his arms, placing her hands on her hips. "What was I supposed to do? I didn't have any sisters."

Xander winked at me, and I could see why the locals thought the Wilde brothers were the ultimate bachelors. "That's what you had friends for. What are you ladies up for tonight? The bar, the club? We have a game room-slash-bar-slash-grill too."

"Wow. That's more than I remembered when your parents ran the place." I remember there being a fast-food-type option and a family-style dinner service.

Everything had been renovated since then. It had this warm, cozy lodge feeling with couches and chairs spread throughout the lobby.

"We've upgraded. My oldest brother, Oliver, is in charge of the numbers. I guess you could say he's the CEO, and then Eli is in charge of hotel management, and I'm all about sports and recreation. Killian helps when he's in town."

"He's not around much. He's always traveling between competitions and endorsement deals. He's quite the celebrity, I guess," Kylie said.

"I'm happy to be back, and I'm impressed with what you've done with the place."

"I can give you a tour." Xander grabbed my hand and placed it in the crook of his arm while we walked through the lobby.

There was a fancier sit-down restaurant on one side and a more casual bar and grill with foosball and pool tables and wall-to-wall windows with a mountain view. Standing in front of the windows, I said, "I didn't realize how much I missed the mountains when I lived in South Carolina."

"You can't get the mountains out of your soul, you know?" Xander said.

I didn't know Kylie's brothers well. I was aware of their love of danger and sports. They certainly lived up to their last name.

Xander checked his phone. "Someone needs to talk to me about scheduling for tomorrow. You guys okay?"

Kylie nodded. "We're going head to the club next."

"I'll talk to Eli about keeping an eye out," Xander said as he backed away from us.

"I don't need my big brothers protecting me," Kylie called after him.

Xander narrowed his eyes. "In that outfit you do."

Kylie wore a short black dress, perfectly acceptable club wear, but I could see why her brother would take issue with it. Kylie linked her arm with mine. "He'd go out with a girl dressed like this, but it's not okay for me."

"We can go somewhere else if you want." I didn't realize her brothers were still so overprotective of her. The boys in high school were afraid to ask her out. Frankly, I was surprised Kylie returned home to live, even if it was for a short while. She'd always wanted to escape her family and the resort.

She shrugged. "That's my brothers, but I love them."

I heard the affection in her voice. "Is that why you came back? You missed them?"

"Something like that." Kylie had been working for a hotel in France. "I'd need alcohol to talk about it."

"Do your brothers know what happened?"

Her face was grim, and she shook her head. "Absolutely not. They'd go ballistic."

"Are you okay? Did someone hurt you?" Kylie was strong, but she had a heart of gold under it. Someone could easily take advantage of her.

"I wouldn't let anyone do that. Don't worry." She patted my arm, but the worry for her didn't dissipate. "I'm just happy we're living in the same town again."

I let it go, but I made a mental note to keep an eye on her.

The bouncer waved us into the club. We wound our way through the throngs of people dancing. I slid onto an open barstool, and we ordered drinks from the bartender before I asked, "Do you know what you're going to do?"

Kylie sighed. "No idea. I like being home, but at the same time, I feel like I'm bursting out of my skin."

Even in high school, Kylie was desperate to see what else was out there. She'd gone to college, then studied abroad, fell in love with Europe, and gotten a job in Paris after graduation.

"You don't want to help run the resort?" I asked her, accepting the glass from the bartender.

Kylie thanked him and fiddled with the napkin. "There's nothing for me here. Oliver and Eli run the business and hotel side of things. You heard Xander say he's in charge of the outdoor activities, and he expects Killian to join him when he retires from snowboarding. Although, I hate to break it to Xander, but that's not happening anytime soon."

"You could help with the hotel management since that's your expertise."

Kylie rolled her eyes as she swirled her drink with the tiny straw. "My brothers don't take me seriously. They think I was partying my way through France all this time. Not working hard to learn a business."

"Why don't you tell them then?"

She sipped her drink. "Trust me. I've tried. I'll always be their irresponsible little sister who runs headfirst into trouble."

"You've never been that though."

"I was the one chasing after them, getting hurt, and in trouble with Mom and Dad. Then I left Telluride. I didn't help out with the family business, so now they see me as unreliable."

"Are you interested in the business?"

"Maybe. I don't know if there's a place for me here."

"That's too bad." Did her brothers realize Kylie would leave again if she didn't have a reason to stay? I'd just returned home, and she was my best friend. I wanted her to stay, but it would be selfish of me to influence her decision. "I just want you to be happy."

"I will be. Don't worry about me." Kylie smiled as she finished her drink. Then she grabbed my hand. "Come on. Let's dance."

I looked back at my glass, and Kylie said, "The bartender will get us fresh ones when we're done. That's the advantage of clubbing at your family's resort."

It was nice to know we were being looked out for and could let go a bit.

People parted for us as Kylie led the way through the crowd to the middle of the dance floor. Men eyed us appreciatively. I think it had something to do with two women holding hands—and also Kylie. She had this energy about her that drew others to her. Plus, she'd lived abroad for so many years that her style and her mannerisms appeared worldly. Next to her, I felt a little frumpy.

We danced and took frequent breaks to grab drinks. As the night went on, I felt lighter and freer. My body had this floaty feeling to it, and I felt good. More than good. Great even. Some part of me recognized that I'd be hurting tomorrow, but I couldn't bring myself to care. I hadn't let go in forever. Probably since before Delaney was born. I needed this.

Not even Mac's grumpy concern about me going out could bring me down.

Occasionally, a man would sidle close to Kylie and ask for a dance, but she always shook her head no and said she was there with her friend. It felt great that she put me first.

"You know you can dance with someone if you want. I don't mind." I was getting tired and probably needed to head home anyway.

Kylie linked her arm with mine. "I'm here with you."

Eventually, we switched to water before calling it a night. Kylie waited with me until the driver pulled up in front of the lodge and hugged me. I'd have to call a car service to pick mine up tomorrow, but it was worth it. "Let's do this again soon."

"Absolutely." I thought of myself as a mother first. Ever since Carter walked away, I needed a way to support myself. I couldn't rely on his income anymore or even the child support. I wanted to be independent. Then Kylie saw the old Victorian for sale and suggested I buy it and open a B&B. It sounded crazy but amazing at the same time.

When the driver pulled up to the house, it was dark. It was late. I was sure Mac had gone home. I walked around to the rear of the house where the private entrance to the owner's suite was located.

Inside, Miranda was watching TV on the couch.

"How was she?" I asked her when I'd closed the door and put my purse on the table by the door.

Miranda stood, gathering her things. "She was great. We baked cookies, and she played some games with Mac."

"Mac stayed?" I wasn't sure he would.

"Delaney asked him to play a game, and I was baking cookies. He couldn't resist."

I wasn't sure how I felt about Mac playing games and baking cookies with his mother and my daughter on a Friday night.

"But enough about us. How was your night?"

"It was really nice to see Kylie and to get out."

"I remember those days when you're in the thick of it with the kids. You never make time for yourself, but you should."

I smiled softly, still feeling the effects of the alcohol. "It was nice. I'd almost forgotten what it was like."

Miranda patted my shoulder. "I'm happy to babysit whenever. Delaney's delightful."

"Let me pay you," I said, pulling cash out of my purse.

Miranda held up her hands. "I don't need payment. I love watching kids. There are cookies on the counter for you. I let Delaney have two before bed."

"I can't thank you enough," I said as she opened the door to leave.

"Why don't you come to family dinner on Sunday evening? That will be thanks enough."

"Of course, we'll come. Let me know if I can bring anything."

"Just that lovely girl of yours. I'll text you the address."

"See you then," I said, shutting the door behind her. I couldn't believe she thought that a thank-you for babysitting was me coming to family dinner.

She wasn't matchmaking, was she? No, that would be ridiculous. Anyone who was around Mac and me could see we didn't get along. He was perpetually irritated with me, and I was in no position to date.

If his mother thought we were a good match, she was way off base. Her son wasn't interested in commitment, and neither was I.

More nights like tonight would be fine, though. It had been good to get out and talk with friends. In South Carolina, everyone seemed to already have their group of friends or family nearby.

I sighed as I lay back on my bed, letting out the pent-up tension in my body. I was home. Even if my parents weren't living here anymore, this was where I grew up and where I'd raise Delaney. It felt right. I liked Alice and Sam, and now Miranda. They'd welcomed me into their family, and I loved it. Being interested in Mac as anything other than my contractor would mess everything up. My business, the renovation, and my new friendships.

Soon, I'd have a B&B to run. My days would be busy, and Mac wouldn't be underfoot every day. I'd forget about him. This invitation to his family dinner was a onetime thing. A way to thank Miranda for babysitting. I wouldn't let it become a weekly thing. I needed to keep my distance from Mac.

My phone buzzed, and I pulled it out of my pocket.

Mac: You make it home okay?

Natalie: I called a service.

Mac: Good.

Natalie: You know, you don't have to worry about me. Kylie has four older brothers who already look out for us.

Mac: Good to know.

I don't know why I told him that. It wasn't to make him jealous. It was to put his mind at ease. I wasn't his responsibility. Just because I was single and alone didn't mean I needed him to make sure I was okay. But it felt really nice.

Had Carter ever checked in on me when I went out with friends when we initially started dating in college? I didn't think so, but then, we were young. It didn't mean Mac was a better man than him.

But I liked it a lot. Without even changing my clothes, I drifted off with the knowledge that people cared about me. That I had a home here, and things were going to be fine.

CHAPTER 6

MAC

I didn't know what possessed me to text Natalie last night. I had her number for professional reasons. I couldn't fall asleep because I was worried she'd drive home or that some asshole would come on to her in the parking lot.

I couldn't call one of the Wilde brothers and ask; they'd give me shit for it. But I was glad to see that they'd looked after her and Kylie. They were protective of their little sister, and I was glad it extended to her friends, at least when they were in the bar or the club on their property. If Natalie was going to go out, that was the safest place for her to go.

I spent the weekend getting caught up on paperwork for the business, making sure the supplies and things we needed would arrive in time so we could stay on the proposed time line. I didn't want Natalie to worry.

I wanted all my customers to be satisfied and for the projects to be completed on time, but I felt extra pressure with the B&B. I knew Natalie needed the money that would come from reservations.

I avoided going to the site and doing any work, even though I could have used the distraction. I wasn't ready to run into

Natalie and explain why I needed to know she arrived safely home the other night.

On Sunday, I headed over to my parents'. When I got there, Mom greeted me with, "Maggie's still recovering from a stomach bug, so they won't be here."

"What?" I came to family dinners to get my Maggie fix. Now that Sam wasn't working on the B&B, I didn't see Maggie as often. Alice only occasionally brought Maggie into her new shop.

Then I came up short when I saw Natalie and Delaney in the kitchen.

When Delaney caught me staring, she said, "Mac. I brought my game for you."

"I didn't know you were going to be here."

"Your mother invited us," Natalie said.

Mom bustled into the room. "She wanted to pay me for babysitting, which is absurd. I loved hanging out with Delaney, and we made amazing cookies. You going to help with the cake later?"

"Sure," Delaney said, a little shyly.

"Perfect. I love having helpers."

"What am I?" I asked, pretending to be hurt.

"You help with a lot of things, but you're not great in the kitchen."

"That hurts."

"I can't wound your overgrown ego. I don't even worry about it."

Natalie laughed, and I couldn't take my gaze from her. She wore a soft-looking blue sweater over light-colored jeans and boots. She looked soft and comfortable. I wanted to curl up with her on the couch. I ran a hand through my hair. Where had that come from?

Delaney tugged on my hand. "Can you play with me?"

"Absolutely." I missed Maggie, but I was happy to play with

Delaney and get to know her better. I told myself it had nothing to do with her mom.

She pulled me to the living room, where we sat on the floor and sorted the cards.

"A rematch?" I asked.

"Are you up for it?" Delaney asked, handing me the green card that saved me from the exploding cards and the other five cards.

"Absolutely."

We played for a few minutes before I asked her, "What grade are you in?"

"Third."

"That was a fun grade."

"It was?"

I thought back to that time. "I have memories of playing football at recess."

"That's what you remember?" Delaney asked.

I smiled. "I think gym class was fun, as well."

Delaney laughed at that. "It's my favorite too."

"I think it's everyone's favorite." I wasn't sure if we had anything in common, but she was more mature than Maggie. She had thoughts and opinions, and I wanted to get to know her better.

"What's your favorite subject? *Real* subject," I added when I suspected she was going to run through classes like art and P.E.

"Math," she said, then she used her *see in the future* card to check the top three cards on the pile. Lifting them so I couldn't see them, she grinned at me, then turned them back over.

"What do you like about it?" I asked, wondering if I should use a *skip* card. Was Delaney tricking me into thinking there was an exploding card at the top of the pile? Taking a chance, I took the top card and breathed a sigh of relief when it was a *taco cat*.

Delaney giggled at my reaction. "Math's easy. I'm in GT."

I raised a brow when she used a second skip card. "Wow. That's impressive."

"Mom says so."

"Your mom is super smart."

"I know," Delaney said as she waited for me to make my move.

"Should I skip or take my chances?" I asked her, keeping a close eye on her expression.

She giggled, and I still wasn't sure if she was tricking me or not. "Are you scared?"

Irritated by her very familiar taunt, I said, "No," and grabbed the top card. It was an exploding kitten. "Good thing I have a *defuse* card." It was the only card that saved a player from an exploding card.

"I bet that's your only one though," Delaney said as she set down another skip card.

My hand hovered over the deck. "Is this one an exploding kitten too?"

She just smiled.

I double-checked my cards, but I didn't have any skip cards. I must have been mistaken. I turned over the card, and Delaney erupted into a fit of giggles. I threw the card in the air and fell over. "You got me."

"You're a much better sport about this when you're not playing your brothers," Mom said, coming into the room.

"Oh yeah, I would be wrestling them right now," I said, sitting up.

Natalie smiled as she followed my mom and moved to sit on the couch, observing us.

"You wrestle your brothers when you lose?"

I shrugged. "Well, yeah. But in my defense, they cheat."

Mom snorted. "That's what the loser always says."

"It's true. Tyler hides cards under the couch, and Sam used to stack the deck."

"Mmm," Mom said, her lips twitching.

"I'd love to see you three interact. I bet it's entertaining," Natalie said.

"It's something, all right," Mom said.

I feigned shock. "You're supposed to be on my side."

Mom stood and headed toward the kitchen. "I'm on Alice's side. I need you and Tyler to meet someone so I'm not outnumbered."

Thankfully, she left the room so I didn't have to answer. Usually, I reminded her I was done with women. She understood why. I'd been hurt the few times I'd tried, and I couldn't take a chance on someone else. Besides, I was happy in my house and with my business. I didn't need someone to share my life with. I ignored the pang in my chest whenever I thought that.

"Will you play with me again?" Delaney asked sweetly.

"How can I say no?" Delaney had me wrapped around her finger, and I'd just met her.

Delaney handed me the deck. "Can you shuffle? I have to go to the bathroom."

"It's on your right," I said, pointing in the direction of the kitchen.

"I heard you stuck around on Friday night," Natalie said when Delaney was gone.

"There were cookies," I said by way of explanation. The truth was a bit more complicated than that.

"Thanks for playing with her. I think she's a bit starved for male attention with her father gone. Although we didn't see him much when we were together, either."

"Sam's in a similar situation. It sucks, and you hate that for your kid, but they have one parent who's got their back, along with friends and family."

"I thought I was crazy for coming here and not having any family in the area."

It might make my life more difficult, but it was worth it for her and Delaney, so I said, "You've got us."

Natalie sighed as her shoulders relaxed. "Thank you. I know you'd probably rather not mix business and pleasure—"

Something in my head exploded at the word "pleasure." The only connotation I could think of was giving her an orgasm. A better one than I was sure her ex gave her. I had a feeling he was more concerned about his own desires, not his wife's.

"But I appreciate it," she said as she leaned over and kissed my cheek. Tingles erupted over my skin as Delaney skipped into the room and came to an abrupt stop in front of us. "Did you shuffle?"

I shook my head slowly, sifting the cards in my hands. "Sorry, I was distracted."

Delaney looked from me to her mother and placed a hand on her hip. She looked like a mini-Natalie in that pose. "Mom. Stop distracting him."

Natalie laughed, and again, I couldn't take my eyes off her. I wanted to hear that sound more often. I wanted her to be comfortable in Telluride. I wanted her to be happy.

I handed the shuffled deck to Delaney as she sat cross-legged on the ground again. I needed to figure out why I felt so strongly about this woman. Maybe it was because, up until a few years ago, she was exactly my type.

The front door opened, and I heard Tyler talking to Mom in the kitchen.

"Who's that?" Delaney asked as she counted out the cards.

"He's my pain in the—" Natalie kicked me, and I cleared my throat. "He's my brother."

Tyler came into the room, a huge smile on his face as his gaze swung from Natalie to Delaney. "I heard we have guests."

"Want to play with us?" Delaney asked him by way of greeting.

"Don't be rude," Natalie said to Delaney.

"It's okay," Tyler said as he sat with us. "I'd love to play. What's the game?"

"Exploding Kittens," Delaney said as she handed him five cards.

Tyler raised his brow. "That's what kids are playing these days?"

"What can I say? It's fun."

"You'll have to explain the rules to me," Tyler said to Delaney as he pointed a thumb in my direction. "You have to be careful of this one. He cheats."

"Like you don't," I said.

"You didn't let him shuffle, did you?" Tyler asked Delaney in a conspiratorial tone.

Delaney shrugged. "I had to go to the bathroom."

Tyler sighed. "That was your first mistake. You can't take your eyes off this one for a second."

Delaney looked from Tyler to me.

I slapped Tyler's arm. "Give her a break. She doesn't have brothers."

"You're not missing anything," Tyler said. "This guy's an as—"

I punched him in the arm again to stop him from swearing.

"Sorry," Tyler said to Natalie.

"Don't worry about it," Natalie said.

"You're the one who's renovating the B&B in town?"

"That's right."

"Everyone in town is excited about the opening. They keep giving me sh—a hard time about when it will be finished. But Mac's working overtime to get it done in time."

I was glad that Tyler had been so positive about the B&B. I knew Natalie was worried about it.

"Is that why you're working nights and weekends?" Natalie asked me.

"I enjoy working when it's quiet," I said, not sure why I was so uncomfortable with Natalie thinking I was a good guy.

"Sure you do," Tyler said, and I shot him a look. I wasn't sure what he was trying to do. Why did he care if Natalie saw me in a different light?

I cleared my throat. "Delaney, you want to teach him how to play?"

I tuned out her explanation as I snuck glances at Natalie. Had she read anything into what Tyler said? I ignored the voice in my head saying I didn't work nights and weekends on other projects. I'd never gotten so invested in something like this before.

Delays and issues were inevitable. That's why we worked extra time into the schedule and budget. I was acting differently with Natalie, and the worst part was, my brothers knew it.

I had a bad feeling about it because Natalie and Delaney stirred up my desire for a family and a home filled with people I loved. I enjoyed going to Sunday dinners at my parents', but I wanted more.

I'd just pushed those desires down deep because they hadn't worked out in the past. But what if I just hadn't met the right person yet? What if that person was Natalie? Goose bumps danced over my skin at the thought.

When I was younger, my brothers teased me that I was a romantic, always looking for a love match. The problem with that was most younger adults weren't looking for commitment. Maybe it was bad timing, and I was premature to cut things off with all women. To assume it could never work out.

But the realistic side of me, the one that had been hurt time and time again, reminded me what the pain felt like when it inevitably didn't work out. It wasn't worth the trouble.

"Do you normally invite guests to family dinner?" Natalie asked.

"Occasionally, we do," I said, to make her feel more comfortable. But the truth was, we didn't. It was our time to hang out as a family, and other than the recent addition of Alice, it was just us.

Tyler gave me a weird look but asked, "Who goes first?"

"The youngest." That's how we always played with Maggie.

Delaney used one of her cards to pick one from Tyler's pile and then picked one for herself.

Tyler looked over her shoulder. "Was it an exploding kitten?"

Delaney rolled her eyes. "No. And besides, everyone has one *defuse* card to start the game."

"What kind of game gives you a guaranteed *get out of jail* card? Or in this case, a stop-you-from-exploding card?" Tyler asked, shaking his head.

"A kids' game, I guess."

We played several rounds, teasing and joking around. Delaney seemed fascinated with the idea of having siblings. I wondered why Natalie hadn't had more kids. Had she wanted them and her asshole ex hadn't been supportive?

I tried not to let that bother me because I'd always wanted a big family. I loved the way my brothers and I interacted and how we teased but stood up for each other. I wanted the same for my kids. I mentally shook my head. I was getting ahead of myself. I'd decided it wasn't in the cards for me. Meeting one mom and her adorable daughter wouldn't change my mind.

Mom paused in the doorway. "It's time for dinner. You want to set the table?"

Tyler stood, brushing off his pants, and said to us, "No peeking at my cards."

"I don't cheat. That's you." The old retort fell easily off my lips as I turned my cards over.

Tyler headed into the kitchen without responding.

Natalie stood and said, "Come on, Delaney. We can help."

I held up my hand to her. "You're guests. You don't need to."

Natalie followed me. "It's refreshing to see men helping out around the house. It's nice for Delaney to see how a real family interacts."

I heard Mom asking Delaney what she wanted to drink.

I paused, a little surprised at her characterization. "You saw how my brothers and I interact, right? That was just a small taste. We fight, we wrestle, we swear. We're not angels."

"I didn't say you were. But you seem to love each other, and you help your parents. That's a plus in my book."

My chest warmed from her compliment. "Thank you, but I can't help but think your ex was an asshole." I tensed, worried I'd overstepped.

She laughed. "You're absolutely right. He thought the house was my domain. It was my fault for not pushing back on that assumption. I've always believed women should be able to work and have children. That their husbands should be their partners. The mental and physical load shouldn't rest on just the mother's shoulders. That's not how our marriage worked though."

"I agree." I'd spent a lot of time imagining how I wanted my family to be, and what she'd described was it. "When I was younger, I wanted the same. A partner. We'd have a big family and divide the household chores."

"You want a big family?" Natalie asked.

I could hear Tyler laughing at something Delaney was saying. As usual, our house was filled with love and laughter. My heart ached to have that for myself. Natalie was bringing up these old desires, things I thought I'd put behind me. "I did."

A crease appeared between her brows. "You don't anymore?"

"It hasn't happened, and I decided it wasn't for me."

Natalie opened and closed her mouth before she finally said, "That's sad."

I shrugged. "It is what it is. Don't feel sorry for me. I have a great life. A successful business. A close family. I'm happy." But was I?

Finally, Natalie smiled, moved closer, and patted my chest.

"There's someone out there for you. I'm sure of it."

Warmth flooded the area where her hand touched me. I wanted to cover it with mine. I wanted to lean down and taste her. There was a roaring in my ears, but she didn't seem to sense the turmoil because she turned on her heel and entered the kitchen.

I took a second to suck in a breath before I went into the fray.

"'Bout time you showed up to help," Tyler said.

"I like having Natalie and Delaney here. They're going to smooth your rough edges," Mom said, patting my shoulder as she set a pitcher of water in the middle of the table.

"I like my rough edges, thank you very much, and the women do too." Tyler smirked and then sobered when his gaze landed on Delaney. But she wasn't listening to us. She was sitting next to Dad as he told her a story about finding a snake in the yard.

Mom smacked his hand. "Don't be crass."

"Yeah, no one wants to hear about your conquests," I said.

"We have a child present. Behave," Mom hissed before heading back to the counter.

"Yeah, behave," I repeated to Tyler.

Tyler gave me a look. "She was talking to you."

"She was not."

"You guys act like kids when you're here," Natalie said, her tone amused.

"It's adorable, isn't it?" Tyler said, breaking off a piece of bread and tossing it into his mouth.

"It's something, all right," Natalie said.

I guffawed. "You're going to fit in around here." She gave as good as she got. I loved it.

"Where did your parents move?" Mom asked as she sat at the opposite end of the table as my dad.

"They moved to Arizona. My father has bad arthritis, and

the doctor said dry heat would be good for him."

"That must be tough to not have them here."

Natalie's expression softened. "I felt a little weird moving back here without them. It didn't feel like my hometown anymore."

"I hope you know you're welcome here, and everyone is tickled pink to have a new B&B in town."

When Dad went into another story about sighting a bear, I leaned in to tell Natalie, "You're something else, you know that?"

"Why do you say that?" Natalie asked.

"You hold your own with my family. You moved to a town where you didn't know many people anymore and opened a business. That's pretty badass."

Natalie stilled; her gaze flitted up to meet mine. "It is, isn't it?"

She hadn't thought of herself that way, but I had, from the moment I heard she was a single mom, moving to the area and opening the B&B. At first, I thought it was a little crazy. But you didn't do crazy without balls, and she had them in spades.

I leaned over to whisper in her ear. "Anytime you feel insecure, just remind yourself that you're Natalie Fucking Anderson, and you're a badass."

Natalie smiled widely, despite my cursing. "I like that."

"Sorry for cussing. I'm not usually so bad about it, but Tyler brings it out in me."

"Blaming me for your bad manners again, brother?" Tyler asked with his mouth full.

I raised a brow and said, "You know it."

"I don't know if I want brothers. You argue a lot," Delaney observed, and the whole table burst into laughter.

The rest of dinner went on like that, good-natured teasing and ribbing, jokes and laughter. I loved my family, and I didn't mind sharing them with Natalie and Delaney.

CHAPTER 7

NATALIE

*D*inner was an experience. A good one. I couldn't remember the last time I'd felt so happy. My stomach and cheeks actually hurt from smiling and laughing so much. Carter had a big family, but they didn't interact like this with so much love and respect for each other.

His parents looked at the boys with affection in their eyes. They loved them, and I had a feeling they would, even if they hadn't all gone into business together.

Carter's family gave the illusion of happiness, but once inside, I realized they were devoid of any emotion or connection. They hugged because it was required, not because they wanted to. They met for dinner because that's what everyone did, not what they wanted to do. There were high expectations and guilt trips.

But there was none of that with the Fletchers. They genuinely enjoyed each other's company. "Thank you so much for inviting us. We had the best time," I said to Miranda while she packed us up a to-go box.

"I'm just sorry we never got around to baking that cake. Maybe you could bring Delaney by another time and we could do it. Do you have any plans to go out with your friends, or maybe a man?"

I took the plastic container of chicken and potatoes. "Oh, I'm not dating. I'm not ready. I'm not sure I'll ever be."

"I wouldn't shut yourself off. You're a beautiful young woman. Any man would be lucky to have you."

That felt good to hear. After your husband left you, it was hard not to feel like there was something defective about you. Something inherently unlovable. That reality was that I'd chosen wrong. Carter wasn't the guy for me.

"Are you in the market for a date?" Tyler asked as he walked in.

"No," Mac said, following behind him. "She doesn't need someone like you or your friends."

Tyler rested a hand over his heart. "What are you talking about? I'm a perfectly nice guy."

Mac smiled wide so I could see his perfectly white teeth. "For that one night, you are."

Miranda sighed. "Boys. I don't need or want to hear about your love lives."

"Oh, I wasn't talking about love," Mac continued.

"It's a good thing Delaney's in the backyard with Waylon. I don't need her to hear you talking like this."

"Yeah, grow up," Tyler said to Mac.

Mac smacked him, but when he caught their mother's glare, he dropped his hands and fell silent.

"Good. Mac, walk Natalie out to her car. I'll go out back and get Delaney."

"Oh, that's not necessary," Natalie said.

"I taught my boys good manners. I know it might not seem like it, but I did my best." Miranda hugged me and said, "Come back next week when Sam, Alice, and Maggie are here. It'll be even more fun."

I found myself saying, "I'd love that."

It was nice to have a family here to visit with, even if it wasn't my own. And there was no pressure because I wasn't dating one of Miranda's sons. She was a friend. Warmth flooded my chest. I was grateful that Kylie had suggested I move back.

Mac opened the door for me to slide past him.

My shoulder brushed his chest, and it tingled with awareness. I felt like I got to know him better tonight. He wasn't grumpy with his family. He was open and loving, playful even. I loved seeing this side of him. "Thanks for having me over."

"That was all my mom," Mac said as he let the door shut behind him.

"Has she done that before?" I asked him, trying to keep the conversation going. This felt like he was walking me to my car after a date, and my heart rate was already picking up in anticipation of whether he'd kiss me at the door.

When we stopped at my car, he turned to face me, shaking his head as he chuckled. "Not quite like this."

I felt lighter than I had in years as I teased him. "I must be special."

Mac straightened, and his expression sobered. "You are special, Natalie. I hope you know that."

I licked my lips, trying to come up with a response because I had so many questions. *Why do you keep saying nice things like that? Do you like me? Do you want me? What the hell is happening here?* But his mother came around the side of the house with an arm around Delaney's shoulder.

"You come back and bake that cake, you hear? I need your help," Miranda said.

"I will, Ms. Miranda."

"Oh, it's just Miranda now. You're practically family."

My eyes widened as I caught Mac's amused face. He mouthed, "I told you so," and I felt the ridiculous instinct to giggle.

Instead, I tempered my smile as I thanked Miranda and

Waylon, who'd followed Delaney to the car, and promised to be back.

They stood together as a family, waving while we drove away. It was nice.

"Can we come back next week?" Delaney asked hopefully.

I met her eager gaze in the rearview mirror. "I don't see why not. They were fun."

"Tyler and Mac are so silly."

"They sure are, for grown men. Silly and a little ridiculous." I didn't think they were acting either. If anything, they were censoring themselves because they had guests. But I found them entertaining. It was like they fell into their old roles as kids when they were in their parents' house, and Miranda and Waylon were all too eager to let them. They loved their bickering as much as we had.

"I wish I had a brother or a sister." Delaney sighed wistfully as she gazed out the window.

"I know you do." I hated that I couldn't give her that, but soon after I had Delaney, I realized Carter wasn't going to be the father I'd hoped for my children. I kept holding out, hoping he'd change, but he didn't. He lost more interest as she got older.

I was glad we didn't have more kids. I wanted to have more children with someone who loved me and who'd stick by my side through everything. I wanted the family. The house with the white picket fence. I still wanted the dream.

"I didn't have any siblings either." I remembered how lonely I was. How much I adored Kylie and her big family. I wanted to disappear into hers. I liked to imagine I was her twin where her older brothers were mine too. Not that they paid us any attention. It was a great dream, but I always came home to my parents' empty house.

They worked a lot and didn't see a need to be home for things like dinner and homework. I was on my own. Eventually,

I concluded they either didn't want kids or decided that after one, they didn't want more. They were good parents, just not particularly engaged ones.

I couldn't complain. They checked in with me on occasional phone calls, but I wasn't expected to visit. Not even when I had Delaney. That's another reason why Carter's family had been important to me. I wanted Delaney to have a close relationship with at least one set of grandparents. Now I felt like she just got shafted all around. We had each other, and it would have to be enough.

"They're so nice. Grandma can be kind of mean." Delaney's voice was soft, as if she were afraid to admit that out loud.

"How so?" My heart stuttered as I waited for her to answer.

"She criticizes me."

"I'm sorry." I'd overlooked that, hoping that having one grandmother was better than none. But now, I was glad we'd moved. When Carter left, they defended his actions, saying he was following his heart. They never said what he did was selfish or wrong. They never acknowledged he betrayed me and abandoned his daughter.

As I entered the town limits for Telluride, I felt content. Everything was going to work out because it had to. I'd sunk my divorce settlement into the old Victorian, and I couldn't afford to keep it without paying guests.

I'd do anything to ensure Delaney felt loved and supported. Providing for her was my top priority. Meeting Mac's family was a nice development, and I wasn't going to avoid them, even if Mac was occasionally grumpy about it.

I couldn't help but wonder how he'd be in bed. I kind of preferred his growly voice to his playfulness with his brothers. I wanted him to press me against the wall and have his way with me.

But that was even more out of the question now that I was friends with his family. I couldn't lose a good babysitter, but more than that, they'd become friends. I needed that in this town, where most people were new to me. My high school friends had left, leaving only Kylie, and who knew how long she'd stick around?

That night, I had trouble getting Delaney settled for bed. She was hyper from her evening at the Fletchers', but it was good for her to meet new people, to see how other families interacted.

When she finally quieted down, I started a bath. I was looking forward to escaping into a good book. I worked hard but needed time to recharge, and Sunday evenings were it for me.

Each time my heart longed to be part of Mac's family, or for him to desire me, I reminded myself I was a recent divorcée. I had no business dating. I needed time and space to figure my life out. Besides, I wasn't sure marriage was something I wanted anymore. I had Delaney to think about.

It wasn't about what I wanted anymore. I couldn't upend her life any more than it already was.

THE NEXT WEEK, I worked on the B&B's website, going back and forth with a local designer, Piper. Alice recommended her as soon as I mentioned needing to create a website, and we immediately hit it off. She was fun and engaging and masterfully put my ideas on the website.

I wanted to get the website finished so I could start taking reservations for the spring.

Something could go wrong at any time and set the time line back. But I needed to plan for the future. I didn't want to lose customers to the other hotels and inns in the area.

Piper's brother, Henry, owned Mountain Haven Lodge, which catered more to the outdoorsy types who bought his adventure packages and tours. There were other B&Bs in town, but hopefully, there was room for more. Miranda had mentioned that townspeople were excited about the addition of another B&B, and I hoped that equated to paying guests.

The ski resort had the main lodge and cabins. But that attracted a different clientele than those who wanted to be in town, close to shops and restaurants.

My ideal customer was someone who wanted to visit the town but not necessarily ski or hike while they were here. There were already plenty of lodging options for those seeking outdoor adventure.

I wanted to draw in newlyweds or couples celebrating anniversaries and who wanted quiet time. I also wanted to make a communal space for those who wanted to dine with other couples for breakfast or sit around a fire at night. I wanted a romantic atmosphere. I wouldn't exclude families, but I wanted to cater to couples.

Maybe I could advertise it as the perfect space for a wedding party. They could rent out the whole B&B just for one family or a bridal party. I could offer a discounted package for it. My mind churned with ideas.

Piper had told me to think about ideal customers and the feeling I wanted to convey, and I think I'd finally settled on it. I might not believe in love for myself, but my romantic heart wanted it for others.

I tried to think of what would draw couples in, like amazing rooms and luxurious bathrooms. Mac had been great about adding details, such as trim and paint, that made the rooms more elegant. I wanted people to feel pampered while they were here. As if they were staying in a five-star resort and receiving the one-on-one attention they craved.

I tried not to think about what that would mean for my life. I needed a profit before I could even consider hiring more help. Thankfully, I had an arrangement with Alice. I offered her reduced rent on the room in the front in exchange for her covering the front desk at times.

Early in the renovation, Sam suggested creating an amazing outdoor space as an advertisement for his new branch of the business. He'd wanted to do it for free, so I'd said yes. But now, I was wondering if it wasn't the perfect draw for a romantic stay. I was beyond lucky that he'd offered.

I couldn't afford to pay for it, but it would make for amazing pictures once it was completed. Sam wouldn't start work on it until the rest of the renovations were complete. Mac said landscaping was done last, which meant we wouldn't have pictures for the website for a while yet.

It was discouraging, but I could still feature the room and bathrooms when those were completed. Of course, nothing was picture-ready yet. How was I going to entice people without any interior pictures? My head ached. I'd been turning this idea in my head over and over all week. Each night, when Delaney was asleep, I'd get out my notebook and laptop and brainstorm ideas.

Tonight, I sat at the front counter, hoping the location would inspire something. I finally dropped my forehead onto the wood surface, wishing I already had it figured out.

The key turned in the lock, and I lifted my head. It was too late for Alice to be here. She was at home with Sam and Maggie.

Surprised to see Mac holding boxes as he kicked the door shut behind him, I asked, "What are you doing here?"

"I wanted to drop off a delivery we got at the main office. It was supposed to come here," he grumbled.

I hurried around the counter. "Do you need help?"

"It's just a few boxes. You sit down while I bring them in."

"Are you sure?"

"I am." He set the box next to the counter with a thump. "Besides, you look exhausted."

"I am," I said, sinking back onto the high stool by the counter.

"Give me a few minutes," he said.

"Take your time." I tried to pay attention to my screen, but the words were floating in my vision.

I was vaguely aware that he was coming and going. Finally, I gave up all pretense of work and watched him as he flexed while carrying the heavy boxes and carefully placed them next to the counter.

"Whew, those were heavy," Mac said when he'd lowered the last box and closed the front door.

"What's in the boxes?" I asked as he headed toward me.

"The fixtures for the bathrooms and kitchen."

"I was just thinking about pictures for the website and how nothing is ready for a photographer yet." My shoulders lowered.

He came around the counter, crowding my space. Then he began to knead the tight muscles. "Is this okay?"

I let my head fall back. "Oh my gosh. Yes."

He worked his magic on my shoulders and upper back until I practically melted onto the stool.

"Come sit on the couch." Mac had moved it into the space shortly after I moved in. He said it was for me to relax on nights when I needed a break from the owner's suite.

"I don't know what I'm going to do once guests start arriving. I won't be able to enjoy all of this by myself anymore."

"You can block out time for you to have off or go on a vacation with Delaney."

I closed my eyes as I rested my head on the back. "I don't see that happening for a while yet. I need the business."

"My dad said you always overwork at the beginning of a business, stressed you won't turn a profit. But he wished he'd relaxed. That was when we were young, and Mom was overwhelmed with raising us. It was a tough time for them."

"I can imagine," I said, opening my eyes to observe him while he talked.

He grabbed a wineglass and a bottle of wine. I'd bought it to relax on evenings like this but was always too exhausted to uncork it. Besides, I couldn't drink the entire bottle by myself. It was better when you had someone to share it with.

He returned with two glasses, handing one to me, raising his for a toast. "To finishing the renovations and taking your first reservation."

"I'll drink to that." I touched my glass to his.

We each took a sip, and I wondered what we were doing drinking wine together.

"Why are you up so late?"

"I was trying to figure out how to advertise a construction zone."

Mac winced. "That's tough. You can't wait until everything is done?"

"I need to start taking reservations soon. I need to know that I'll have customers. I'm freaking out a little. Is doing this completely crazy? I've never owned a business or run a B&B. I've never even worked at a hotel before."

Mac gave me a look. "I told you what I think. What you're doing is brave. But it's also smart. I don't think you'll have any issues booking this place. It's right on the main drag. It's charming, and Sam's going to create that amazing outdoor space."

"I can't believe he's doing that for free."

"It's an investment into his business. It's the same thing you're doing here. You're believing in something that isn't finished yet."

"That's the hard part." How did people know that everything would work out? I didn't think I'd survive the stress.

"It's called faith."

Something passed between us then, an understanding. "I just need to believe it will work out, even when I can't see it yet?"

"That's exactly it."

"Have you ever had to do that?" I asked, curious to know more about him.

He drained his glass and looked away. "There's an opportunity, but I haven't taken it yet."

I wanted to know what he was talking about, but something told me it was personal.

He stood and left his empty glass in the sink. "I should go. I just wanted to drop off the boxes so we had them in the morning."

"Thank you for stopping by," I said, following him to the front door.

With his hand on the doorknob, he reached out to gently tuck my hair behind my ear. "It's all going to work out. Don't worry."

Tingles danced under the skin where Mac had touched me, but before I could respond, he'd opened the door and walked through it. I heard his distant, "Night, Natalie."

I wanted him to stay. I wanted to keep talking about my worries and fears and our dreams and desires in front of the fireplace while we sipped wine. It felt great to have someone to talk to, to have their support. And there was something else there, simmering just under the surface, an attraction, a desire for more.

I wanted him. I wanted to lose myself in him, no matter how irresponsible it was.

CHAPTER 8

MAC

Every time I walked through the family room at the B&B, I remembered the night I shared a glass of wine with Natalie on the couch. I liked listening to her concerns and fears, but the overriding urge was to kiss her.

That's why I drained my glass and got out of there. She was a single mom with this renovation on her hands. She didn't have time for a distraction. Besides, I wasn't the guy she'd settle down with in the end. It never worked out for me, and it wasn't likely to now.

At the door, in a moment of weakness, I touched her hair, and it was just as soft as I'd imagined. I'd wanted to pull her in to my body and feel her pressed against me. But I didn't give in to temptation. I didn't want to take the chance that she wasn't over her ex.

I didn't feel great about walking away, but that didn't stop me from avoiding her. Every time I thought about talking to her, or wanted her company, I reminded myself why women never chose me in the end.

I headed upstairs to the bathroom, desperate to work in solitude so I could escape my thoughts. But at the end of the hall, I drew up short, because Delaney was sitting on the deep windowsill, her knees bent as she hugged them tightly.

I hesitated, unsure what to do. Was she looking for a second to herself, or was she upset? I wasn't sure whether I should stay or get her mother. Before I could decide, she looked up. Her eyes glimmered with tears.

I sat gingerly on the other edge of the window. "Is everything okay?"

She looked at a paper on the windowsill between us that I hadn't noticed until now. I picked it up gingerly, unsure what I'd find. What would get a nine-year-old this upset?

It was a school flyer about a daddy-daughter dance. You could bring a dad, a grandfather, or any special person in your life. "Do you want to go?" I asked tentatively, nervous about stepping into an emotional minefield.

She nodded and bit her lip.

"Is your dad—" I couldn't finish that sentence because I knew the answer. As long as Delaney and Natalie had been living here, he'd never visited. I never heard them talk about him. It was like he didn't exist.

"I called to ask him, but he said he was too busy to travel." Her voice was rough from the emotion clogging her throat.

My heart broke for her. "Does your mom know?"

Delaney shook her head slowly. "I haven't talked to her yet."

"You should. Moms are good at this stuff." That was a Band-Aid because I wasn't sure how to handle this situation, and it was Natalie's place to say the right things, not me. No one could replace her father, and she'd always feel the sting of that abandonment. I hated that I couldn't erase that for her.

"And your grandfathers?"

"They live so far away. I couldn't ask them to travel to see me."

"That's sweet of you to consider that." She was empathetic

for such a young child, but then maybe she was getting used to giving others around her excuses.

"It says you can bring any special person." I read from the paper, trying to think of the right thing to say.

"Would you go with me?" For the first time, her eyes cleared, and her shoulders lowered.

There was only one answer, and it felt right in my soul. "Are you sure you want me to be your special person?"

She nodded as she swiped the tears away.

My heart contracted at her response. "You know, you could take your mother."

"There's already an event for mothers and daughters. Besides, everyone's going to be there with their dads."

"You know you're not the only one in this situation," I said gently.

Her lips quivered.

"Does your dad normally come to events like this?" I wasn't sure which was worse, a stand-up dad who disappeared or one who'd never been there at all.

"I've never had a school dance before, so I'm not sure."

I wanted her to feel better and forget about the people who'd let her down. "I'd be happy to go with you. What should I wear? A tux?"

Delaney's lips twitched as she lowered her knees and scooted closer to me so she could read the flyer. She pointed at the paper where it said it wasn't a black-tie event.

I tapped my chin with my finger. "I have just the thing."

"No jeans or T-shirts," Delaney said seriously.

"What do you take me for? I'm a gentleman. I'll pick you up and—" My mind was already whirring with ideas. She'd need a bouquet of flowers.

"Where are you taking my daughter?" Natalie stood in front of us, her hands on her hips.

My heart raced in my chest as I handed her the flyer. I completely forgot we needed to run this past her mother.

"He's taking me to the daddy-daughter dance," Delaney said, excitement tinging her voice as Natalie read the form.

When she lifted her gaze, she asked, "Are you crying?"

Delaney shook her head. "I was but not anymore."

"Honey, I think you should ask your father first," Natalie said.

Delaney's expression fell. "I did."

"He said no, didn't he?" Natalie's jaw tightened, and her fingers tightened on the school form.

"He said he was busy." Delaney's voice was small and full of pain.

"I'd like to take her if that's okay with you," I said to Natalie, desperate to get Delaney's mind off her father's rejection.

"Delaney, why don't you go to our room and get started on your homework. I need to talk to Mac."

"Mom—"

"I'll be there in a minute. Go."

"Ugh. Fine," she huffed and then jogged toward the steps.

"I'm sorry. I should have discussed it with you before I told her I'd go." This was just one more reason why I wasn't a good bet for a single mother. I didn't know how to handle these situations.

Natalie sat on the windowsill next to me. "I should have known this was coming and prepared her father for her invitation."

"Would it have changed anything?" I asked her.

Natalie sighed as she leaned against the window. "Probably not."

"It's not your job to prepare him for a call from his daughter. He could have made a different decision." He could have made a lot of different ones. His bad decisions were why Natalie and

Delaney were here, and I couldn't be upset with him about it. My life seemed more interesting with them in it.

"I don't want her to be hurt."

"He's going to do things that hurt her feelings, and there's nothing you can do about it other than be there for her. If you want to take her to the dance, I'll step aside. But honestly, she seemed happy with the idea of me taking her."

"It would be amazing if you could, but I can't ask that of you."

I wanted to go with Delaney. "I want to. I'm excited about it."

"You are?" Natalie asked, her voice tentative.

My mind tripped over to that list of things I'd need to make the night special for Delaney. "I already have my suit picked out. Are you taking her shopping for a new dress?"

"I can," she said, carefully considering me.

"I think I'll—" I didn't want to tell her all my plans. I wanted some things to be a surprise. "We'll go big. Maybe I could take her to dinner before."

Natalie shifted so that she was sitting cross-legged on the windowsill. "You don't have to do that—or any of this. It's not your job to fix things after her father crushed her."

"Maybe not, but I want to. I want to make that girl smile. I want her to be happy. I don't want her to be the only girl in that room without a dad." My heart ached for everything she was feeling, a sense of loss, confusion, abandonment, and doubt.

Natalie gave me a sad smile. "You know she won't be."

"But she'll feel like she is."

Natalie sucked in a breath. "You're right. It doesn't matter if someone else is in the same situation. It matters that she is."

I touched her knee. "Let me do this for her."

"If you're sure?" she asked, her eyes on mine.

I stood, determined to make this night special. "I haven't had a date this important in years. I'm going to make her feel special."

Natalie stood close, placing the palm of her hand on my cheek. "You're kind of amazing, you know that?"

Our gazes caught and held. My breathing felt erratic. I couldn't slow the beat of my heart.

"I can't believe you haven't found your person yet," Natalie said wistfully as she dropped her hand and stepped back.

"I don't know if everyone gets that. But I plan on being the best uncle to my niece and friend to Delaney." I hoped that didn't sound as pathetic to her as it did to me.

Natalie made a move to leave. "I can't thank you enough. I'm going to tell her the date is on."

"When I saw her crying by herself, I couldn't take it. I'd do anything to make her smile."

Natalie touched my chest. "You're a good man, Mac."

I didn't know about that, but she'd already walked away.

I tried not to think about how, if one of my other relationships had panned out, I'd be going to my daughter's dance. That wasn't in the cards for me, but I could make Delaney happy. She was a part of my protected circle. I'd do anything for her.

When women broke up with me in the past, they'd said we didn't want the same things. But I took that to mean they didn't want me. I'd accepted that I'd be alone. So why did my heart ache for something more with Natalie? She was no different from my exes.

It was shortsighted to start something with her, knowing my history. I thought I had successfully shed any romantic notions of relationships and morphed into a realist. Now, I wasn't so sure. But I could make a difference in Delaney's life by going to this dance, by showing her she was the most important girl in my life. She deserved it, even if her idiot father didn't understand the damage he was inflicting on her.

If Natalie's ex ever showed up in Telluride, I wanted to have a word with him. But I didn't even know his name. I couldn't imagine my father walking away. He'd always been there for us.

We went into business together. Delaney didn't deserve any of the things that were happening to her, and I'd do my best to create a magical evening for her.

* * *

THE NEXT DAY, I tracked Delaney down outside the B&B after school. She was on the swing the guys had hung on the mature tree in the backyard.

"Mac," she said with a hint of a smile on her face when she saw me.

"Do you have any favorite colors?"

"Pink and purple," she said without hesitation.

"Yeah? That will work perfectly." Last night, Alice had shown me a few bouquets of flowers that would be pretty for a little girl, and I'd fallen in love with the peonies. It wouldn't be easy to get this time of year, but I would.

"For what?"

"Mmm. It's a surprise." After I put my phone away, I asked, "Where do you want to go to dinner before the dance?"

She planted her feet on the ground to stop her momentum. "We're going to dinner?"

"A man should always take you to dinner before a dance," I said seriously.

"And I can pick anywhere I want to go?" Her eyes were wide.

My heart skipped a beat. Had I gone too far? "Uh-huh."

"So, I could say pizza or burgers?" she asked slowly.

"You're my date, and I'll take you wherever makes you happy."

Her eyes lit up and then dimmed. "What if I said I prefer salmon?"

My eyes widened at that. "I'd be impressed with your taste."

"Then I'd like to get salmon and watch Irish dancers."

I'd already thought of a fancier restaurant that served

amazing salmon, but she'd thrown me with the Irish dancer request. "Are you serious about the dancers?"

"They were at an assembly last year at school. They were fun to watch. It's okay if you don't want to."

I held up a hand. "Let me do some research and see what I can figure out. If I can't find something in town, we can find something for our next outing."

"What are you two up to?" Natalie asked as she came outside.

"We're just settling our plans for the big dance. Delaney requested salmon and Irish dancers," I said.

Natalie frowned. "Delaney—"

"It's fine. I asked her what she wanted to do. I like to plan the perfect evening for my dates."

Natalie's eyes sparked with interest. Was she thinking about what it would be like if I took her on a date? I'd always gone overboard in the past, and women had said it was too much. But with a nine-year-old, I was confident *too much* was just right.

"I'm a little jealous about your night out," Natalie teased Delaney.

"You need to go out too, Mom," Delaney said, her words tugging at my heartstrings.

Natalie smiled. "That would be nice."

I wondered if she was thinking about how long it had been since a man had taken her out, brought her flowers, or bothered to find out her preferences.

"I'm sure you two have things to do. I'll go clean up and get out of your hair." The crew had already cleared out for the day.

"Why don't you join us for dinner?" Delaney asked. "If you're going to be my date to the dance, we should probably get to know each other better."

Natalie laughed. "She has a point."

I looked toward the house, uncertain how I should play this. "I don't expect you to cook for me."

"Why don't we go out to eat?" Delaney asked, excitement filling her voice.

"We haven't eaten out since we moved here," Natalie said.

"Then it's a date. I'll run home and shower, and we'll get out of here. If that's okay with you?" I asked Natalie.

Natalie smiled softly. "That sounds great."

"Perfect. You two ladies think of the perfect spot."

"We don't know any of the new places here," Natalie said.

"Think of what you're in the mood for, then. I'm up for whatever," I said, before heading home to clean up.

I rushed through my shower, wanting to get back to them. Delaney had made a good point that we needed to get to know each other better. I wanted her to be comfortable, but I couldn't help but think she might have an ulterior motive for going out. Did she sense something between me and her mother? At this point, I wasn't sure I could stop myself from falling for both her *and* her mother.

I wanted to take care of both of them. I wanted to take them out and give them a good time. Tonight would be casual, but I'd love to take them to one of the fancier restaurants.

On the drive home, Sam called. "Hey, just checking in."

"Everything's going good," I said as I signaled to make a turn.

"Hopefully that continues." Sam's deep voice filled the cabin of my truck.

"I want to get the B&B done so Natalie can start taking reservations. She mentioned she can't take pictures of an unfinished project."

"No. She can't. We're working as fast as we can. I can pull more people from other projects if you need it."

"Don't worry. I've got this."

"You want to come over for dinner tonight? Maggie missed you on Sunday."

"I wish I could, but I have a date."

The truck was silent for a few seconds. I checked to make

sure the call hadn't disconnected when Sam asked, "What did you say?"

"I said I have a date, but don't get too excited. It's with a nine-year-old. Delaney asked me to go to the daddy-daughter dance with her, and I said yes. She asked if we could go out before to get to know each other."

"You're taking her to the dance?" Sam asked, his tone cautious.

"She was crying because her dad couldn't or wouldn't come. The flyer said she could take someone special to her. It didn't need to be a dad or grandfather, so I said I'd go."

Sam whistled before he asked, "Are you someone special to her?"

My jaw tightened. I didn't like where he was going with this. "Not yet. That's why we're hanging out."

"Are you sure this is a good idea?"

A muscle ticked in my jaw. "Why do you ask?"

"It's just... Natalie's a single mom. They've been through a lot—a divorce, moving across the country—"

"You don't need to tell me what they've been through. I know. I was the one who found Delaney crying."

The cabin fell silent.

"This is some serious shit, you know. You can't just swoop in and out of their lives. If you're going to be invested, you need to be there."

"I intend to." I clenched my teeth.

"As friends or something else?"

"As friends." For now. There was no denying that I was attracted to and intrigued by Delaney's mother.

"What if Natalie starts dating someone else? I overheard Alice asking to set her up with a blind date."

"Are you serious?"

"She's single. Why not?"

"You said yourself she's not ready. She just got divorced." I didn't know the time line on that, but it had to be somewhat recent.

"But she's ready for you in her life?"

"As a friend."

Sam was quiet for a few minutes as I pulled into the driveway and shut the truck off. "I don't want you to get hurt either."

"How would I get hurt?" I asked, already knowing what he'd say. My family had been concerned about me after the last breakup because I'd sworn off relationships. It was so unlike me, but it was necessary if I wanted to protect my heart.

"There was a time when you wouldn't have hesitated to ask Natalie out. Those two are perfect for you."

I shook my head, even though he couldn't see me over the phone. "Not after what happened last time. You don't have to worry about me."

"Rae went back to her ex," Sam said.

"That's right." I was a diversion. I'd swooped in and tried to save someone who didn't want or need to be saved.

"You fell in love with her kid too."

I rubbed the all-too-familiar ache over my chest. "That won't happen this time."

"Kids are easy to love. I think Alice fell in love with Maggie before me." His tone was filled with affection.

"Of course, she did. I still don't know what she's doing with you."

"Shut up. We're talking about your situation."

"I don't want Delaney going to that dance alone. Besides, I already agreed to go. I'm not backing out now."

"Of course not. I just want you to be careful. You have a big heart."

"I used to have a big heart." Now it was wrapped up in barbed wire, or at least that's what I liked to think.

"I don't think anyone changes that much. You've always wanted a family."

"I'll get the dog. That'll satisfy my need to care for others."

"You know that's not enough."

"Are you done? I promised someone a date."

"Just be careful. I love you."

"Love you too." Warmth flooded my chest because we rarely said we loved each other. My parents said it freely, but my brothers and I liked to pretend we hated each other. It was a good reminder that I already had an amazing family; I didn't need to build one for myself. I'd be fine as the perennial bachelor with the house and a dog but no wife or kids. I'd be the best damn uncle and friend there was. That had to be enough. Because there wasn't another option for me.

CHAPTER 9

NATALIE

*D*elaney insisted on changing her outfit to a dress over leggings, and I took extra care with my appearance. I felt flutters in my stomach as we got ready. I never felt like this when I went out with Carter during our marriage, but maybe that was normal in a long-term relationship.

Delaney wanted to go to the brick-oven pizza place, which was fine with me. This was a good way for Mac to get to know Delaney better.

As we waited for Mac to return, I couldn't help but think that he'd be an amazing father. He was a great uncle, and he was amazing with Delaney. He was sweet and conscientious. The day I found him soothing Delaney, I thought my heart was going to burst out of my chest.

He said he wanted to make her feel better by attending the dance, but he'd been genuinely excited about going. It was clear he wanted to plan something special. Who knew the way to my heart was through my daughter's?

Mac had softened my resolve with that one act. His resistance must have been stronger than mine because nothing had changed between us. Maybe he'd written off all women because of a past experience.

I hoped he wouldn't hurt Delaney. It was only natural he'd drift away when the renovation was complete. As much as I needed this renovation to be done so I could start taking reservations, I enjoyed having Mac in my space.

I was hyperaware when he was on-site. I loved listening to the rumble of his voice while he talked to his crew, giving instructions or joking around. If I was being honest with myself, he was the reason I worked at the front counter. I wanted to be near him, even when something more between us wasn't logical.

When a soft knock sounded on the door, Delaney dropped her book and jumped up to answer it.

I saw Mac's silhouette through the door, so I didn't stop her.

"You're here," my daughter said to Mac, and my heart contracted. His hair was damp from his shower, and he smelled faintly of aftershave. It was a heady combination.

Mac's gaze met mine over her head, and my face heated at where my mind had gone—Mac naked in his shower, water flowing over the hard angles of his muscles. Had he thought of me?

Mac winked at me before stepping inside. "I said I'd be here, didn't I?"

Since the updates, he'd been to our personal quarters one other time when his mother was babysitting, and I'd forgotten how his presence seemed to take up all the available space.

Delaney merely nodded, but I sensed the insecurity swirling inside her.

Mac dropped down to her level, meeting her gaze, and said, "I always keep my promises."

Delaney tilted her head to the side as if she were considering him.

He smiled softly, and my heart ached. "You don't have to believe me yet. I'll prove it to you."

I looked forward to that. A man who didn't let us down would be a nice change. Carter frequently said he'd be somewhere and then didn't show up. We stopped expecting him to after a while.

Mac stood without waiting for her response and revealed a bouquet of flowers he'd hidden behind his back.

"For me?" Delaney asked hopefully.

Mac smiled wide. "Yes, for you, beautiful girl."

"They're gorgeous," I said, moving a chair to get the vase I'd placed in the seldom-used cupboard above the fridge.

"I'll get it," Mac said, easily opening it, finding the vase, and pulling it down. "Is this what you wanted?"

"Yes, thank you." I filled the vase with water and took the arrangement from Delaney so I could trim the stems and place them carefully into the water.

Delaney sniffed the petals once I'd set the vase on the counter. "These smell nice."

"Beautiful flowers for beautiful girls."

I let out a sigh at his words. I could close my eyes and almost imagine he was here to take us out for real. I let his words settle over me like the stars blanketing the sky on a clear night.

"Want to see my room?" Delaney asked, holding her hand out to him.

"I renovated your room, remember? I can't wait to see what you've done with it." Mac turned back to me with a wink as he let her lead him down the hall.

My heart pitter-pattered in my chest. I wouldn't survive this. How could there be this seemingly perfect man in our lives who had valid reasons not to get involved with a woman and her daughter? Yet, here he was, taking us out to dinner and escorting my daughter to a school dance.

He was interested but wouldn't let himself make a move? I

wish I knew more about him. I had a feeling that, even if I knew all his reasons for him staying away from us, I wouldn't be able to change his mind.

My reasons for waiting to pursue something went out the window when he was sweet-talking my daughter or bringing us flowers. He'd done so many thoughtful things already: renovating the owner's suite so we could move in, arranging for a couch to be delivered to the family room of the B&B, and introducing us to his family so I'd have their support too.

He was a good man, and he'd be perfect for any woman. Why couldn't he see that? Or was it me he didn't want? I didn't like that thought.

Mac and Delaney returned to the kitchen, laughing about the number of stuffed animals on her bed. "How do you even have room to sleep?"

"I move them to my chair," Delaney said, her sweet face upturned to his.

Mac raised a brow. "Your chair is covered in stuff animals too."

"There's plenty of room," Delaney insisted.

"If you say so," Mac said lightly to her before asking me, "You ready for dinner?"

"I am." But the thumping of my heart was telling me a different story. I wanted more with Mac, despite my recent divorce, my daughter, and the B&B.

Delaney covered her stomach. "I'm starved."

"You're always hungry." I ruffled her hair.

"Are you a bottomless pit? That's what my mom always said to me," Mac said.

"Yeah?" Delaney asked as they headed out the door.

I grabbed my purse and keys, taking a second to myself to recover from the sweetness that was Mac with my daughter.

"I'll drive," Mac said when he saw me head to my SUV.

"Oh, that's okay. I'm sure you want to head home after

dinner. I bet you're tired. Your job is so physical." Then I blushed because I'd essentially admitted I was aware of his fit body. He'd reduced me to a girl with a crush.

"When I say I'm taking my girls out, I'll drive."

"Please? I want to see his truck," Delaney pleaded, and Mac was already opening the back door to his truck.

I couldn't resist these two when they wanted something.

His truck was an extended cab with a car seat in the back.

"I bought this so I could take Maggie with me."

"Do you babysit her often?" I asked to cover the effect his admission was having on my system. I felt warm all over.

Carter never had a car seat in his car. He said it would ruin his leather seats. It was a great excuse for him to never take Delaney anywhere by himself.

"I love spending time with her, so I don't see it as babysitting. She's my niece, you know?" He gave me a soft look that had my heart flip-flopping in my chest.

He was literally killing me.

Then he lifted Delaney into the backseat, and she sat on the leather. "This is so cool."

"You need help with the seat belt, or do you have it?" Mac asked while I struggled to suck in air.

"I got it," Delaney said as she reached for the seat belt.

Mac waited until it was secure before closing the rear passenger side door and opening mine.

"You need a boost?" he asked, his voice amused, as if he knew what was running through my head.

There was a running board, so I said, "I've got it." I wouldn't survive with his hands on me. I'd combust into tiny pieces he'd have to put back together.

He waited until I was in and then shut the door.

My heart was pounding in my chest. What had I gotten myself into? Was this a friendship? If so, I wouldn't survive it. I was falling more and more for him with each word and soft look. He was the man I would have imagined for myself if I could conjure up the perfect one.

In the cab, his scent pervaded my senses, making me feel a little weak in the knees. It was a mix of soap and sawdust. As I looked around to distract myself, I was impressed he kept his work truck so clean. Was his house the same? Did he live in an apartment or a house?

"Do you live in town?" I asked, wanting to know more about him. Where did he go when he went home at the end of the night? What did he do in his spare time? Or did he fill it with work because he was lonely?

"I built a house near my parents' home a few years ago when it looked like—" He glanced at Delaney in the rearview mirror.

"When it looked like what?" I asked.

He glanced over at me, then returned his attention to the road. "Marriage wasn't in the cards for me."

"Why would you say that?" I couldn't stop myself from asking. He'd mentioned this when I was at his parents' house for dinner, but he hadn't explained his reasoning. I was dying to know the answer.

He shrugged. "It didn't work out, but that's a story for another time."

I understood he didn't want to talk about it in front of Delaney.

He flashed a smile at me, then at Delaney in the back. "My house is nice, but it feels empty."

"I can help you with that," Delaney said from the backseat. "Mom said I fill every room with my infectious energy."

Mac chuckled, reaching over to squeeze my hand and quickly letting go. "Is that right?"

I smiled over my shoulder at Delaney. "Our house never feels quiet or empty."

Delaney nodded. "Except when I'm in school."

Turning toward the front, I teased, "I don't know. I can feel your presence even then." I spent twenty minutes after the bus picked her up, cleaning up the mess she'd made from her room to the kitchen, then to the living room. She was a human tornado.

Mac met Delaney's gaze in the rearview mirror. "I'll have to have you over sometime so you can fill my place with this energy."

I admired the cut of his jaw and the line of his throat. His shirt was a polo that opened, revealing a light dusting of chest hair and tan skin.

"I can come over," Delaney said sweetly.

I loved my daughter. She was so caring and kind. I hoped that meant I was doing something right with her and that her father's actions hadn't irrevocably changed her.

"Perfect. I can't wait. I have this amazing outdoor space where you can make s'mores."

"Did Sam build that for you?" I asked him.

Mac nodded as he stopped at a red light. "He's practiced on our houses. He started with his own, then did mine, and now he's pressuring my dad to do his."

"Your family's great." I couldn't help but love how different they were from Carter's.

"I know I'm lucky. I think they were what made me want something similar for myself. But I'm starting to think that kind of love and acceptance is rare."

"Maybe." I was divorced and hadn't found anything like what Mac's parents had either, so I wasn't an expert. I tended to have a positive outlook on life. Now that Carter was in my rearview mirror, I wanted someone for myself at some point. It didn't have to be now, but I couldn't help but think Mac might be the one.

Mac drove to the brick-oven restaurant and found a parking space on the street nearby. He helped Delaney down. She stood between us, holding our hands as we walked on the sidewalk. To anyone else, we looked like a happy couple.

It was dangerous because I could see us doing this again. Despite what Mac said, he was born to be with someone. He wasn't like any other man I'd met who was anti-commitment. So he was telling himself he couldn't have it, and I'd love to know why. It couldn't be just that one woman who'd hurt him.

Besides, he had an amazing example of a good relationship with his parents. They seemed so happy and in love.

The hostess sat us by the window.

"I love this little town. I didn't realize how much until I moved back."

"I'm glad you did. Your B&B will be perfect for the town, and I think you're going to love it here."

"I can't wait to see snow," Delaney said, staring out the window at people walking by.

"We didn't get any snow in South Carolina."

The waitress stopped to take our order, and we ended up getting two pizzas because we couldn't agree on a topping.

"Have you been skiing yet?" Mac asked as he gathered the menus and handed them to the waitress.

"Nope," Delaney said.

"I can take you. I know your mom hasn't been either."

I raised a brow at Mac. What was he doing? First the dance, then dinner, an invitation to his house, and now skiing? It sounded like he wanted to spend time with us, even if it was just as friends. He thought we were lonely, and he was stepping in to help. Or maybe his mother put him up to it. My stomach dropped at that idea.

"Can we? Please?" Delaney asked.

"I don't want to take up too much of Mac's time. He's already taking you to the dance."

"I don't mind," Mac said.

"Are you sure? I don't want to be a burden." I couldn't stop thinking about how Carter wouldn't have wanted to spend time with us.

"I enjoy hanging out with you."

At his words, we both relaxed. Delaney chatted happily about what a ski lesson at the Wilde Resort would be like. Then Mac pulled out his phone to show her the lift that ran from a barn in town up the mountain to the resort.

"There's a restaurant midway up the mountain. I should take you there sometime." Mac showed her the picture of the restaurant.

"I've never been there," I admitted.

"It's really cool. I'd love to show you."

When the food arrived, the server handed us each a slice, and we dug in. Delaney talked about the news at school and how the fifth-grade anchors were hilarious. I was a little surprised when Mac listened attentively and asked questions. He seemed genuinely interested. He even asked if he could see a video of it online.

When the bill came, Mac paid it.

When we walked out, I said, "Thank you for dinner."

"It was my pleasure."

I couldn't stop thinking of the night we'd gotten soaked with the leaky faucet. What would have happened if we'd let go and acted on our instincts?

We rode home in silence. Delaney was probably tired. At home, I sent her to take a shower and get ready for bed.

Mac hovered by the door.

"Thank you for dinner. It was nice to get out."

"You have my mom to babysit if you want to go out with your friends, and I'm always happy to spend time with you two."

I stepped closer to him, my heart pounding in my chest. "I had a nice evening, but what is this? Are we friends?"

"I'd say we are."

"Are you ever going to tell me why you don't believe in

marriage?" I asked softly, in case Delaney stepped out of the bathroom.

Mac looked away, clearly uncomfortable with the question. "Let's just say... I dated a few women who weren't for me."

"So you've written off all women?"

His lips pressed into a tight line. "Something like that."

The why didn't matter because I wasn't prepared to offer him anything.

"I wanted more than they wanted to give. I wanted marriage, family, and the house with the white picket fence. I wanted everything."

That admission sent a pang through my heart. "And they didn't?"

He shook his head. "One said she wasn't ready for that yet. To be fair, we were young, just out of college."

"Plenty of people get engaged their last year in college or soon after."

"Obviously, she wasn't the one for me. Then I dated a single mother who was recently separated from her husband. That was my mistake."

I winced. "She went back to him?"

"She was just biding her time with me." His tone was bitter.

My heart ached for him. "You thought it was something more."

"I thought we had a future. But it didn't mean anything to her. I was just a distraction."

"I'm sorry, Mac. You didn't deserve that."

I could see him so clearly now. His heart was huge, and he was easily hurt. So much so that he'd withdrawn. Maybe even believed there was something wrong with him, not the women he'd dated.

He stepped back, and the physical distance between us felt like a chasm I couldn't cross. "It's getting late. I'm going to head out."

I had so much more to say, but he was retreating. I was going to let him, but this conversation wasn't done. I walked him out the door. "Thank you for tonight."

"Anytime."

I opened the door. "You're great with her, you know."

Mac grinned, looking younger, more carefree. "Kids love me."

"They do, but you make an effort, and she sees that."

Mac shook his head. "Don't get me started on her dad. He's—"

"Not even worth talking about."

"That's for sure." Then he waved a hand at me. "Enjoy the rest of your night."

"We will."

I stood there, watching him go, when Delaney suddenly appeared in her pajamas. "Mac?"

He turned. "Yeah?"

"When can I see you again?" She looked up at him with so much hope in her eyes.

"Delaney—" I reached for her, but she was running across the grass in her bare feet and nightgown before I could stop her.

He reached down and gathered her in his arms. He talked to her in a tone too low for me to hear. Then he set her down. "Now, get to bed before you get me in trouble with your mother."

"It's cold," I chided. "Get inside."

"I just wanted to say good-bye," she said.

"Next time, put on some shoes and a coat."

"Listen to your mother, Del."

"Yeah, yeah," she said, slipping inside.

"Mind your attitude."

She looked back at me. "I don't even know what that means."

I let out a breath and met Mac's amused gaze. "Good night."

"Night, Natalie. Sweet dreams." He turned and walked away as I closed the door.

"What were you thinking running out there like that?" She'd run into his arms like she'd expected him to catch her, which he had, but still. What made her so confident in Mac? Or was that the eternal optimism of young kids?

Delaney shrugged. "I just wanted to say good-bye before he left."

"What did he say to you?"

"That I should listen to you, and he'd see me soon."

Warmth spread from my chest to every inch of my body. Mac was getting to me. "He's right. Now, let's get you tucked in."

I followed her to her tiny bedroom, and we settled onto the bed to read a book. I barely registered the meaning of the words because I couldn't get the picture of Delaney running to him out of my head.

It was some kind of crazy trust exercise to believe he'd catch her, and he kept surprising me. He was giving her exactly what she needed: male attention and respect. He said he never made promises he couldn't keep. I hoped that was true.

I couldn't handle one more man breaking my little girl's heart.

CHAPTER 10

MAC

Tonight was the daddy-daughter dance, and I was nervous. Sam and Alice had come over with Maggie while I was getting ready. They were a good distraction. Escorting Delaney to the dance was a big deal, a privilege I didn't take lightly.

Sam kept trying to tell me to remember that, but I couldn't forget it, even without his constant reminders. Delaney needed someone in her life, and I didn't mind being the man she could count on. I didn't know what it meant for Natalie and me, but I would be there for Delaney, regardless. I never went back on my word. I knew all too well how it felt when someone let you down.

Alice came into the bedroom to help me with my tie.

"No jumping on the bed, Maggie," Alice said, her attention on my tie.

"But Mac says it's okay," she said without missing a jump.

Alice paused and raised one brow at me.

I cleared my throat, knowing I was in trouble. "I didn't know it was a hard no."

Alice returned to her task with jerky hands. "Let me spell it out for you, Mac. Jumping on a bed is always a no. She could fall and hurt her head."

"Maggie, you heard your mother." I paused because I'd called Alice her mother when she wasn't, but neither Alice nor Maggie said anything. Maggie's actual mother, Felicia, didn't visit often, and maybe Maggie saw Alice as her mother. I already did.

Maggie jumped from the bed to the floor and raced out of the room to her father, who gave in more easily than Alice.

"That was nice to hear," Alice murmured as she finished the knot and stepped back to admire her work.

I moved to the mirror, satisfied with the results. "Thank you for the help. Maggie doesn't mind? It just slipped out."

"Not at all. She's already asked if she can call me that."

"What does Sam say?" I turned to face her.

"He said it's her decision as long as it's okay with me."

"And it is." There was no question that Alice adored Maggie, and she had from the beginning when she took the job as Sam's nanny. We teased Sam that he wouldn't be able to resist his young, hot nanny, but Alice was so much more than that. She was exactly what Sam and Maggie needed in their life.

Alice patted my shoulder. "Have fun tonight. Treat Delaney like a princess."

"Oh, I intend to. I have a bouquet of flowers and a corsage. Hopefully, I didn't forget anything."

"What about the necklace?" Alice asked as she opened the box for the corsage.

Panicked, I asked, "What necklace? Was I supposed to get something?"

Alice laughed as she lowered the box and closed it. "No, silly. I was just teasing."

"That wasn't very nice," I grumbled. I wanted the evening to be perfect for Delaney. I didn't want her to have even a moment where she wished her father were present.

Alice sat on the bed while I searched the closet for my dress shoes. "You're really invested in her, aren't you?"

"Delaney?"

Alice smiled softly. "Did you think I meant Natalie?"

"Of course not," I said from the closet. I grabbed the shoes I wanted and sat on the foot of the bed to put them on. "I found Delaney crying about the dance one day, and I couldn't not say yes to going with her. Besides, I'm excited about it too. It will be fun."

This was what I envisioned when I thought about being a dad. Doing this with Delaney fulfilled that need for me. At least that's what I told myself.

"You want a family," Alice said, picking at the stitching on my comforter.

"Sure," I said, standing in front of the mirror to pull on my suit jacket. I didn't get many opportunities to dress up. I usually saved suits for fundraisers the company was invited to, and I was expected to appear with my dad. My younger brothers usually didn't attend those events.

"If you've bonded with Delaney, does that mean you're interested in Natalie?"

"Being interested and acting on something are two different things," I said gruffly.

"So you are interested, but you're not going to make a move?" Alice asked, disbelief tinging her words.

I nodded, my jaw tight. "That's right."

Alice's forehead wrinkled. "Why not?"

My jaw felt tight. "I'm not the right guy for her."

"You want a family, and I'm sure she wants the same. She wants to be with a guy who loves her and her daughter."

"It's more complicated than that."

"If it's so complicated, explain it to me."

I stretched my neck to work out the kinks and sighed.

"Women don't see me as a family guy. I'm just a way to pass the time. I'm a good boyfriend but nothing else."

"Bullshit."

I startled at her curse. I didn't think I'd ever heard her swear before. She'd spent a lot of time with her niece, Amelia, and now Maggie. But I think it was something she was raised not to do. She was born into a rich family and called herself a socialite. Not that she was anymore. You don't break old habits like those.

"You're making excuses without even trying."

"That's not it," I said, even though I suspected she was right.

"You're closing yourself off. Trust me, I recognize the signs. I did it for years, pretended I didn't have desires because I didn't trust my judgment."

I didn't know the whole story with Alice, but there was some guilt about how she'd treated her sister, almost breaking up Elle and Gray. She'd tried to make amends by watching their daughter, Amelia, when she was little. Sam mentioned she didn't think she was worthy of a good man like him. She didn't see herself as a good person. It caused some friction between the two of them before she got over it. "How do you get past it?"

Alice smiled sadly. "You forgive the people who hurt you, and more importantly, you forgive yourself."

I ignored the latter because I was not in the right space for that. "How do you excuse their behavior? If Rae thought she'd get back with her ex, why did she string me along?" I'd felt like such a fool.

"You're not excusing their behavior. You forgive them to free yourself."

I'd never heard it explained that way before, and it sounded strangely enticing. Before I could ask what that looked like, Maggie ran into the room. "Are we going home to watch the movie now?"

"We promised her a movie if she'd come over to see you off,"

Sam said with an apologetic smile as he followed her into the room.

"I see how it is. You have to be bribed to come to Uncle Mac's house."

Maggie climbed onto the bed and held her arms up to me. I couldn't refuse her, so I lifted her into my arms, ignoring her suspiciously sticky hands. Then she patted my cheek. "I love you, Uncle Mac."

"I love you too, sweetness."

She smiled widely. "You're the best uncle ever."

It was a running joke between Tyler and me. She usually only said it when one of us was present. "Don't let Uncle Tyler hear you say that."

She squirmed to get down. "Oh, he's my favorite too."

She hopped out of the room while we laughed.

"Kids are the best," Alice said, following her out.

"They sure are, aren't they?" Sam asked with a knowing look.

"Not you too. Alice already gave me a hard time."

"Alice sees herself in you. She wants to help you avoid the heartache she went through."

"I'm doing just fine on my own, thank you very much."

"By closing yourself off?"

I growled as I escaped my bedroom. "How am I closing myself off when I'm taking Delaney to the dance? I took them out to dinner the other night, and I invited them to go skiing."

"Oh, so you're dating?" Sam asked.

Alice stopped braiding Maggie's hair to wait for my answer. "Are you?"

"Natalie knows that's not what I want." I'd shut those fantasies down, and I had no desire to open myself to that possibility.

Sam sat next to Alice and Maggie. "You're friends?"

"I guess? I just want to be there for them, especially Delaney. Her dad's a worthless—"

Sam covered Maggie's ears. "Don't finish that sentence."

Maggie shook her finger at me. "No swearing, Uncle Mac. You're going to get into trouble."

She was too cute for words. My heart ached for the millionth time for what I couldn't have. For what I'd never have. I could be close, but it wouldn't ever be mine. Maggie was Sam's, and Delaney was Natalie's.

I gathered up the bouquet and the corsage. "I'd better get going. I have another princess waiting for me."

They walked out with me, and I pushed away the worries and doubts. Tonight was about what Delaney needed, and I was looking forward to showing her a good time.

For the first time, I wished I had something that wasn't a truck. Maybe Delaney would prefer to be escorted in something fancier. I told myself she was just happy I was taking her. I didn't need fancy things to impress her. My presence and attention were enough.

When I pulled up to the B&B, my heart was pounding in my chest. It felt different from any other time I'd been here. I wasn't here to work or take Natalie and Delaney out for a casual dinner. This was important.

No matter what I'd said to Sam and Alice, this thing with Delaney felt big. It wasn't just a favor. I was getting in deep with these two, and I needed to be careful. Not only to protect myself but them, too. I didn't want to disappoint Delaney like her father had.

I knocked on the door, and Natalie answered. Her eyes widened, and her nostrils flared as she took me in. "You look handsome."

"Thank you." I felt nervous, like I was taking a girl out for the first time and meeting her parents. This was important to Delaney; therefore, it was significant to me too.

Natalie stepped back so I could come inside.

"Where's Delaney?"

"She'll be out in a minute. We had a last-minute wardrobe change," Natalie said, her lips twitching in amusement.

"She didn't buy a dress?"

Natalie chuckled. "She bought two because she couldn't decide."

My heart contracted.

"I'm ready. I'm ready. I'm ready," Delaney chanted as she skipped up the hall and came to a stop when she realized I was already there.

"You're here?" Delaney asked as she looked up at me.

I handed her the bouquet. "I told you I would be."

"Look, Mom. He brought more flowers."

"I see that, baby girl," Natalie said as she took the bouquet and arranged the flowers in a jar.

"This is for you too," I said, handing Delaney the corsage box.

"What's this?" Delaney asked.

"It's a flower that goes on your wrist. A guy always brings one for his date to a dance."

Delaney opened the box and pulled it out. "This is so cool. Will you help me put it on?"

I moved closer, helping her wrap it around her wrist. "It looks perfect with your dress." I wasn't sure what colors she was wearing, and apparently, neither did she, so I went with a simple white.

"Beautiful," I said.

Delaney picked up the ends of her skirt and twirled in a circle. "Do you like my dress?"

"It's lovely, and so are you. Are you ready for dinner? We have reservations." I felt a little overwhelmed by the whole situation. I was plagued with thoughts of wanting more things like this in my life.

Delaney giggled. "Oh, fancy."

"Nothing but the best for you," I said as I offered her my elbow and turned to face Natalie.

Natalie shook her head and grabbed her phone. "Uh-huh. Not so fast. I need some pictures."

"Mooom," Delaney said, rolling her eyes.

"Just a few. It won't take long." Natalie posed us in front of the fireplace where she'd placed the bouquet.

After we suffered through the pictures, I told Natalie to send me a pic so I could forward it to my parents.

"Don't be out late."

"Mom," Delaney said.

"What? That's what I'm supposed to say." Natalie hugged her. "Be good. I love you."

Tears sparkled in her eyes. She was probably thinking that it should be her ex here and not me.

Delaney moved through the door ahead of me, and Natalie stopped me with a hand to my arm. "Thank you for doing this. You made her whole year."

Something cracked in my heart. I knew this was a big deal, but hearing her confirm it had my emotions out of whack. "We'll have fun. Don't worry about her."

"I don't worry when she's with you. I know you'll take care of her."

I felt tender toward her and Delaney. I hugged her quickly and kissed her temple. "I'll bring her home safe. Have a good night."

"I'll be here. I didn't want to go out in case she needed me." Her eyes were suspiciously shiny.

I bet she was worried Delaney would be upset that her father wasn't here.

"I'll let you know and send pictures."

"Good. Now go." Natalie waved me off, and I had a feeling she wanted a few minutes to herself.

I'd feel better if Natalie had her friends around her. On the way to the truck, I texted Alice, asking if she'd check in on her, maybe call Kylie and see if she could come over and keep her company. Alice immediately responded by saying she was on it, then asked for a picture. I sent the obligatory photos to my parents and Alice and Sam before helping an eager Delaney into the truck.

"Where are we going?" Delaney asked.

"It's a seafood place that serves your favorite."

"Salmon," she said with a smile.

She buckled up, and I closed the door. I drove her to the restaurant with Delaney talking a mile a minute in the back about the theme of the dance and whatever her teachers had been telling her all week about it.

I had a feeling if I lived with her, I would have heard these stories many times already. I thought of my empty house and the string of unsuccessful relationships and felt lonely. Could I really go my whole life without a child of my own?

We parked and headed into the restaurant. This time, Delaney held my hand, and I could almost pretend she was mine. She looked up at me with so much adoration.

"I couldn't find any Irish dancers."

Delaney shrugged. "That's okay."

We ordered cider and salmon and talked about school and her hopes and dreams of being a vet when she grew up. I was impressed because I had had no idea what I wanted to do at that age.

"Daddy said getting into vet school is really hard, so I should do something else."

I shook my head, not liking that her father had discouraged her from pursuing her dreams. "You can do it if you want to. You can do anything if you want it badly enough."

"Did you want to do construction?" Delaney asked in her sweet voice.

"Dad encouraged us to go to college and pursue our own

interests. It just worked out that we wanted to be in the family business."

Then we talked about the kids at school and her friends, which kids were nice and which I should avoid. I listened, making appropriate comments about being nice to everyone, even if they were mean, hoping I wasn't overstepping. I sent Natalie a picture of us at dinner.

Natalie: Salmon?

Mac: She said it was her favorite.

Natalie: You spoil her.

Mac: She deserves it.

I didn't hear from Natalie after that, and Delaney was eager to get to school and play with her friends. I had a feeling it was less of a dance and more of a social event after listening to her talk. We stood in line to sign in, and I wondered if I was the only "special friend" here.

After we registered, we got in line for official pictures. The theme was Under the Sea, and the entire gym was decorated with silver and gold fish. The decorations sparkled with the overhead lights. The DJ was playing familiar music, and a group of kids were hanging out in the middle of the dance floor.

"I see my friends," Delaney said, and then she was off.

Another dad moved closer to me. "We're just the chauffeurs."

"Yeah?" I asked, feeling a little uncomfortable because I wasn't her real dad. I hadn't thought about needing to speak to other parents.

"First time?" he asked me.

"That's right." I held my hand out to him. "Mac."

"Chad. Mine is the one in the frilly pink dress."

To avoid telling him she wasn't mine, I said, "Delaney's wearing the white-and-purple dress with the corsage."

Chad smiled. "Oh, nice touch. I thought you said it was your first time?"

I chuckled along with him. "I just wanted to make it special for her."

"It's my daughter's favorite event all year, even if all I do is hold her stuff," he said, lifting a small pink sweater. "Sometimes she mixes it up and tells me to stand in line for the picture station." He pointed to the photo booth where there was a line of dads.

"You stand in line while she has fun with her friends?" I asked him.

Chad nodded. "Now you're getting it."

I let out a breath, looking around at the dads standing on the outskirts of the action and the girls running around the dance floor, talking and laughing and screaming if a good song came on. I worried that Delaney would forget I was there, but she came over to grab my hand. "Can we do the photos?"

"Sure. We can do whatever you want. It's your night."

She pulled me over to the line, and I waved good-bye to Chad. We took serious and silly pictures and waited for the string of photos to print out before heading to the food and drink table. I helped Delaney fill a plate and her glass and took it to one of the many tables in the corner.

I couldn't help but think this was what I'd always wanted. Kids, a family, soccer on Saturdays, and dances on Friday nights. I wanted it all.

Then I thought about holding Natalie in my arms and kissing her. I wanted more. It was probably reckless, but I wanted to pursue this thing with Natalie and Delaney, even if it didn't work out.

No matter what happened, I'd stay friends with Delaney. I'd never walk away from her. Not like her father had. I tried not to think about what would happen if Natalie didn't allow it. The old fear reared its head again, and I tapped my fingers on the table.

"What's wrong, Mac?" Delaney asked me as she popped

another grape into her mouth.

"Nothing."

"Are you thinking about my mom?"

I cleared my throat. "Why would I be thinking about her?"

"Because you like her?"

My mouth dropped open because I wasn't even sure she knew what was going on between me and Natalie.

Delaney shrugged. "What? It's not a big deal."

It's not a big deal? Was it that simple?

She got up to throw out her plate and cup. "Will you dance with me?"

It was a slow song, and dads were on the floor with their daughters. "I'd love to."

On the dance floor, I showed her how to hold my hands, and I led her through the steps, twirling her occasionally because she loved it. Someone nearby took a picture of us and asked for my number so they could forward it. When the song ended, I stood on the outskirts and looked at the picture while she danced with her friends. It was perfect. Delaney looked happy. It was what I wanted, even if I was a little sad I wouldn't get to be the person in her life who always did these things.

Then it hit me as I forwarded it to Natalie. I'd felt so out of control in other relationships, and that's why I refused to let go with anyone new. But wasn't I the one who decided whether to pursue something with Natalie? I couldn't control the outcome, and maybe that was the real fear holding me back.

What if it didn't work out? What if I never saw Delaney again? What if I fell in love with Natalie and she broke my heart?

But nothing in life was guaranteed. I'd taken a chance by offering to help Delaney. I made good decisions. I could trust my judgment. I was attracted to Natalie, and she felt the same. We could figure it out together.

I just hoped I wasn't making another mistake.

CHAPTER 11

NATALIE

I felt weird being in the house by myself. On the rare occasions I hired a babysitter, I wasn't home. I was worried that Delaney would get upset when she saw the other kids with their dads. I kept my phone on my lap and frequently checked it.

Mac sent images throughout the night. It looked like Delaney was having a good time, and that's all I could ask for.

Around eight, someone knocked on the door. I opened it, wondering if it was Mac because Delaney wanted to come home early.

Had she finally realized her father wasn't here for the big events and might not ever be? That it would only ever be me and her? Or was that me projecting my feelings onto her?

Instead, it was Kylie and Alice, carrying take-out bags. "Surprise!"

"What are you doing here?" I asked as they filed in.

"We brought takeout and ice cream because I have a feeling you didn't eat." Kylie gave me a pointed look, just as my stomach rumbled.

"I was too worried about Delaney." The knot that had taken

up residence in my gut remained, but the tension in my shoulders eased slightly now that my friends were here.

Alice smiled as she pulled out the ice cream carton. "She's in good hands with Mac. He's gone for that little girl."

"He is, isn't he?" I smiled, the knowledge that he loved my girl filling me with a glow from the inside.

Alice nodded. "We were there when he was getting ready, and he was nervous."

I pulled out plates and silverware. "Why would he be nervous?"

"He wanted the night to be perfect, and he was worried Delaney would prefer her father over him."

I sighed. "I was worried about that too."

"From the pictures he sent, it looked like she was having fun," Alice said.

"Let me see the pics," Kylie said, looking over her shoulder.

"Did you see the one with them dancing together?" Alice asked me, scrolling through her phone. "It's precious. I'll send it to you."

Kylie's eyes widened when she saw the image. "You should post it online."

I hadn't touched my social media accounts since the divorce. Carter had posted pics with his new girlfriend, but I hadn't wanted to make any public declaration. "Are you sure that's a good idea? What if Carter sees Delaney with another man?"

Kylie shrugged. "Hey, he had his chance. He said no."

I paused as I spooned out the rice and chicken, my heart heavy. "You're right. He did."

"He lost the right to complain or feel hurt," Alice agreed. "I'll post it for you real quick. It's too good not to share."

Before I could protest, Alice grabbed my phone, which I'd kept unlocked all night, and pulled up the image she'd texted. When she handed it back to me, she smiled. "There, it's done."

I opened the picture and zoomed in on Mac's expression. He

was looking down at Delaney with so much tenderness and affection that I felt a pang in my heart. That's how her father was supposed to look at her, but it was Mac.

He wasn't doing this solely out of obligation or a sense of duty. He liked her. He wanted to make her happy. It was all a mom could ask for.

Not sure what I should do about the situation, I tucked the phone away.

"Let's eat in front of the TV," Kylie said, already taking her plate piled high with food to the couch. "I put the ice cream in the freezer for later."

"I've got the wine," Alice said, pouring three glasses.

"Thank you for coming over. I didn't know how much I needed the company until you were here."

"That's what Mac said when he texted, but we would have checked in on you regardless," Alice said.

"What do you mean, Mac texted you?" I asked, balancing the plate on my lap.

"He asked me to check on you and to get Kylie to keep you company."

I wasn't sure how I felt about it, but everything in my chest was warm. "That was nice of him."

"Are you guys a thing now?" Kylie asked as she picked up the remote and turned on the TV.

"We're just friends." We hadn't put a label on it, but that's the only way I could describe it.

The living room was too small for socializing. I only had one couch and an end chair, but it was fine for the three of us.

Kylie nodded at my phone. "Well, after looking at the picture, I think Mac's in love with your daughter."

"It's sweet." It was all I could manage because I was thinking the same thing.

"He's always wanted a family," Alice said carefully.

"He said something about that but that he doesn't anymore," I said, moving the food on the plate around with my fork.

"I think he's just scared. The right woman should be able to get past his defenses. Tyler and Sam always say that he's the romantic. He always wanted a girlfriend, even in high school. He was never interested in hookups or one-night stands," Alice said.

That was something I didn't know, but I could see that about him. I loved that he was into relationships. It was rare to find a man like that. "He said he's not the same man."

"You don't change that much. It's still there, underneath all the scar tissue," Alice said, and I wondered if she felt a kinship with him.

My shoulders tightened. "I don't know if I want to start anything right now. I just got divorced."

Kylie pointed her fork at me. "It's been a year since Carter told you he was done."

"It has been." It took me a few months to get my bearings and deal with the divorce on my own since Carter wasn't interested, then I bought the B&B and moved here. "It feels shorter."

Kylie shook her head. "There's no manual on how long you have to wait to date someone else."

"What about Delaney? I don't want her to get hurt."

Alice chewed and swallowed before she said, "Mac's not the type to walk away from someone he cares about. Besides, you're both part of the family now."

Kylie flipped through the channels, settling on an old comedy sitcom we were all familiar with. "He's a good man."

"He won't hurt you," Alice added.

"I don't want to hurt him either." By getting involved with someone before I was ready. By thinking I could scale his walls when they were impenetrable. But thinking about him dancing with my daughter had me melting all over again. Anytime I remembered our encounter in the kitchen, I remembered how my body reacted to his. I wanted him.

"You should go for it," Kylie said.

"I'm not like you." I wasn't reckless. I thought about things before I did them.

Alice set her plate on the coffee table and sat back on the couch. "Do what feels right, then."

If I did what I wanted, I'd jump him as soon as he came home and Delaney was tucked into bed. I just wasn't sure if he'd be into it or if it was a good idea. Sometimes, being a responsible adult sucked.

"You deserve this time to figure things out and explore what you want."

"Yeah, but this isn't some guy I picked up at a bar." Not that I ever did that, but it had to be said. "This is Mac. Your future brother-in-law, your family friend, and he's renovating my house. He's clearly bonded with Delaney, and I can't mess that up."

"What if he's the one for you? What if those other women didn't work out because you were meant for him?" Alice asked.

"And I was married to someone else? That's some twisted fate." I didn't want to listen to what she was saying because it was convincing. I wanted a reason to pursue Mac, and she was giving it to me.

Kylie waggled her brows. "You're here now—and single."

"Between us, we have enough baggage to fill a plane," I said, brushing crumbs from the fortune cookie off my lap.

"What does your fortune say?" Kylie asked as she made a grab for the piece of paper I hadn't unfolded yet.

"*Your wildest dreams are about to come true.*" Kylie's voice raised as she read each word.

"See? It's meant to be," Alice agreed.

"I don't know if a fortune cookie proves anything," I insisted, even as I felt myself giving in to the possibility. What would

Mac do if I kissed him tonight? Would he push me away? Would he say he wasn't interested, or would he kiss me back? The thought sent a tingle down my spine.

"Is this why Mac sent you over, to butter me up for him?" I teased.

Alice rolled her eyes. "He's just as resistant as you. He insists that you're friends."

"He's just there for us." And it felt good. Too good.

"Oh, I love this part," Kylie said, turning up the volume on the TV. We finished eating, and I cleaned up the trash while the girls watched the show. It was nice to have friends who'd come over like this. It had only been a short while, but I was settling in here. Making friends and a home for myself. Did I really want to pursue something with Mac that could risk everything I'd worked so hard for?

I wasn't like Carter. I wasn't irresponsible.

When I received a text from Mac saying they were on their way home, I refrained from asking how Delaney was. I wanted to hear it from her. It was funny how it was nice to have a few hours to myself, but it made me miss her more.

Shortly after, I ushered the girls out, thanking them for coming. They didn't say anything else about what I planned to do with Mac. I preferred to see how things went tonight. I knew how I felt, and if he made a move, I wouldn't put a stop to it. I was teetering on the edge, and one small nudge would send me over.

I was ready when the knock came because I heard the rumble of Mac's truck. As soon as I opened the door, Delaney burst in and hugged me. "It was so fun. I wish you could have come too."

I laughed, looking over her head at Mac. "Then it wouldn't be called the daddy-daughter dance." I tensed, hoping I hadn't just reminded her of her absentee father.

"Tell me everything," I insisted as she pulled away and flopped onto the couch.

"It was amazing."

"Did you have fun too?" I asked Mac.

"It was great. I even met some of the other dads. Apparently, I was there to hold her things while she danced with her friends and to stand in line for the photo booth."

He'd said it with a smile, but I was concerned about how Delaney treated him. "Did you make Mac stand on the sideline when you played with your friends?"

Mac held up a hand. "That's what the other dads did. Delaney stood in line with me."

My stomach fluttered at his casual reference to dads. Did he consider himself to be a father figure? I liked that a lot. To cover my reaction, I said to Delaney, "It's time for bed. Why don't you get changed and brush your teeth."

Not wanting Mac to leave just yet, I said, "You want a beer while I tuck her in? I want to hear all about it."

He waved me off. "I'll get it. You take care of our girl."

Our girl. I bit my lip against the smile that threatened to spread over my face as I followed Delaney to her room. I waited while she changed in the bathroom, then tucked her in. "Was it everything you hoped for?"

"It was so much better. He took me to a fancy dinner and let me order whatever I wanted. He didn't ask whether I was really going to eat it or worry about me wasting it."

I winced at her reference to Carter. He had money, but he was stingy with it and never failed to complain when we wasted it on frivolous things. But I was proud of her for eating healthy, even if salmon was expensive. "Good for you for ordering what you want. How was the dance?"

"My favorite part was dancing with Mac." She fell silent for a few seconds before she asked, "You don't think Dad will be jealous, do you?"

"Why would he?" I felt uneasy because Alice had posted it on my account, and there might be questions.

Her eyes fluttered closed. "I don't know. I'm tired."

I leaned over and kissed her forehead. "I love you."

"Love you too," she murmured before turning to her side.

I turned off the light and walked the short distance to the living room.

In the living room, Mac had taken off his suit jacket and rolled up the sleeves of his button-down shirt, beer bottle in hand. He looked sexy working in his jeans and T-shirt, but in a suit, he was irresistible. I wanted to straddle him, but that was a line he might not be ready to cross.

Mac stood when I entered the room. "You want to sit in front of the fire in the main living room? You only have a little longer to have it for yourself."

"I'd love that." It wasn't late, and I was energized now that I knew Delaney was okay.

I grabbed a couple of water bottles and followed him through the door between the spaces and sat on the couch while he threw some logs onto the fire. "These won't burn too long."

"I'm always afraid to start one because I'm not sure how long it would take to burn out."

Mac gave me a look before he sat next to me. "We'll find out."

"Tell me everything," I said, excited to hear the details. "It looked like she was having fun."

Mac met my gaze and nodded. "She had the best time."

What if Mac was her father? The feeling was so strong I had to look away.

He rubbed his chin. "I felt like another dad. It wasn't awkward at all."

My shoulders lowered at his admission. "Oh good. I was a little worried about that."

117

"No one asked who I was, and I didn't say anything. We just did our thing."

"That's good to hear."

"I loved that I was the one who got to take her. That probably makes me the bad guy."

My mouth dropped open as my attention turned to him. "Why would you say that?"

"Her father should be here." Mac's voice lowered to a hush, even though we'd closed the door between the two spaces.

It would be unlikely that Delaney would get up in the middle of the night and come looking for me, but I loved being in the B&B space and imagining everything it could be.

I pressed my lips into a straight line. "He made it clear he didn't want to be. Did Delaney seem upset?"

"Not at all. She had a great time."

"You looked like you were enjoying dancing with her."

"I couldn't help but wonder if that's how it would have been like for me if I'd had kids." He took a swig of his beer.

"You can still have kids. It's not over for you," I said, a little shocked that's what he thought.

"I gave up on the idea a long time ago."

"It doesn't seem like you have." My fingers itched to touch him, to soothe him in some way.

"It still hurts, you know? When you want something so badly but you can't have it." His voice was raw as he set his empty bottle on the floor.

Were we still talking about kids, or was it something else?

Then he stood and paced the small space in front of the couch. "I've been telling myself that you're off-limits, that you don't want anything to do with me." He stopped to face me. Meeting my gaze, he said, "Tell me I'm wrong."

Not able to break the connection, I stood and closed the distance between us. I placed my palms on his chest, not breaking eye contact. "You're wrong."

I wasn't second-guessing this because I wanted him. I was intrigued by the heart I saw under this man who was afraid to pursue what he wanted. I wished I'd met him when he was younger, less jaded, and open to possibilities. But something inside me wanted to peel back the layers and find that guy again.

Mac cradled the back of my head as he gazed at me with so much tenderness and wonder. "Are you sure?"

"I've never been surer of anything." It was a combination of what he'd done for us, the expression on his face when he danced with Delaney, and what he described he'd given up on. I wanted to see the man underneath.

CHAPTER 12

MAC

I've never been surer of anything.

Natalie's words pumped through my veins, urging me on. This was the right move. I wanted Natalie, and she felt the same.

When Natalie's lips parted, I lowered mine to hers, gently exploring, giving her a chance to pull away, to tell me this was a mistake. But when she didn't, I pulled her closer to me with a hand on her hip.

It was a heady feeling to have her pressed against me. She moaned, opening up for more.

I usually only slept with women I was in a relationship with or intended to be with. This was the first time I wasn't sure, but it felt right.

I backed her up until her knees hit the edge of the couch, never taking my lips from hers. I turned us so that I sat on the couch, looking up at her.

I tugged her arm, and she came willingly, straddling my hips. When her warm center touched my aching dick, I almost lost it. Nothing felt as good as her in my lap.

She rose up over me, her hands tangling in the hair at the

base of my neck, her lower body undulating over my dick. I felt constrained by our clothes. I eased back slightly and raised a brow as I played with the hem of her shirt.

"Please." Her voice was husky, and I wondered how much lower it would go when my mouth was on her pussy.

My dick twitched at the thought. She must have felt the movement because she bit her lip, and her eyes glazed over with lust.

I slowly pulled the shirt over her head, marveling at her breasts that threatened to spill over a blush-colored bra. Sweet and feminine, just like her.

I cupped her breasts, rubbing a thumb over the already hard bud.

Natalie's breath hitched.

Keeping eye contact, I moved closer so I could suck on the material covering her nipple. She arched her back as if she enjoyed my mouth on her.

Her fingers twisted in my hair as she dropped her head back. She was so responsive, so passionate. I couldn't imagine why her ex walked away unless he wasn't the man for her.

Maybe there was no chemistry, maybe he didn't see what he had, but I did. I never wanted to let her go. I chilled at the thought of commitment and what that meant. Being vulnerable and allowing someone else to decide how your life got to be.

Then I pushed those negative thoughts out of my head. This was Natalie. It wasn't my past. I wouldn't let it taint this moment with her. It already felt different, special even. Like nothing could compare.

I pulled her head down to kiss her. I felt my heart opening with each slide of my tongue and touch of my fingers.

Needing more contact, I maneuvered us so that her back was on the couch. Lowering my body over hers, I pulled down the cup of her bra and sucked her nipple into my mouth.

She held the back of my neck as if she were in control of

keeping me there. I laved one with attention and then the other. I'd never get enough of this woman. How had I ever thought she couldn't be mine? She was perfect.

I ignored any niggling doubts. I refused to hear them. Not now. Not when she was ready, willing, and pliable in my arms.

I unsnapped her jeans, and she moved to help me ease them over her hips and down her long legs, leaving her in tiny lace panties. As much as I loved seeing her in lace, I wanted her naked.

When I moved to hook my fingers in the straps, she stopped me with a hand on my wrist. "You're still dressed."

I reared up to a kneeling position, anxious to get back to her. With jerky movements, I attempted to unbutton the shirt. She moved in front of me, and the sight of her kneeling in front of me, with her breasts glowing in the light of the fire, had me swallowing hard.

She was gorgeous. Her skin, her body, and the desire I saw in her eyes… I'd never seen or felt anything like it before. I wondered if I'd bared myself to her more than any other woman so that our coming together was more emotional.

She swiped my hands away and took over the task. I let her do a couple of buttons before the temptation was too much, and I cupped her breasts, my thumbs grazing over her nipples. She faltered, her breath hitching, as she looked at me.

"You're beautiful."

Her eyes drifted closed as I plucked her nipples. Her fingers stalled as they tangled in my shirt.

"Look at me."

When she slowly opened her eyes, they were dark with lust and something else. Before I could decipher the emotion, she said, "I need you."

I ripped off the shirt, the buttons skidding over the hardwood floor. I'd have to search for them later because there was zero chance I was stopping now. Then I stood to push my slacks and briefs down. I grabbed my wallet to pull out the condom I'd placed there after that late-night faucet incident at the B&B and ripped the wrapper.

When I returned to the couch, Natalie was naked as she lay with her legs spread, one foot on the floor, the other resting over the back cushion.

Her plea that she needed me played on repeat in my head. I moved over her, nudging her entrance with my cock.

She pulled me down to kiss her, and my cockhead slipped inside. I tried to move slowly, allowing her to accommodate to my size, but she moved her hips, urging me deeper. I couldn't resist.

She felt so good. Her nipples brushed my chest, her fingers running up and down my back and then my ass, pulling me deep.

I lifted up slightly to watch her face as I filled her. Her eyes were slightly glazed over as she bit her lip.

"Move," she said, and I complied, pulling out to the tip and thrusting into the hilt, over and over. The position was a little awkward on the couch, so I flipped us so that she was on top. She smiled as she lifted herself over me.

I palmed her breasts, loving the view from this position. I wasn't sure if I'd ever be with her again, and I wanted to enjoy every second. When I felt myself barreling closer to a huge orgasm, I moved one finger to her clit and pressed hard.

She detonated, spasming and shaking, as she fell forward onto my chest. I thrust up once, twice, a third time before I let go. I held her tight to me, wishing we had the comfort and space of a full bed. Wishing I could stay the night. I wasn't done with her.

Eventually, she eased off me so I could take care of the condom. When I returned, she was already dressed.

Disappointed, I followed suit, taking my time buttoning my shirt. "You're not having regrets, are you?"

"Of course not." But she'd said it too easily for that to be believable.

When I finished the last button, I knelt in front of her on the floor. "I want to stay the night with you."

"I can't. Delaney—"

"I know, but I wanted to tell you where my head is at. That was amazing, and I want to hold you all night and explore this thing between us."

"We can't." Indecision flashed in her eyes.

"We can't tonight. But will you let me take you out?"

She smiled softly. "I'd like that."

I returned her smile despite knowing I couldn't stay overnight. I didn't want her to let her good sense return and realize we couldn't pursue this. But the suite was too small for me to stay. Delaney's room was right off Natalie's. Maybe Mom could babysit her for a night sometime soon, and I could take Natalie back to my place. Or I could invite them both over. Delaney would love that, and I could show them my house.

"Are you okay with what just happened?" I asked her.

"I knew what I wanted, but I wasn't sure about your intentions."

"I'm not going to lie and say I'm not scared because I am. I can't predict what's going to happen, but I want to try. I like you."

"Well, I would hope so," Natalie teased.

I stood and held out a hand to draw her into my body.

"I've never felt like that during sex before," Natalie murmured against my chest.

I had a feeling she wasn't just saying the sex was good but that we had chemistry. Because I'd felt it too. "I knew something was special about you from the beginning."

She smiled up at me, and it was so wide and bright that it pushed out everything else—the doubts and worries, the what-ifs.

Natalie was worth the risk of a broken heart. If I didn't pursue this, I'd never know if she was meant for me.

CHAPTER 13

NATALIE

I woke up the next morning with a sense that there'd been a shift overnight. I felt lighter, happier. Mac and I had sex, and it was amazing. It was exactly what I hoped it would be. It was exactly what I needed.

I was a little worried he'd had too much time to rethink things overnight. Would he regret it? Would he retreat to protect himself? I mentally prepared for any scenario.

I went for an early morning walk with Delaney since it was Saturday, and we picked up books from the library. I loved that we were in town and could walk most places.

When we returned, I was surprised to see Mac standing on the porch with his ever-present tool belt over worn jeans and the black company T-shirt. He looked too good to be true standing on my porch.

Mac rumpled Delaney's hair. "My mom's inside. She wants to take you home to bake that cake."

"Seriously?"

"If that's okay with your mom," Mac said, deferring to me.

Delaney turned to me as I said, "Of course, it's fine, but remember to be polite."

"I will." Delaney headed inside, and we were alone on the porch.

"Come here," he commanded.

When I was within reach, he drew me into his body. "I missed you."

I laughed against his chest. "You were inside me last night."

"Shh. How will that sound if my mom overhears us?" I heard the smile in his voice.

"Mmm. Probably not good, but then, you're not exactly hiding anything," I said, looking up at him. This was a great way to start the day. "Did you have a hand in your mother coming over?"

"That was all her. She called bright and early this morning to ask when she could bake a cake with Delaney. Maggie's fun, but she's only four. She can't do the same things Delaney can. It has the added bonus of allowing us to get some work done this morning." He brushed a strand of hair off my forehead. "How do you feel about a picnic lunch?"

"I'd love that." My heart was galloping in my chest. This was real. He wasn't backing out. If anything, he was moving forward. I was excited to get to know the real Mac, the one who'd been holding himself back, protecting himself from heartbreak.

"Was there something that changed your mind last night?" We'd discussed it a bit, but I was curious about his thought process.

"I realized I couldn't run from this. I couldn't escape who and what you represent in my life."

"And what's that?"

"Something amazing. Maybe even my future. If I don't pursue this, I'll never forgive myself."

Tingles erupted over my skin despite the unseasonably warm weather for March in Telluride. "You have a way with words."

"I've been holding them inside."

I got it then. He was afraid to speak his truth because it had been thrown back in his face so many times. He was a good man. He deserved someone who'd cherish him. "You don't have to be afraid with me." It came out as a whisper because I was positive he didn't want anyone to hear him being vulnerable.

"I'm working on it." He kissed me lightly and then said with a wink, "Let's start with lunch."

"Do you need me to pick up food?" I asked him.

"I've got it covered. You just need to show up in the backyard at one."

"How romantic," I teased as I walked toward the front door.

He held a hand over his chest. "I'm trying here, but I'm in the middle of this huge renovation for a high-maintenance client."

I tipped my head to the side. "High maintenance, huh? Is that how you see me?"

He moved toward me, and my heart picked up again. "Not at all. You're perfect."

"We should get to work." My body was on board with sneaking him into my suite and having my way with him, but I wanted him to make the next move. I wanted him to be sure.

"You're distracting," he said.

"And you love it," I said, holding my breath that he would take it for the lighthearted words I meant. Carter had always been very serious, not interested in flirtations or romantic gestures. He loved to say he was a realist, and I didn't realize how much I hated it until now.

"Absolutely," he said as he kissed me again.

The morning flew by as I tried to concentrate on work while reminiscing about what happened last night. I only wanted to date a man worth my time, and Mac seemed like he was worth the effort. He was a family man who kept his promises. He'd proved he would put Delaney first, and I was looking forward to seeing where this could go.

I was lost in Piper's recent template for the website, making notes and thinking about the best way to present everything, when my phone buzzed.

Mac: Did you forget about lunch?

Glancing at the clock on the computer, I saw it was 1:10. "Oh no."

Natalie: Sorry! I'm coming.

I closed my laptop and stored it in the locked drawer before hurrying through the house and out the back door. It was even warmer than it was this morning on the porch. It was the perfect day to eat outside.

Instead of eating on the picnic table, Mac had spread a blanket on the ground nearby. Hurrying over, I said, "I'm sorry. I lost track of time."

Mac kissed me. "Don't worry about it. It gave me time to set everything up. Come sit. I'm starving."

"Me too," I said, sitting next to him.

Mac opened the picnic basket and pulled out strawberries, cheese, crackers, sandwiches, and a box of chocolates.

"You thought of everything," I said as he handed me a sandwich.

"I hope you like turkey. If not, I got ham." He held up the second sandwich.

"Turkey's great." I unwrapped the sandwich and took a huge bite. "This is perfect. I usually whip up an omelet or something quick at home."

"It feels like spring."

"It sure does. Delaney's going to expect it to be this warm every day now."

Mac smiled, shaking his head. I loved that we could talk about Delaney. That he had equal affection for her.

"I wonder what they're doing."

"Mom said she was teaching her to sew while the cake baked."

"That's amazing. I don't even know how to do that."

"How did you end up in South Carolina?" Mac asked as we ate.

"My ex was from there. I got pregnant soon after we graduated from college, and he got a job at his father's business. It only made sense that I go with him. I had Delaney and wanted to stay home, but now, I see that was shortsighted. I should have been smarter about being independent and saved money for myself."

"You did what you thought was best, and I'm sure Delaney loved the time she had with you."

"I enjoyed staying home with her."

"Then you made the right decision. No use in second-guessing it." He rested on his side, propped on an elbow, while he popped strawberries into his mouth.

"Even if I regret my ex?" I asked with a wry smile.

"You don't regret Delaney."

"Nope."

"Do you ever talk to him?"

"In the beginning, I encouraged him to see Delaney. I said it wasn't good for her to feel like she was abandoned. He claimed she didn't feel that way unless I was the one who told her she should feel the way. His parents weren't like yours. They saw Delaney solely as my responsibility. I decided to have her, so I should do all the work."

"And what about their son? Doesn't he have the same duty?"

I laughed. "Not when you think child-rearing is the woman's job, and you baby your only son."

Mac scowled. "Both parents should be involved. That's how I see it anyway."

"I always did too. To be fair, Carter's parents never said they wanted to have a relationship with Delaney. She was more someone they could brag about if she did something remarkable. Although I'm not sure she's done anything to meet their high expectations yet."

"She's smart and kind. That's not enough?"

"Not in their eyes. They like tangible things like grades and trophies."

"Yikes. I can't imagine growing up that way."

"Somehow, Carter came out spoiled. They make excuses for him all the time, even when he cheated on me. I wasn't giving him enough attention. I didn't keep myself up."

"Fuck that. You're gorgeous." He leaned over and kissed me, sealing his words on my lips.

"Thanks," I said when he pulled away.

"I can see why you moved."

"There was nothing for me there."

"They tried to tell me to wait for Carter to move back."

"So, you're supposed to put your life on hold and wait for him to come back to you?

"I have too much self-respect for that. Besides, I was just done with him and his family. Being there wasn't good for Delaney or me."

"I have to agree."

I smiled at him. "You're just happy I moved here."

He nodded. "Over the moon."

I laughed. "Who knew there was a sweet guy under all that grumpiness?"

"I'm not grumpy."

"You were." But maybe he hadn't been in a long time.

We'd finished eating, leaving our trash scattered on the blanket. He pulled me to standing. "We have the house to ourselves."

Feeling out of breath, I asked, "When is your mom bringing her back?"

"Not until four."

"You're kidding?" I felt giddy inside, like we had all the time in the world.

He raised a brow. "Want to take this inside?"

"Yes." I didn't think we'd get this time alone. When Delaney was at school, the crew was usually here. I hadn't counted on his mom coming through for us the day after we decided to take a chance on something.

He lifted me bridal-style and carried me to my door and waited for me to turn the knob and push it open. "Home sweet home."

"It is now," I said as he carried me to my bedroom, closing the door and locking it behind us in case his mom returned earlier than we thought.

CHAPTER 14

MAC

I lowered Natalie to the bed, not quite believing we had a few hours to ourselves. I should have been working, but I wanted this time with her. It was all I could think about after I went home last night. I couldn't believe I'd finally made a move, and it felt so good.

But the reality was, I was dating a single mother, and I needed to be careful. If something seemed like it was too good to be true, it probably was, so a part of me was still waiting for something bad to happen. For Natalie to tell me she wasn't ready for a relationship. I told myself I was being cautious, not holding back. But I wasn't so sure about that.

Instead, I poured my feelings into my kisses. Even though we had all afternoon, there was a sense of urgency. We tore at each other's clothes, not pausing until we were both naked.

Natalie laughed as she looked up at me. The afternoon light poured through the windows, warming us and illuminating her face.

She was gorgeous.

My breath caught in my throat as she placed featherlight touches on my skin.

Then she lifted her head to kiss me. "We don't have all day."

"I wish we did." My voice was guttural, my muscles tight with the effort to hold back and savor this moment. How often would we have the luxury of an afternoon in bed?

So, I kissed her mouth, then her jaw, her collarbone, and lower still, needing to taste her. I paused on her nipples before moving downward, placing light kisses on her soft stomach. Her legs spread for my shoulders, and I didn't waste any time licking her core and sucking her clit. When I added my fingers, her body arched off the bed as I continued to drive her higher. I didn't let up until she was writhing, her fingers twisted in the comforter.

When I increased the pressure of my tongue and added a second finger, she went off. I rode the waves of her orgasm, not moving up her body until she was resting flat on her back again.

"That was—"

"Amazing, indescribable?" I smiled against her lips.

Her arms wrapped around me. "All of the above."

I'd give anything to be with her like this forever. I felt like I could forget about the rest of the world and lose myself in her. Forget about my past, the worries and anxieties, the old fear that said a future with a woman wasn't for me.

My cock slid through her folds, and she was so sensitive she practically bucked off the bed. It felt so good, better than it ever had. Then it hit me. "Fuck. A Condom."

Her hands cupped my ass, and I wanted nothing more than to slide inside her, to be enveloped by her sweet heat. My muscles trembled with the effort to hold back. We couldn't be reckless. Natalie already had a child. I wouldn't be so careless with her.

I reached over the bed to grab my wallet and pull out the condom I placed there this morning after my mom called. I'd been hopeful.

I lined up with her entrance and eased inside. It felt as good as last night. It wasn't a fluke. There was something here. Something bigger than I'd ever felt before. I wanted to sink inside her forever.

Natalie reached for me, and I had this sensation of never feeling close enough to her. I lifted her and sat back on my heels so that I cradled her in my arms, and she straddled my hips. She bit her lip as she sank down on me.

I went so much deeper in this position. It felt shockingly intimate. I guided her as she rose up and then down, kissing her and holding her close. Her breasts were in my face, so I latched on to one nipple, teasing it into a hard peak before moving to the other.

She lost her rhythm then, and I took over, lifting her and slamming her down. It was something but not enough. Lifting her off me, I flipped her to her hands and knees and entered her again from behind. The sight of her on her knees almost made me lose control.

She pushed back against me, intensifying the sensations. I wouldn't last long in this position. I reached around and circled her clit until she spasmed around me, pulling my own release from me. I kissed her back as I eased out and collapsed onto the bed.

"Was I too rough?"

"It was perfect." She shook her head and pulled her hair out of her face. She looked freshly fucked and adorably rumpled. Her skin was flush, and her hair knotted. I wanted to see her like this all the time. I wanted morning sex and night sex and quickies in between. The emotion threatened to overwhelm me, so I got up to get rid of the condom.

I splashed cold water on my face, pausing to rest my palms on the sink. I told myself I wouldn't get this deep with another person again, that I could do something casual with Natalie while still being cautious. But I wasn't sure it was possible. I was already falling for her.

I dried off and returned to the bedroom, where Natalie had pulled the sheet over her body. I slid in next to her, holding her against me. We must have fallen asleep because I woke to the sound of my phone buzzing.

Shifting to my back, I grabbed the phone I'd left on the nightstand. "Shit."

"Is it your mom?"

I dropped the phone on the bed and ran a hand through my hair. "Yeah, they're on their way."

Natalie jumped up, grabbing the clothes we'd carelessly thrown off before. "I can't believe we fell asleep."

I wanted to pull her back into bed and take our time waking up, but we didn't have that choice. Any moment together would be like this, stolen moments, and if we were lucky, a few hours here or there.

I was worried one or both of us was going to freak out over the intensity between us. But she didn't acknowledge it, too busy stepping into her clothes and going into the bathroom to fix her hair.

I moved a little slower, taking the time to remake her bed. It wouldn't be good if we told my mom and Delaney we spent the day napping.

I headed into the kitchen, wondering if I should pretend to be working. By the time I could work out what was right, there was a knock on Natalie's door.

She sailed past me to open the door. "Miranda."

Delaney hugged Natalie. "Mom, look what I made."

"Oh, that's amazing. Did you sew that?"

"Ms. Miranda showed me how." They came into the kitchen, and Delaney placed a few things on the table before coming to me. "I made this for you. To thank you for taking me to the dance."

"You don't need to thank me."

She handed me a small blue dolphin.

"Did you make this?" I asked her.

"Your mom taught me."

"It's amazing. Thank you." I pulled her in for a hug, not even thinking about whether it was appropriate. I was acting on instinct, and the fact that she'd made something for me had my heart contracting inside my chest. When I thought about having kids, the first thing that came to mind was crayon drawings on the fridge. But this dolphin was small and soft, and I could keep it in my pocket when I worked.

Delaney held up the string of rainbow-colored stars. "Can we hang it in my room?"

"Of course. Above your bed?" Natalie asked.

"I'll get my hammer and some nails." If Mom wondered why I was in Natalie's apartment and not working in the main house, she didn't say anything. I was grateful for that because I wasn't ready to talk about what was happening between me and Natalie.

I was almost too scared to hope for the best. There were so many factors to consider: Delaney, Natalie's ex, and my hang-ups.

I gathered what I needed and met Delaney in her bedroom, where she showed me where to hang it. I could hear Mom and Natalie talking in the kitchen but not their exact words.

"You have fun?" I asked Delaney, as I had her hold the string up so I could gauge the best height.

"Oh yeah."

I showed her how to hammer in the nails, carefully watching her so she wouldn't hurt herself. My mom could show her the domestic things, but I could pass on my love for fixing things and making things out of wood. It was what my father had done with my brothers and me. A sense of contentment stole over me.

Natalie came into the room, and Delaney jumped off the bed. "Mac showed me how to hammer."

"You hammered the nails?" Natalie asked Delaney, looking from her to me.

"Uh-huh. It was fun. Almost as fun as sewing."

I held a hand over my heart. "Hammering is way more fun than sewing."

"I like creating pretty things," Delaney said earnestly. Then she left the room, probably in search of my mom.

"Thanks for letting her help," Natalie said, sitting on Delaney's twin bed.

"You aren't mad?" I asked her.

Natalie tipped her head to the side. "Why would I be?"

"Because she could have gotten hurt."

Natalie frowned. "I knew you wouldn't let that happen."

"You trust me with her," I said softly, the realization hitting me hard in the chest.

Natalie rose to stand in front of me. "I think you've proven yourself trustworthy."

I gathered her into my arms, right there in Delaney's pink bedroom, and kissed her. I wanted to show her how her declaration made me feel. I felt like I could take on the world if I had her supporting me.

All too aware that we weren't alone, I pulled back. "We should go out there."

She smiled. "Yeah, we should."

I felt like I should have said something more about what her words meant to be, but the moment was lost because Delaney led Mom down the hall, and we stepped apart. Delaney showed her the stars, and they chatted about what other things they could make together.

I walked Mom out, worried she'd say something.

At her sedan, she held her hands up. "I don't think I want to know what's going on. You're both adults. I just hope you know what you're doing. Those girls in there are vulnerable. Just moved to a new town, opening a business. If you're not serious about them—"

"When have you known me not to be serious about a girl I was dating?"

Mom patted my cheek. The familiar gesture was comforting. "You're right. That's not what I meant. I'm worried about you. I don't want you to get hurt. You give everyone your whole heart, and there's nothing wrong with that."

But I read the concern on her face. "I'm trying to be careful."

"You need to be honest with her," Mom said, nodding toward the house.

"I have been. She knows my past."

"I think she's good for you," Mom said with a small smile, getting into the car.

I held on to the frame of the door. "You do?"

"I really like her."

I liked her for me too. "You don't think I'm moving too fast?"

"If it feels right, then you're not," Mom said.

"It does." It was my fucked-up past screwing with my head and making up worst-case scenarios in my head that was the problem.

"Then you can't go wrong. You were always so open, so quick to fall, and I never thought it was a bad thing."

"Really?" It certainly felt bad when it didn't work out.

"It's what makes you—well… you. I love you more for it, and the right woman will too. You're a special man, and she'd be lucky to have you."

"Thanks, Mom." I closed the door, and she pulled away from the curb.

I liked how she thought of me, but she was my mother. Being too open had hurt me in the past. I wasn't sure I was ready to be that guy again.

Inside, Delaney was on the couch, watching a cartoon.

"I'm going to try to get some work done."

"We were hoping you'd join us for dinner," Natalie said.

I looked at Delaney watching TV and Natalie standing in the kitchen and said, "I have a better idea. What do you think about helping me pick out a puppy?"

Delaney looked over at me. "Are you serious?"

"I could use the help."

Delaney shut off the TV and ran into the kitchen. "Yes, yes, yes. I want a puppy."

Natalie held up her hands as if to fend her off. "No, *we're* not getting a puppy. Mac is."

"You have to help me pick out the best one."

Delaney sobered, nodding. "I can do that."

I ruffled her hair. "I knew you could. That's why I asked." Then I asked Natalie, "As long as you're okay with this?"

"I'd love to help you pick out a puppy, but are you sure this is what you want?"

"I've been putting it off, but I think it's finally time."

Delaney was a bundle of energy while she waited for us to get ready. I needed to put away my tools. When we were in my truck, I couldn't help but think this was right. They belonged here with me.

"Where are we going?" Delaney asked.

"Good question. Let me call my friend Gray and see if he has any ideas. He's the local veterinarian."

I dialed the number and let the ringtone fill the cab.

"Gray here."

"Hey, how are you?" I could hear his daughter, Amelia, in the background, asking to be picked up.

Natalie smiled over at me.

"Good. Someone's climbing me like I'm a tree." Gray's voice went in and out as he presumably moved the phone around his daughter.

Suddenly, the cab filled with Amelia's giggles. He must have picked her up.

"You want to go out?" he asked, his voice louder.

"Not right now. Maybe soon, though." I hadn't gone out with the guys in a while, and I liked Gray. "I want to get a puppy, and I'm hoping you know somewhere we can get one on a Saturday night."

I wanted to get one eventually. But when I returned to Natalie's apartment, the thought of working alone and then heading back to my empty house wasn't appealing. I wanted to fill it with something. And if the puppy drew Delaney and Natalie over to my place, even better.

"I'll text you some options. What are you looking for?"

The background was quiet now, and I wondered if Elle took Amelia into another room. "I want a nice family dog. Lab or golden retriever. I don't care which."

From the backseat, Delaney called, "Golden retriever. They're rainbows, sunshine, and cotton candy."

"I'm not sure about that," I said to Delaney, amusement tinging my voice, and then to Gray, "I'm getting a request for a golden."

"I think we have some things to catch up on," Gray said, clearly having heard her.

"I'm with Natalie and her daughter, Delaney. She's the one fixing up the old Victorian into a B&B."

"Yeah, I heard something about that. She's friends with Alice."

"That's right."

"Give me a minute, and I'll send you the information on a farm that has goldens. It's not a mill. They have a nice breeding operation going on there. You can't go wrong. The mom and dad have great dispositions."

"Great. Thanks." I knew Gray would know where to go.

"They have a wait list but always reserve a few for local buyers. They want to keep the puppies close so they can keep an eye on them."

"That's nice," Natalie murmured from next to me.

"Listen, I have to go. Someone wants me to play horsey." Gray's tone was irritated but full of affection. He loved his daughter more than anything, and I knew it was because, like me, he didn't think he'd ever have a family because of his past.

Handing the phone to Natalie, I said, "Direct us to the farm when Gray sends the info."

Natalie cradled the phone in her hands. "I don't know Gray."

"He moved to town a few years ago and took over Telluride Animal Clinic." Gray had an interesting backstory. When he was eighteen, their home was raided, and his father was arrested. He was currently serving time in federal prison for his money-laundering crimes. Gray moved here, hoping to escape his past, but it eventually followed him. Thankfully, the townspeople only cared that he was a good man and an even better vet. "He married Elle, Alice's sister. She owns the barbershop in town."

"That's right. Alice said something about that. It sounds like a nice place."

"It was Elle who introduced Alice to Sam. She knew he needed a nanny and told her about the position."

Natalie relaxed into the seat. "Sounds like fate."

I wanted to say I didn't believe in that, but Delaney was listening intently to our conversation. "What should we name the dog?"

She tapped her chin. "Princess?"

"Yeah, no." Maybe it was a bad idea to involve Delaney in the naming.

Natalie covered her laugh with her hand.

"Glitter, Fluffy, Bailey..." Delaney listed them on her fingers.

"Bailey's a possibility." It wasn't so girly. I hoped that this thing with Natalie and Delaney would last, but if it didn't, I didn't want to be stuck with a dog named Princess. "It might be a boy."

Delaney gave me a face. "Why would you want a boy?"

"Just keep thinking boys are bad," I said, getting an image of her as a teenager.

"But you're a boy," she said incredulously.

I met her gaze in the rearview mirror. "I'm a man. That's different."

Before Delaney could ask how, Natalie interrupted, "What about picking a name that means something to you?"

Delaney nodded. "It'll come to me when I see her."

"You're fairly confident it will be a girl," I said.

"Oh yeah. You don't want a boy dog. They lift their leg to pee."

We burst out laughing at her serious reasoning. Getting a puppy with these two was the best decision. It beat drinking a beer on the couch while I watched TV alone for the millionth time.

CHAPTER 15

NATALIE

I couldn't believe Mac was getting a puppy. Delaney wanted a pet, but Carter was against it. It wouldn't be possible to keep one at the B&B.

We were at the farm Gray suggested, which was about thirty minutes outside of town. The land was beautiful. I didn't think I appreciated the view of the mountains when I lived here growing up.

Delaney sat on the ground, the puppies playing with each other and climbing on her lap. She giggled each time one fell off her lap and onto the ground. They weren't steady on their feet. "They're so cute. I want them all."

"I was worried this would be a problem," I said to Mac.

Mac unloaded the puppy he'd been cradling into my arms. With a challenge in his eyes, he said, "See if you can resist."

Everything inside me softened when I caressed the puppy's head, his fur tickling my chin.

"We should name him Butter because he's yellow," Delaney said.

"I don't know if you should have put her in charge of names," I teased Mac, knowing he had to be regretting his decision.

"Cookie?" Delaney asked.

"That one's not bad. But we have to pick one first," Mac said diplomatically.

He was so good with her. I felt all my defenses falling. If I'd bothered to make a list, he was everything I ever wanted in a man: good with kids, responsible, hardworking, conscientious, and a family man.

I wasn't ready for this day to be over, and I was happy he'd suggested this outing. Even if we didn't get to bring a puppy home today, it was one of my favorite days.

"These puppies aren't quite ready to leave their mother, but I have one that just returned. She's four months old," the owner, Tina, said.

"Are you serious?" Delaney asked. At Tina's nod, she asked, "Where is she?"

"It's a boy. I kept him separate in case you wanted a true puppy."

"Why did the owners return him?" Mac asked.

"They found out their toddler was allergic, which is a common issue. You have no idea until you get the puppy home. They went to doctors, but there isn't much they can do at that age. They felt really bad about it and insisted he go to a forever home next time. Do you think you'd be a good fit for him?" Tina asked Delaney.

Delaney nodded solemnly. "Oh yes. I'm very responsible."

"The puppy will live with me, but Delaney will visit often," Mac said.

"This puppy adores kids," Tina said, heading inside the barn.

"He does?" Delaney asked, following the woman.

"Are you sure you want an older puppy?" I asked Mac, putting the puppy I'd been holding into the pen to play with his brothers and sisters.

Mac shrugged. "Honestly? I don't care. I just want a dog, and the younger they are, the more you have to get up with them in the middle of the night."

"They're a little like babies in that way," I agreed.

Delaney squealed inside the barn, and Mac said, "I think she found it."

"Mommy, come see. He's adorable."

I bumped Mac's shoulder lightly with mine. "Just so you know, I don't think she's met a puppy she didn't like. You'll be lucky to get out of here with just one."

Mac linked his fingers with mine and winked. "I'll keep that in mind."

"Can we get him?" Delaney asked before we'd even arrived at the stall.

Standing in the doorway, this puppy's feet and head were large, but his fur was soft. His feet were on Delaney's shoulders while he licked her. Delaney squeezed her eyes shut and hugged him tight. The puppy didn't seem to mind. He planted his butt in her lap and leaned hard against her chest as if he wanted to sink into her.

When she opened her eyes, she said, "I want him."

If Delaney noticed us holding hands, she didn't mention it, but then the dog was a good distraction.

"This isn't our decision," I gently reminded her, but the way she held this one, I knew I was going to be getting it if Mac didn't.

From the look on Mac's face, I knew he was a goner. This was his dog. He squatted next to Delaney and the puppy, holding his hand out to him. He sniffed it for a microsecond and then licked it.

The puppy moved out of Delaney's hold to get closer to Mac. Mac held his hand out in a stop motion and told him, "Sit." The puppy's butt hit the ground, but his tail wagged on the ground.

"They worked on basic training, but you'll need to continue it," Tina said.

"What do you say? Want to take her to basic training with me?" Mac asked Delaney.

Delaney's eyes widened. "Uh-huh."

Mac scratched behind his ear, and the dog tipped his head in ecstasy. Then he rolled onto the ground, showing his belly. "You said we can take her today?"

"She's yours if you want her," Tina said with a smile.

"What do you say? Want to come home with us?" Mac asked the puppy, but Delaney said, "Yes, yes, yes!"

I moved to snap a picture of the puppy, but then Delaney rested her head on Mac's shoulders, and I couldn't resist taking that one. It was the perfect picture of the three of them. If this ended up being something permanent, this was a picture I'd frame for the wall. I'd always wanted Delaney to have this kind of relationship with her father, but I guess it didn't matter as long as she had someone who stepped up. I just hoped Mac stuck around and didn't break both of our hearts.

The image was on my phone when Tina left to get the paperwork, and Mac asked, "You okay with this?"

I put the phone away, not wanting him to see the screen. I wasn't sure if it would freak him out that we looked like a family. "Absolutely. Besides, it's your decision."

"It feels like *our* decision. I invited you here for your advice."

"I don't think you can go wrong with any of them. They're fluffy and so sweet." But I never owned a dog, so I wasn't sure how much work they'd be.

"They pee in the house and chew your furniture," Mac said, more for Delaney's benefit than mine.

"It's your house she'll be peeing in," I reminded him. No matter what transpired between us in the last twenty-four hours, we were still new.

"Will you help me get everything she needs and get her settled at home?" Mac asked Delaney.

"Can we, Mom?" Delaney asked.

"I don't see why not." It was Saturday. We didn't have anything to do. I'd gotten a little lonely with it being just me and Delaney at home on the weekends. I was used to the noise of the crew during the week.

Delaney played with the puppy while Mac handed the woman a check and filled out the paperwork with promises to send updates and pictures.

Mac gently placed the puppy next to Delaney in the back-seat. "Can you hold his leash so he doesn't get into trouble?"

Delaney buckled her seat belt and took the leash from Mac. Nodding solemnly, she said, "I've got him."

In the front seat, Mac asked, "You mind if we head to the pet store? I don't have anything for a dog."

"Not at all."

I twisted around to check on Delaney, who was enamored with the puppy. He was trying to bite the leash, and Delaney giggled and kept moving it out of his reach.

"We have to come up with a name, but I can't decide on anything," Mac said as we pulled down the long lane.

"I bet it will come to you," I said.

"It better because calling him *Puppy* might stick," Mac said, looking into the rearview mirror at Delaney.

"We can't call a full-grown dog *Puppy*."

I almost wished we could get a pet for the B&B, but it wasn't practical. Our place was small, and the only needs I could manage were Delaney's and the guests'.

It was something I hadn't considered when I bought the place, that our lives might be limited by the guests' needs and desires. I thought it would be convenient to live in the same house, but now, I wondered if that meant I'd never escape work, and Delaney wouldn't have a real home of her own. When it opened, we'd share the backyard with guests. Someone new each week.

"What's wrong?" Mac asked, glancing over at me.

"I'm rethinking living in the owner's suite."

"You might want to hire someone to manage the place for you. You can offer them a free place to live. That's a great incentive."

"Business goals, right?" It could be years before the B&B was doing well enough to justify hiring employees. By then, Delaney would be a teenager.

"Don't worry about it. We'll figure it out," Mac said, pulling into the lot of a pet store.

We climbed out, and Delaney was thrilled to take the puppy into the store. Mac kept a close eye on her hold on the leash, reaching out to help when another dog walked by. So far, the puppy seemed content to sniff. He didn't seem aggressive, but then he was a puppy. His full personality probably hadn't developed yet.

We picked out dog beds, a crate, and bowls. Mac deferred to Delaney on the choices, only refusing her suggestion of anything pink.

While Delaney tested out toys for the puppy, Mac read the labels for the dog foods, searching online for the best options before finally settling on a brand. "We need to schedule a vet appointment too."

"Can I come with you?" Delaney asked when Mac rang up his purchases.

"If your mom is okay with it, and you don't have school."

"You still up for helping me get him settled at home?" Mac asked Delaney in the rearview mirror.

"Uh-huh," Delaney said from the backseat.

"We've come this far, might as well." I wanted to see Mac's house. I had a feeling it might give me more insight into him.

He drove out of town to a newer neighborhood, where the homes were spread out. Each one seemingly had a few acres, and the entire neighborhood backed to woods and the mountains.

His house was a large colonial but not exactly what I pictured for a bachelor. When he pulled into the driveway, he said, "Home sweet home."

"This is nice," I observed as we stepped inside. The space was large and open with wood floors, an office, a dining room, a large kitchen, and a sunken family room.

"It seems empty when I'm here alone," Mac said, his footsteps echoing through the house.

Maybe that's why he wanted a puppy.

Delaney was chasing the puppy through the house, his mouth on a squeaky tennis ball she'd wanted him to have.

"Let's take him outside," Mac said to Delaney.

He opened the French doors, and the puppy ran through them. "It's good the yard is fenced. He'll have plenty of room to play."

We followed him out onto a large deck, with steps going down to the yard. The puppy raced around the deck before skidding to a stop by the steps as if he'd never seen them before. Delaney began coaxing him down with a treat she must have grabbed from one of the many bags we'd bought.

"You really want Delaney to come to training?" I asked Mac, wondering why he wanted to ingrain us more into his life when he didn't want anything long-term.

"I know she'll love it, and it's a good idea if she's going to be around. He needs to listen to the smallest member of the family."

"Is that what we are?" I asked him, my heart thumping wildly in my chest.

"I'd like to think it's the start of one," Mac said hesitantly.

I liked the sound of that.

When Mac lifted his arm, I instinctively cuddled into his side to watch Delaney with the puppy.

She threw him a ball and begged him to bring it back.

"The dog's good for her. We always had one growing up. We

were in charge of training and walking it. It taught us responsibility," Mac said.

"I almost wish we could get one."

"You can come see him as much as you want. Now, what do you say about ordering pizza for dinner?"

My stomach rumbled at the mention of food.

"Pizza it is. I'll call it in. Just keep an eye on them. I trust Delaney, but the dog is new. We don't know if he'll nip at her."

"I'm on it." I descended the stairs to the yard. Each time the puppy returned the ball to Delaney, he jumped around and nipped her hands until she threw it again. I told him no, but it didn't seem to faze him.

Mac returned shortly after he placed the order and observed the interaction, then handed Delaney a toy. "When he nips, hand him a chew toy. Always keep one in your pocket so you can do that. If he jumps, knee him in the chest. You can't hurt him. He's a sturdy guy."

"You know a lot about dogs," I said.

"When we were kids, Mom claimed we kept the dog exercised and entertained with all of our energy."

"That's probably true." I could imagine a younger Mac tasked with playing with a dog, taking him for walks, and feeding him meals. I bet he was a responsible kid.

We played with the puppy in the backyard until the pizza arrived, and then we ate on the deck.

"I almost never eat out here. It doesn't make sense when it's just me."

It hit me then as I took a large bite of the greasy pizza. Mac was lonely. He wanted to fill his house with energy and laughter but hadn't found someone who fit into his life. Did we?

I hadn't intended to move on this quickly after my divorce, but when the right person comes into your life, you take the leap. I just wasn't sure where Mac's head was at. Was he still cautious because of his history with women? Or was he finally putting it behind him?

After dinner, we cleaned up and headed into the family room because the night air was cool. Mac put on the TV to something Delaney would watch, and we sat on the couch while Mac set up the puppy's bowls and crate. He filled a small basket with his toys.

Once the puppy ate dinner and Mac took him outside to pee, the puppy curled up with Delaney on the couch. Mac started a fire, and we sat on the couch, reminiscing about the day. When it was close to Delaney's bedtime, I said, "We should get going."

Mac smiled and pointed at Delaney, who was curled up on the couch, asleep. "Why don't you stay the night? I can move her into the guest room."

I hated to wake her. It would be hard to get her back to sleep if I moved her now. "If you're sure?"

He grinned. "I'm positive. Let me make up the guest room, and then I'll move her."

He disappeared, and I wondered what I was getting myself into. We'd helped him buy a puppy, then supplies, and now we were staying the night at his house. It was wonderful and domestic, but was Mac someone we could count on?

When the B&B opened, I'd be tied to that place, forced to be on call twenty-four hours a day. The thought didn't hold the same appeal it did when I was contemplating this new step in my life.

Mac returned and said, "All set." Then he lifted Delaney's sleeping form into his arms. The sight did some crazy pitter-patter thing to my heart. I followed him up the steps and down the hallway into a bedroom. There was a double bed, a nightstand, a bookshelf along one wall, and a dresser.

He'd already pulled back the covers, so he lowered her down and pulled the comforter over her.

I leaned over to kiss her forehead, wondering what she'd

think when she woke in a strange bedroom. "Do you have a nightlight for the hallway so she can find the bathroom if she has to get up in the middle of the night?"

"I'm sure I have one somewhere." He scrounged in the drawers of the bathroom, lifting the lights when he found them. He plugged one into the bathroom socket and one in the hall-way. "How's that?"

"Perfect," I said as he pulled me into his side. We returned to the family room where the fire was still going strong.

"Are you sure it's okay for us to stay?"

"I like having you here. You and Delaney fill all the empty spaces."

My heart warmed at that. I liked being what Mac needed. We were probably moving too fast, but I couldn't seem to put on the brakes because I liked him, and I wanted him to be happy. It was a different sort of relationship than what I'd had with Carter. We'd met in college at some party. We never intended for it to be long-term. We should have given each other space before settling down with each other.

Mac picked up the remote and flipped through channels as we snuggled together on the couch. I rested my cheek on his chest, listening to the steady beat of his heart. When it got late, he clicked off the TV, taking the puppy out to the yard and settling him in the crate for the night. Then he held out his hand. "Ready to go to bed?"

I placed my hand in his, more than ready to spend the night with him. Who knew how many opportunities we'd get for something like this? Or maybe we'd get lucky, and Delaney would be okay with overnights. At least until the B&B officially opened. Then everything would change.

A lamp cast a muted glow over the room. He handed me a T-shirt and shorts, and I cleaned up in the bathroom before joining him in the bed.

"Should we behave ourselves since Delaney is just down the hall?" Mac whispered in my ear.

I surprised myself by saying, "Can you be quiet?"

He took that as a challenge and rolled me onto my back, settling between my legs. He shifted his hips so that his cock ground into my center. "Can you?"

I gasped at the contact, not entirely sure I could make that promise. Not with him.

"Let's see." Then he was kissing me. The thought of needing to be quiet spurred our desire until we heard a whimper.

Mac lifted his head. "Is that—"

Then another.

"I think it's the puppy."

Mac dropped his head to my chest. "I'm being cock-blocked by a dog."

I giggled, my fingers tangling in his hair.

He rolled to his back and threw his arm over his forehead. "Should we get him?"

"You've been a parent for a few hours and you're already caving."

"If we put him in the bed, he'll feel better."

"The guy at the store said crates are like a den to them. They make them feel safe."

"But he's crying," Mac said, like the sound pained him.

I propped myself on my elbow so I could see him better. "You are a huge softy, aren't you?"

His expression pained, he asked, "How can you listen to him?"

I laughed. "I have a child. I'm used to crying and whining. You can't give in or you'll have a bigger problem. Besides, he's not a baby that needs you to hold him when he cries."

"Should we put the crate in here?" Mac asked.

"It might make him feel better to be with his pack."

Mac moved the crate and puppy into his room and then

turned off the light. After a few minutes, the puppy finally curled up and went to sleep.

Mac let out a breath. "Who knew having a puppy would be this much work?"

"I think you're up for the challenge." The puppy would be good for him, filling his house with noise and energy when we couldn't be here.

CHAPTER 16

MAC

The puppy woke me once in the middle of the night and then again early in the morning. I enjoyed getting up early in the morning and drinking my coffee. I just wondered what I'd do when I needed to go to work. Maybe he could come with me? Or perhaps he could stay with Natalie?

Once the puppy did his business, I fed him and got started on breakfast, pulling out eggs, bacon, and pancake mix. I wasn't sure what Delaney and Natalie ate for breakfast.

Delaney woke up first and wandered into the kitchen in her wrinkled clothes with her hair knotted. "Morning, sweetie. You find the bathroom okay?"

She sat on the stool, looking a little confused. "We're still here."

I nodded. "You fell asleep on the couch last night. We didn't want to move you."

"Are you making breakfast?" she asked, perking up a bit.

"Eggs, pancakes, and bacon. Which do you prefer?"

"Can I have a little of everything?"

I held my hand over my heart. "A girl after my own heart."

When she giggled, she stole another piece of my heart.

I pulled out the orange juice and poured her a glass. When her eyes got big, I thought to ask, "Is your mom okay with you having juice?"

"Uh-huh."

"Are you telling me the truth?" I had a bad feeling about it.

Delaney grimaced. "Juice isn't good for your teeth. Mommy only lets me have it when I'm sick or on vacation."

I swiped the glass away, dumping it into the sink. "Thank you for being honest. Milk?"

She nodded, looking disappointed.

"Hey, this won't work if you're not honest with me about what your mother would do. I don't think she'd appreciate me giving you something that she doesn't want you to have. She has her reasons."

Delaney sighed. "I know."

When I put a plate of pancakes, eggs, and bacon in front of her, she asked, "Can we stay here again?"

"That's up to your mother." I was a little worried I'd already messed up with the juice. What else didn't I know?

I sat next to her and dug into the food I prepared. Delaney chatted with me about the puppy and everything he needed to learn. It was sweet, and I enjoyed her company.

When we were finished, I stood to clean up the dishes when Natalie wandered in. "You're both up. I haven't slept this long in ages."

"That's because I'm always up early," Delaney said with a smile.

"I made breakfast. Delaney told me juice wasn't a good idea."

Natalie sat on a stool. "This is quite a spread. I didn't expect you to watch Delaney or make breakfast."

"I was up with the puppy and figured you could use the sleep."

"Thank you," she said simply as I piled a plate high with food and slid it across the counter toward her.

"Would you like coffee or toast?" I liked how they looked in my kitchen.

Natalie smiled. "Coffee would be great. Thanks."

Delaney hopped down to play with the puppy and his new toys.

"You sleep okay?" I asked Natalie.

"I slept great. Your bed is amazing, and this house—it's so cozy and inviting."

I looked around at the mostly empty walls. I had a few landscape pieces with views of the mountains, but that was it.

"It's better than living in an apartment. That's all I meant. You have a home."

"Are you regretting moving into the owner's suite?" I braced my elbows on the counter and watched while she ate slowly, considering her words.

"You need the manager on-site to handle any issues that might come up with the building and the guests."

"But you don't have to do it yourself. You could hire a manager."

Natalie frowned. "Not yet. It will be a while before that's a reality."

"It's fairly busy year-round here with tourists. I think you'll be booked in no time."

"How can you be so sure?" she asked me.

I wasn't positive about anything when it came to interpersonal relationships, but business, that I understood. "I'm confident because you're opening a B&B on Main Street. When we're done with it, the accommodations will be inviting and luxurious. There's no way you won't be booked year-round. Especially after Sam is done with the outside."

"I can't thank him enough for helping me out."

"It's a mutually beneficial arrangement. Besides, you helped out Alice, providing her the space she needed for her store at a reasonable price."

"She's helping me with the front counter."

"We help each other out. That's what we do. Our family will help spread the word when you open for business."

"I'm so lucky that I hired your family's business and got to know you better. It's been good for me and Delaney."

"You're a part of our family now." I meant the Fletcher family collectively, but I wished we were talking about starting our own family—me, Delaney, and Natalie. I wanted it all.

"I hope you're right."

When she finished eating, I cleaned the dishes while they played with the puppy in the living room.

"We need to name him. We can't keep calling him *Puppy*," I said to them.

Delaney looked outside where there was a beautiful view of the mountains. It was the sole reason I bought this house. "What about Rocky? Mom said to pick a name that meant something to you, and you have this view of the mountains. I know it's not the Rocky Mountains, but—"

A sense of rightness flowed through me, and it wasn't just that Delaney had named my dog. "It's perfect. What do you say, Rocky? You like that name?" I dropped to the floor, and Rocky wagged his tail excitedly as he kissed my face.

"He likes it!" Delaney exclaimed, moving to sit next to me.

"He loves you," I said as Rocky climbed into her lap, scrambling to get her to pet him. When she complied, he licked her face, and she giggled. There was nothing better than puppy kisses and giggles.

I met Natalie's gaze, and I winked at her. I hoped she understood my meaning. I wanted more mornings like this.

"You want to take him for a walk?"

Delaney's eyes grew wide. "Can I hold the leash?"

"I don't see why not."

"Can we stop at home and get showered and dressed?" Natalie asked, still cradling her mug of coffee.

"We can walk around town, maybe grab some lunch. A few of the restaurants are dog friendly if you sit on the patio." I held my breath, wondering if this was the moment Natalie pulled back or decided I was pushing too hard. But she didn't.

She smiled at us and said, "That sounds great."

"But there's no rush. Finish your coffee."

"If I were you, I'd never get tired of this view."

This house was the perfect one to raise a family. There was room to grow. We could add a playground or even a pool if that's what they wanted. But I couldn't get ahead of myself. I'd done that too many times before. I needed to chill out and take things slow.

I was falling hard and fast for Natalie and Delaney. The years of holding myself back hadn't changed anything. I was still the same romantic at heart. I wanted a wife and a family, and Natalie and Delaney fit. I liked them. But I didn't want to ruin it with unreasonable expectations.

My head was a mess as I drove them to the B&B and waited for them to get ready. Then we walked downtown. It was a treat because it was the first time Natalie or Delaney had wandered the town.

They were excited over each new shop, eager to go in and peruse the wares. I waited outside with Rocky, content to just spend the day with them. We stopped at a deli for lunch and took the food to the park. It was a nice day, cool but not unbearable. When Delaney was tired, we headed home.

When I didn't get out of the truck, Natalie said, "Come inside. I want to make you dinner."

"I don't want to intrude on your evening. I'm sure you need to get ready for the week and school." She probably had laundry and cleaning to do.

"I'd really like to make you dinner to thank you for everything. Unless you need to get Rocky home."

"I brought him small bags of food because I wasn't sure how long we'd be gone."

"Then come inside," Natalie said with a smile.

And then Delaney said, "Please," from the backseat, and I caved. There was nothing I wouldn't do for them.

I helped Natalie cut the veggies for dinner, and then Delaney showed me how to sew, using her little kit. I never thought I'd let a nine-year-old girl teach me to sew, but I couldn't say no. It was more fun than I thought it would be. Although my skill must not have been up to Delaney's standards, because when I showed her my attempt at making the snail, she said, "Don't worry. You just need more practice."

I held it up. "I didn't think it looked too bad."

Delaney made a face. "Eh."

My stitches were gaping at parts and overlapping at others. "You'll have to keep teaching me."

"Maybe Miss Miranda can help. She taught me."

I set my needle and snail aside. "I think you might be more talented in this area. It's my fingers. They're too big for these tiny needles."

"Your fingers are too big? That's your excuse?" Natalie teased from the kitchen, where she was keeping an eye on the chicken cooking on the stove.

"Have you seen this needle?" I held it up so she could see it.

"You always make excuses when things aren't perfect?"

"I guess it's a habit with having two brothers. We do tend to do that. We rib each other."

"I'd love to have brothers," Delaney said.

"You can have Tyler and Sam. I'll gladly give them to you because they're a pain in my—"

"Don't finish that sentence!" Natalie yelled in her mom voice from the kitchen.

"Butt," I finally whispered in a conspiratorial tone, and Delaney giggled.

When she recovered, she said, "Mommy doesn't like when I say potty words."

"'Butt' isn't a potty word, is it?" I twisted around to see the disapproval on Natalie's face.

Natalie shook her head, but her lips twitched. "If you let a kid say something like that, it's all they'll say in the most embarrassing situations, so no, I don't allow it."

Ensuring that Delaney's attention was on the TV, I stepped behind Natalie and kissed her shoulder. "I have a feeling that's going to be an issue with Delaney hanging out with me and my family."

Natalie shrugged, her expression vulnerable. "It's good for her to have more people around her, supporting her."

She'd moved to a town she hadn't lived in for years, not knowing most people. She was lonely. Trying to lighten her mood, I teased, "So, it's okay if I say 'butt'?"

She smacked me, but I used her open stance to pull her into my body. "You didn't say no."

"I think I made myself clear."

Keeping an eye on Delaney, I kissed down her neck. Natalie's eyelids fluttered closed as she tilted her neck to give me access.

"When will dinner be ready? I'm starving," Delaney whined.

Natalie jumped back from me, and the moment was broken. I knew what we had was fragile, but it would be nice when Delaney knew about it. I didn't want to hide what was going on between us forever. But I could be patient. I understood that Natalie was trying to protect her.

She already had one man walk out of her life and didn't need a second to do the same. The thought of walking away from these two was a crushing weight on my chest. I couldn't draw a breath without feeling the heaviness.

Natalie stepped around me to move the pan with the chicken to the back burner. "Can you throw the salad together?"

She'd already chopped lettuce, so I added it to a large serving bowl along with shredded carrots and cherry tomatoes. I grabbed a couple of dressings out of the fridge and placed them on the small, round table.

Their space was small, and they had to share the common areas with guests. I couldn't help but think Delaney deserved a yard for herself. Somewhere she could play and chase a dog.

As we sat down to eat, Delaney yammered on about the funny episode of a cartoon she'd just watched. I could envision Natalie and Delaney sitting at my table for dinner, getting up to let the dog out, and cuddling on the couch to watch TV afterward. It was so clear in my mind.

"Is something wrong with your food?" Natalie asked with a glance at my full plate.

I lifted my fork. "Not at all. I was just thinking about something."

Delaney launched into a recitation of the clubs she participated in at school, and I listened with half an ear. All I could think about was what if I was all in with these two? What if I let it go wherever it would? What if we had a future?

As soon as my heart soared, I reminded myself it was reckless. I knew better than anyone how these things ended. In the end, I was never the man someone wanted. Women were looking for something I couldn't offer. Over the years, my brothers had claimed women liked men who played hard to get, but I didn't like games. I was an open book, someone who knew what he wanted—a woman to love him and eventually a family.

I ate, not really tasting anything, but said, "Good dinner, Natalie," when I finished.

She flushed with pleasure. "Thank you."

From her reaction, I suspected her husband either wasn't present for mealtimes or didn't give her the credit she deserved. I vowed to treat her better, to let her know when I appreciated her, and to remind her how she made me feel.

My vision went a little blurry when I realized how big of a risk I was taking. I was supposed to be protecting myself, not opening myself up for rejection. But I couldn't change who I was at my core, no matter how much I'd tried. I just hoped my family would be there to pick up the pieces when it exploded in my face.

After dinner, Natalie told Delaney to finish her homework, so I volunteered to clean while they sat together at the table, going over some math problems. Every once in a while, Delaney let out a frustrated huff. "Why don't you know how to do this?"

Natalie stood. "It's different from how I learned. Let me see if your teacher sent any instructions."

I squeezed Natalie's shoulder as I moved past her. "Let me take a look."

It was a math problem she had to solve, and she'd drawn a large box in the space provided for the answer. "What's this for?"

Delaney showed me how she was supposed to use the box to show her work, and I immediately understood it. "This is easy peasy. Let's reread the problem and fill it in as we go."

Natalie sat across from us, watching as we slowly went through the problem.

When Delaney got the right answer, she moved on to the next one, doing it by herself. I just nodded my head in approval when she placed the numbers in the correct spot. When she was done, I said, "See? I told you it was easy."

To my surprise, Delaney hopped into my lap and wrapped her arms around my neck. Her breath was hot on my cheek. "Thank you."

Before I could say, *"You're welcome,"* she'd slipped off again to carry her homework to her backpack.

"Thank you for doing that. I struggle with math, and she gets frustrated with me. I'm better at language arts."

"I'm good with numbers. I don't mind helping."

Her shoulders lowered. "They do everything differently now. I'm useless to her."

I was quick to disavow her of that notion. "You're an amazing mother."

"I appreciate the help." She smiled and then sighed when she looked at the clock above the stove. "It's time for her shower."

"I need to get this baby home anyway." Rocky had fallen asleep in a pile of Delaney's jackets by the door.

"Can't he stay with us?" Delaney asked when I picked up Rocky.

"He's Mac's dog," Natalie reminded her gently.

Delaney's face fell.

"You can come visit him anytime, and who knows, I might bring him to work with me."

"You can't do that. He might be scared of the noise or get hurt," Natalie said.

"I'll figure out something," I said, opening the door to leave.

Natalie bit her lower lip as if she was working something out in her head. "Why don't you bring him here? I can keep an eye on him while I'm working this week."

This was what I was hoping for. "You'd do that?"

"Of course. Besides, I love the little guy already." Natalie petted his head, and the puppy sleepily lifted his head to lick her hand.

"So, Rocky will be here when I get home from school?" Delaney asked excitedly.

"Looks like it," I said to her, pleased when she cheered.

"It's bedtime for you. Say good-bye to Mac and Rocky, then get in the shower."

I squatted down with the puppy so Delaney could pet Rocky, but she wrapped her arms around my neck instead. It felt like she was hugging my heart because it contracted. I closed my eyes against the overwhelming sensations. I wanted this feeling all the time. I wanted someone to come home to, someone to love.

The sensation was so overwhelming that I dropped a quick peck on Delaney's cheek and said a rushed good-bye to Natalie so I could get into the relative quiet of my cab. I needed some distance and some clarity. We'd spent all weekend together, and it was messing with my head. I wanted things I shouldn't and longed for scenarios that could never be mine.

I shouldn't be leaving my puppy with Natalie. It would only bring us closer together. It would force me to fall deeper with her. My brothers would say I was an idiot. That I was going to get hurt. It was inevitable when you got involved with a mother right after a divorce. I was just a rebound for her. Not a serious relationship.

Who got divorced and jumped into a relationship with the next guy they met? No one.

I settled Rocky on a towel in the passenger seat. He lifted his head, looking around at the dark interior. "It's just you and me, buddy."

It was a good thing I'd gotten a dog. They were known to be loyal companions. It was the smartest commitment I'd made in years. He wouldn't walk away from me.

CHAPTER 17

NATALIE

For the next few weeks, Mac dropped Rocky off at my apartment each morning, and Delaney had a chance to cuddle with him before she got on the bus. He was usually here when she got home too. She was starting to think he was hers.

I didn't have the heart to tell her that the renovation would be completed soon, and Mac wouldn't need to drop his dog off with us. He'd work at a different location, and we wouldn't see him as much. He'd be busy with something or someone else, and we'd have to get used to being alone again.

Or, at least, alone while we entertained guests at the B&B. The tiling in the bathroom was finally done, and Mac was putting in the fixtures. The crew was working on the smaller things, like the trim and finishing details.

Sam began work on the yard, and it had gotten incrementally noisier. It was just outside my window, so that hadn't helped either. I took the puppy for walks and sat outside a local coffee shop to get some quiet.

I'd ordered furniture for the front porch and rooms. I was

just waiting for everything to be delivered. I'd paid extra for things to be put together on-site. I couldn't move furniture, and I had no business asking the renovation crew to help.

This was my business, and I needed to do it on my own. One afternoon, I sat on the front porch, waiting for Delaney to get off the bus. Rocky sat on the swing next to me, content to rest his head in my lap while I rocked us.

I was happy. I loved this town, and the B&B was finally coming together. I had a lot to be thankful for. I was surprised when a car pulled to the curb, and a man got out of the back. It must have been a private driver because the car left as soon as he was on the sidewalk.

It was Carter.

I stood, my heart beating rapidly in my chest. "What are you doing here?"

"I can't come see my wife?" he asked wryly as he approached with a suitcase.

"You lost the right to call me that when you left me for another woman," I said, not liking the bitterness that seeped into my voice.

"What's this?" he asked, looking at Rocky, who growled next to me, his hair on end.

Flustered, I wondered if I should say it was my boyfriend's. "He belongs to one of the contractors. But the question is, what are you really doing here?"

I was very aware that Delaney's bus would be here any moment, and she'd walk into this little confrontation. She wanted to see her father, but I wasn't sure he was here to see her.

He stood in front of me. "This escapade has gone on long enough. It's time for you to move back. My parents want to see Delaney."

I laughed without any humor. He hadn't said he wanted us back or that his parents missed her. "No."

He flinched. "You're not even going to hear me out?"

"There's nothing to say. We're divorced. There's zero chance I'll ever get back with you. Besides, you have a new girlfriend in Texas, remember?"

His face reddened. "We're not together anymore."

"Let me get this straight. You cheated on me and then moved to Texas to live with another woman, who also left her family—for what? A fling?" I was incensed that they'd impulsively uprooted two families.

He looked away from me. "It wasn't supposed to be."

"If you want to see Delaney, this isn't the way to do it. You need to talk to me before you just show up. I need to prepare her."

He scowled. "She's my daughter. She doesn't need to prepare to see me."

"When she hasn't seen you in months?" I needed the warning so I could prepare.

"Whose fault is that? You're the one who moved to this godforsaken place." He lifted his arms around him.

"This is my hometown. And you left South Carolina first. You expected me to live in that house, so close to your parents, until you came to your senses and realized what you lost?"

The front door opened, and Mac stepped out. His expression was one of concern. "The bus is here."

I brushed past Carter, but he grabbed my arm to stop me. "I'm not done talking."

I sensed Mac move closer, waiting for the right moment to step in, but I could handle myself.

Shaking him free, I said, "I need to get my daughter."

"You mean *our* daughter?"

I didn't bother arguing because I was already flying down the steps in my rush to get to Delaney, to protect her from her father. I didn't want her to get hurt, but I knew I wouldn't be able to stop it.

I met her on the sidewalk.

"What's wrong?" she asked, probably sensing my panic.

"Your father is here. I didn't know he was coming," I said softly, my heart threatening to beat out of my chest.

"He is?" Excitement filled her face as she looked past me. "Daddy!" she cried as she rushed toward the porch, past Mac.

Carter didn't get down on her level like Mac did to accept her hug. She settled for hugging his waist while he patted her head awkwardly.

"How long are you staying? Can we go skiing?" Delaney asked, gazing up at him.

"Maybe," Carter said absentmindedly, his gaze on me. "Can we talk?"

"We have nothing to discuss. I have a snack and dinner to prepare. If you want to talk, you can call or email."

"But I want to see Daddy," Delaney pouted.

The problem was, I didn't think Carter was here to see her. He wanted me to move back to South Carolina, but I had a feeling he was still living in Texas.

"I'll get a hotel room in town. But I'm not going anywhere." He moved off the porch, pulling out his phone, probably to call for a car.

I didn't like the threat that tinged his tone.

Mac ushered us inside. "Did you know he was coming?"

Tears stung my eyes. "No."

"You want to go to my place for dinner? He can't show up there unannounced." Mac's voice was carefully controlled, his body tense with irritation.

"We can't crash your plans," I started, just as Delaney said, "Yes."

After waiting for Carter to leave, Mac gathered Rocky's things and Delaney's backpack and led her to his truck. I followed them, making sure the apartment was locked up. I couldn't believe Carter was here. I never expected him to care what was going on with us after he'd so easily walked away. What had changed?

Mac reached over and interlaced my fingers with his. It didn't feel right. I wanted the comfort but felt like I didn't deserve it, not with my past showing up in the form of my ex. "It's going to be okay."

But those were the words I should be saying to Delaney. I was supposed to be comforting her.

When we got to his house, Mac said to Delaney, "Why don't you take Rocky around to the backyard to let him run?"

Mac followed behind her, helping her to open and shut the gate. He returned to stand in front of me, his expression pained.

"I'm sorry you had to see that. I didn't know he'd show up like that." Carter hadn't given me any reason to think he was interested in seeing us or rekindling our relationship.

"It seemed like he wanted to see you, not Delaney." Mac's voice was low.

My stomach dropped. "You caught that too?"

He tipped his head to the side, his arms crossed over his chest. There was a chasm between us. "Should I be worried?"

"Why would you think I'd go back to him?" I asked, genuinely wanting to understand his response.

Mac shifted on his feet, unable to meet my gaze. "Because he's your ex, and at one time, you must have loved him enough to marry him."

"He left me for another woman. But our relationship wasn't great before that. We'd already drifted apart. For me, it was because he didn't want much to do with Delaney. Then he stopped putting any effort into our relationship. We didn't have more kids. I wasn't sure he wanted them, and I wasn't sure I wanted more with him." I understood Mac's history with women, and I wanted to reassure him. I wasn't sure if he could handle Carter showing up like this.

"I don't know what to think," he finally said, his shoulders lowering in defeat.

I moved into his body, the wind blowing hard around us. There was a storm coming. I wrapped my arms around his waist and rested my head on his shoulder. "I like what we have. I have no intentions of entertaining the idea of getting back with Carter. But you'll have to trust me on that."

He sighed as his arms tightened around me. "I want to."

I looked up at him. "Carter isn't the man for me. He's proven that time and time again. His leaving gave me the courage to go out on my own, to move back home, and to start a business. It was a good thing for me but not necessarily for Delaney."

"She doesn't need her father in her life if he's going to disappoint her."

"I have to agree with that. I wrestled with the concept that he should have access, but what if it's not healthy?"

Mac rubbed my shoulders to warm me. "Sam goes through the same thing with his ex, Felicia. She pops in and out of Maggie's life when it suits her. Sam let it go on for a long time, but now he sticks to a custody agreement. She can't see Maggie without adhering to the schedule."

"Sam doesn't worry that Felicia will change her mind and ask for custody?" I asked as Mac took my hand and unlocked the front door.

"He did at one point, but I think he's fairly confident that being a full-time mother is not what she wants. If she wanted to be a mother, she'd live nearby so she could see Maggie on a consistent basis."

"Oh my god, what if Carter moves here?" I asked, panicking now.

Mac's jaw tightened. "Then we'll deal with it."

I liked the idea of Mac being by my side. I could handle Carter, but I liked his support.

He led me to the couch and waited for me to sink into the cushions before he started the fire. Once it was stoked, he sat next to me. "I'm sorry I freaked out when he showed up. It brought everything back from my ex, who went back to her husband. But I don't want to be that guy anymore, comparing everyone to my ex."

I took his hands in mine. "I don't want that for you either."

"I need to forget about that and move on. I want to be here for you."

Relief flooded my veins. Somehow, everything was easier when you had support. I didn't feel so alone.

Mac pulled me in to his side. "We'll get through this together."

A second later, Delaney was looking through the window on the deck. The puppy scratched at the door.

"I'll let them in." Mac eased out of my hold.

I hated that Carter was here and causing trouble. I would have liked more time with Mac before he felt challenged like this. He'd only recently given in to whatever this was between us. I was worried he wasn't strong enough to withstand whatever Carter's plan was.

When Carter wanted something, he went after it. I just hadn't been the subject of his desires for a long time.

Mac opened the door, and Delaney ran in with red cheeks. "It's so dark. Do you think it will rain?"

"It looks like it."

Delaney did a little dance and said, "I can't wait. I love playing in the rain."

Delaney didn't seem to be fazed by her father showing up on her front porch. I was grateful for that, but she tended to confide in me when I tucked her into bed. I'd need to be prepared for her questions.

My phone buzzed. It was Carter saying he'd checked into

another B&B down the street and wanted to schedule a time to talk. I put my phone away, not ready to deal with him and what his presence might mean.

My life was about to be turned inside out, and I wasn't ready for it. I wished I could close my eyes and transport myself back to the last few weeks when we'd spent our free time with Mac and Rocky, either at my place or at Mac's. We'd gotten close but not close enough to withstand the windstorm that was my ex.

We decided to stay at Mac's all weekend. We'd left some clothes here for weekends when we decided to stay over. Delaney thought it was one big sleepover.

I finally agreed to meet Carter on Monday. He could wait.

We made pizzas and cooked them in a new brick oven Sam installed in his outdoor kitchen. He'd put on the fire outside and turned on a few heaters so we could enjoy the mountain view. Even though it was windy, it never rained.

When it was time for Delaney to get ready for bed, she shrieked from the guest room.

"It's probably a spider," I said as I took off for the bedroom. I paused in the doorway, not sure what I was seeing.

"What's this?" I asked Mac when he joined me.

He draped his arm over my shoulder. "I wanted her to feel more at home here."

There was a wooden loft twin bed over a double, a desk with a lamp, and a round chair for her to read in. Delaney was drawn to a chair that hung from the ceiling. She sat on the small cushion, drawing the curtains around herself. "This is so cool."

"The best part is that it lights up." Mac showed her the switch, and twinkly lights spread over the transparent material. "Sam helped me with it after he installed the oven."

"I can't believe you did this. It's too much," I said when he moved closer, his expression filled with delight.

"She loves it. That's all that matters."

"Well, yeah. But now she's not going to want to live in her

bedroom at my place," I said, feeling a little uncomfortable with his thoughtful gift. It wasn't something I could provide for her right now.

He rubbed a hand over my cheek. "I'm sorry. That wasn't my intention."

There was nothing about the room that screamed Delaney, so maybe I could justify this as a space for Maggie when she visited. But it felt like he'd done this specifically for her. It was more of a tween bedroom than a little girl's. I rested a palm on his chest. "It's amazing. Thank you for making her feel at home."

He squeezed me tighter to his body. "We should talk to her. Tell her we're more than friends."

"I think she suspects, but I agree." Especially with her father around. We weren't careful around her. We held hands and hugged but never kissed. And if it made Mac more comfortable, I'd do it.

I didn't want him to doubt us or what we had. I wasn't sure if we'd make it, but I liked him. He was a good man who deserved happiness. I liked to think I did too.

Just because my marriage didn't work out didn't mean there weren't great guys out there. Mac was one of the best. I'd be lucky to have him in our future.

Delaney hopped out of the swinging chair and opened her drawers. "All of my things are here."

There was even a basket of stuffed animals in the corner that Delaney could put on the bed. He'd thought of everything.

"There's one more surprise," Mac said with a grin.

"What is it?" Delaney asked, her voice filled with anticipation.

Mac flipped a switch that turned off the overhead light and flipped on another one that lit up twinkle lights. They were hung on the bottom of the loft and around the room, crisscrossing to light up the room.

Delaney stood in the room, her mouth dropping open, as she slowly spun in a circle. "I love it."

"What do you say?" I asked Delaney.

Delaney stopped mid-spin and ran for Mac, and unlike her father, he dipped to meet her, lifting her in his arms. Her arms tightened around his neck, and she said, "Thank you. Thank you." Then she placed kisses over his face as his eyes closed.

"You're welcome, sweet girl," he said as he dropped her back to the floor, his throat tight with emotion.

He was falling for my daughter. Maybe he already had.

It took a while to get Delaney calm enough to fall asleep in her made-over room. When she was finally out, we got ready for bed and lay on our backs in Mac's king bed. I loved it here. It was quiet and spacious, and I felt content in a way I hadn't when I was married to Carter.

"We should have twinkly lights on the ceiling," I teased.

Mac rolled to his side so his head was propped on his hand. "It would be a nice addition."

"I can't believe you did that." He'd bought furniture and lights. He thought about what she might like. Emotion clogged my throat.

"I wanted her to feel at home here."

"I don't think she's ever going to want to leave."

He kissed me softly. "That's the idea."

He couldn't be saying he wanted us to move in here. I couldn't with the B&B opening soon anyway. I couldn't believe he'd be ready for something like that anytime soon.

"I like having you here." He kissed me a second time.

The soft kisses turned longer and deeper as he slowly removed our clothes. I savored every touch and soft press of his lips. By the time he entered me, I was soft, pliant, and ready for him. With long, sure strokes, he built me up only to send me over the edge. There was no other way to describe it other than making love.

My chest expanded with emotion, and my mind went to places it shouldn't. I imagined a future with Mac, living here, hiring a manager for the B&B, and maybe even having another child. It was crazy to let myself go there, but I couldn't help it. I'd fallen for Mac despite any logic or reason. I just hoped he was in this with me.

CHAPTER 18

MAC

Over the weekend, we stayed in our bubble, not leaving my house except to go to my family's Sunday dinner. We arrived together, but no one mentioned it.

As it was, I was close to freaking out with Natalie's ex in town. What did he want? To get her back? It was a trigger for me. One I was desperately trying to fight off. It was easy over the weekend when it was just us, but now, Delaney was back in school, and I was at work.

Ever since Natalie left this morning to meet Carter at the coffee shop downtown, I was tense and short with everyone around me. A few times, a member of my crew asked if I got up on the wrong side of the bed.

I couldn't explain it away by saying my girlfriend's ex-husband was in town and attempting to get her back. There was zero chance he was here for Delaney. I'd heard what he'd said on the porch and how he'd greeted her. He'd proven what kind of dad he was already, and I wasn't impressed.

He'd had everything I'd ever wanted, and he'd fucked it up royally. He didn't deserve Natalie or Delaney. But I couldn't help but wonder if Natalie would see things differently. If there was enough history and love that she'd overlook what he'd done so that Delaney could be with her father.

Natalie was a good mother like that. She wanted the best for Delaney, sometimes at the expense of herself. That's why she stayed in South Carolina after Carter left and why she might do something drastic now.

I couldn't control this situation, and it was driving me crazy. I gripped the back of my neck after I dropped the wrench on the floor.

"Boss, why don't you take a break. We've got this," Luis said.

I nodded and followed his suggestion because I wasn't any good to the project right now. I was grumpy and accident-prone. If I didn't break something, I was going to hurt myself or someone else. Then I'd have to explain that to my dad and brothers.

I stood outside for a few seconds before checking the time again. What could they possibly have to talk about for an hour?

"I'm going for a walk," I said to no one as I made my way through the inn and to the sidewalk. I was a man on a mission as I stalked toward the shop they were supposed to meet at.

Why should I stand back and let this asshole steamroll my relationship? He didn't deserve Natalie or Delaney. The thoughts were rolling around in my head so quickly I couldn't find one to stop on.

My head was a mess, and my emotions were worse. By the time I reached the coffee shop, a dull ache was starting at the base of my skull.

I pulled open the door, quickly scanning the space for Natalie and Carter. My heart stuttered when I saw them seated toward the back, to-go cups of coffee on the table between them. It looked cozy.

Before I could think of what I was going to say or do, Natalie's gaze lifted to meet mine. They widened in surprise as her lips parted.

Without thinking, I erased the distance between us, hovering over the table.

"What are you doing here? Is everything okay?" Natalie checked her phone and then put it down when she didn't see any messages.

My heart was galloping in my chest, and there was a roaring in my ears. "You about done here?"

Carter tapped his fingers on the tabletop. "We were having a private conversation."

"I think you need to wrap it up." I made a motion with my finger and wondered briefly why I couldn't rein in my inner asshole.

"I don't have to listen to you. What are you, her new boyfriend?" As Carter leaned back in his chair, a Cheshire grin took over his face as he looked from me to Natalie. "Are you fucking the help?"

"What asshole says *help*?" I asked as I braced my hands on the table to get closer to Carter.

Carter chuckled. "I thought you were reckless, moving here and opening a business when you have no experience, but now you're sleeping with the guy who's renovating it? That's rich. You have no room to complain about what I did."

"You cheated on me for months while we were married. We're nothing alike." Natalie stood and walked out.

I had the brief realization that she was pissed at both of us, but it didn't stop me from leaning in close to Carter and issuing a threat. "Stay away from her and Delaney. They're mine now."

I growled that last part, and Carter didn't even have the decency to flinch. I slapped the table and stood to find Natalie.

I needed to talk to her, to find out what happened, and to apologize for walking in here like a caveman. I finally found her sitting on a bench, her head in her hands. "Are you okay? Did he say something?"

She looked up at me, her eyes glistening with unshed tears.

"We were just talking about things when you showed up like some—" She waved a hand in the air.

"Like a caveman?"

"What were you thinking?"

My jaw tightened. "That I didn't want that asshole around you. That I couldn't stand the thought of you going back to him."

Natalie sighed and stood. "You should have trusted me. I have no intention of getting back with him."

The muscles in my body slowly loosened as I processed what she'd said. "Seriously?"

"He cheated on me, and he wasn't that great of a husband. I thanked him for doing what I couldn't. He moved on, and now I have this amazing new life. I love it here. I love the life I'm building."

Did she love me? Should I tell her I loved her? She was already not liking how I was handling her ex in town, so it probably wasn't the best timing. She'd think I was saying it because he was here, not because it was how I felt.

"What does he want? Why is he here?" I asked, lowering myself to the bench.

"He said he just wanted to make sure I was okay."

"Now?" I couldn't believe he showed up after all this time, pretending to care about Natalie after everything he did.

Natalie shrugged, but her eyes seemed watery. "He seemed genuine."

"He break up with that girl he left you for?"

"He said they're taking a break. She regretted leaving her kids. She's in a tense custody battle with her ex, and she blames Carter for it."

"So he runs back to you when he breaks up with his girlfriend?"

Natalie shook her head. "I don't know what's going on. I'm just concerned about Delaney. I don't want him showing up and showering her with attention and then disappearing again."

This was about Delaney, not about my hurt feelings or concerns about our relationship. Carter was Delaney's father. If I was going to be involved with Natalie, I'd need to get used to him being around. "I'm sorry. You're right."

It wasn't about where I stood in this relationship. Or how insecure I felt in these situations. I couldn't forget that my status was precarious. Anything could change, and I needed to be prepared for it.

Natalie started walking toward the B&B.

"Are you okay?" I asked her, the ache in my skull now radiating pain through the back of my head.

"I will be. It was a shock that he showed up, but I knew it would happen eventually."

My throat tightened. "Does he want to see Delaney while he's here?"

Natalie nodded. "He said he does."

"Are you going to let him?" I asked, my heart stuttering.

"I think I have to. We don't have any sort of visitation agreement. He wasn't interested in talking about it when we discussed the divorce. He gave me primary physical and legal custody. My attorney said that means I make all the decisions."

"So you could tell him no."

"I could, but where does that leave Delaney? I think it would be good for her to see him. Sometimes I worry that she'll forget him."

I wanted to ask if she really wanted Delaney to have a relationship with Carter, but I withheld my opinion. I didn't like Carter because he'd left them. Why let him return now and get whatever he wanted? But it was more complicated than that. He would always be Delaney's father, and some part of her would always long for his approval and attention. I didn't have to like it.

"He doesn't want you back?" I finally bit out as we approached the inn.

Natalie frowned. "He didn't say that. Besides, I'm not interested in reconciliation."

"He wants you back," I said, more to myself than to her.

"Why would you say that?" Natalie paused at the porch of the B&B and faced me.

"Because you're beautiful and amazing, and I can't believe he walked away from you. He has to regret his decision." I would if I did the same thing. Not that I would ever cheat on her, but I was worried enough about repeating my past that I might do something stupid when it came to her.

Should I walk away from Natalie and let her deal with Carter? Maybe it would be better to give her space.

She tipped her face up to mine, and I couldn't put words to what I was thinking. "He's obviously an idiot."

I squeezed the back of my neck. "I can't disagree with that."

Natalie touched my cheek, lowering my chin to look at her. "I like what we have. You have to trust me. I'd never go back to him."

"I trust you." I wanted to, but it was hard to erase the past. I learned valuable lessons from past relationships, and I couldn't just ignore them. Women didn't usually settle for me. I wasn't the right guy for anyone. The old insecurities flared to life, forming a pit in my stomach.

She went up on tiptoe and kissed me softly. "I'm going to get back to work."

She turned on her heel and went inside. My head was a mess. My nerves were shot. I couldn't stand her even talking to her ex; how would I be able to stomach the next eight or nine years that he was in Delaney's life? Even when she turned eighteen, he'd still be there, hovering at the edges, causing doubt and stress. Was it worth it?

There was a reason I vowed never to get involved with a

single mother or divorcée again. There was always the possibility she'd go back to her ex. I couldn't compete with years of history and a shared child. I didn't know why I thought I could.

Luis opened the front door. "Boss? We've got a problem."

I followed him inside, putting everything out of my mind. I needed to focus on my job. I needed to finish this project.

In the kitchen, they were putting in the cabinets and appliances.

The guys stood in a circle around the stove. "The measurements were off. It doesn't fit."

I ran a hand through my hair. "How the hell did that happen?"

I hated to think it had anything to do with me being distracted, but it was a distinct possibility. We measured again, and I took notes of what we needed. "I'll need to see when we can get another one."

The floors and walls were done, and the cabinets and appliances were supposed to be installed today. Then we'd finish the lighting and fixtures.

I went to the backyard to make a call about the stove, but Sam was already there, drinking his water on the newly installed patio. "Everything okay?"

"The stove doesn't fit."

Sam's eyes widened. "Seriously? That's a rookie mistake. Who fucked that up?"

"I'm the one in charge."

"Are you distracted by someone?"

"I might be."

"I heard her ex is in town."

"She met with him this morning." But Carter had nothing to do with a missed measurement. I needed to focus on my job and not so much on the owner.

"How'd that go?" Sam asked.

"He said he just wants to see Delaney, but after seeing them together Friday night, I don't think that's right. He's an idiot for letting Natalie go. Of course, he's going to try to get her back."

"But Natalie's worried about Delaney's father showing up after not seeing him for months. She's worried he'll disappear just as quickly. She's worried about her daughter," Sam said.

"I know that."

"Do you?" Sam's gaze was steady.

"What if she goes back to him?" I couldn't help but express my greatest fear. I couldn't ignore the possibility. I wouldn't be blindsided again.

"What did Natalie say about that?"

"That it wouldn't happen," I grumbled.

"Then you have to believe her. You can't have a relationship without trust."

"I hate that word. Trust. What does it even mean? Blindly believing the person won't leave you? That you're enough for them?" I was emptying my biggest fears into the air between us. I'd never felt so vulnerable.

"There's a certain amount of faith that goes into a relationship. You have to let go of the fears and doubts and believe in your love for each other."

I shifted from one foot to the other. "We haven't said those words yet."

Sam dropped his chin. "But you do, don't you?"

"I love her. But I don't know where her head is." My brothers always teased me that I fell too quickly. That I couldn't know my feelings. Were they right?

"You want something long-term with her?"

I sighed. "It doesn't matter what I want."

"Because you're a victim of circumstance?" Sam asked, his eyes narrowing on me.

"I can't control how she feels or what she wants."

"So you can't go after what you want?" His tone was filled with accusation.

"I can, but there's no guarantee that she feels the same or wants the same things."

"She wants a good man who loves her and her daughter."

"And you think I'm that guy?" In the past, my brothers acted like being a good guy was bad. But maybe Sam had changed his thinking since he met and fell in love with Alice.

"Any woman would be lucky to have you, and only a smart one will grab on with both hands. Is Natalie a smart woman?"

"I think so," I said around the lump in my throat. I needed to tell her how I felt.

"You need to go after what you want. No woman wants a man who feels threatened by her ex. She wants a strong man who can deal with whatever comes your way. And you deal with it together. You're a team."

"Is that how it is with you and Alice?" I was thinking of the times that Felicia popped into town, wanting to see her daughter.

"I'm sure there were moments where she might have felt unsure of her position, but that was when she was my nanny. Now that we're officially together, we're stronger than ever. She doesn't doubt how I feel about her, but then I don't give her a reason to."

Sam's position struck me hard in the chest. His explanation was something I could easily understand. "You're saying I need to show her how I feel."

He clasped my shoulder. "And never let her forget it."

"I can do that." I just needed to tap into the guy I was in my twenties. The one who had no problems showing his emotions.

"If she goes back to a man who cheated on her and left her and her daughter, then she's not a woman you want anyway."

Pain sliced through my chest. I didn't want to think about Natalie doing that. But Sam was right. If she was the woman who was still emotionally tied to her ex, then she wasn't ready to move on with me. That had nothing to do with me. Why hadn't I seen that before? My last girlfriend wasn't ready to move on. It had nothing to do with me being unworthy. It was her issue.

"Whatever happened in the past is on your exes. Not you."

I nodded. "Yeah, I'm getting that now."

Sam smiled. "Took you long enough."

"You guys always made fun of me for wearing my heart on my sleeve." I hated that analogy, but looking back, it was accurate.

"In the right relationship, that's how it is. You want the person to know you love them and will do anything for them. In the wrong relationship, you'll get hurt. Which one is this?"

"I think it's the right kind." As long as she didn't go back to Carter. I couldn't help but think that this was just the start of Carter meddling in our lives. "I don't like him showing up here."

"For your sake, I hope it's a short visit. I can't imagine he's changed his ways."

"She said he's never been that involved. It's why they didn't have more kids."

"Then you have nothing to worry about. You already love Delaney."

"I do." That was easy to admit.

"Then, again, you have nothing to worry about. Be confident in your relationship and what you have."

That was the hard part, but it was worth making the effort. I couldn't imagine my future without Natalie and Delaney in it.

"How'd Delaney like her new room?" Sam said.

"She loved it. Thanks for helping out."

"You'd do the same for me. Now give me a hand out here. You need to get your mind off everything."

I agreed because I needed physical labor to clear my head, to stop thinking about how Carter looked sitting across from Natalie at that coffee shop.

CHAPTER 19

NATALIE

The work Sam was doing in the yard was loud. I couldn't escape the constant pounding. But when I looked out the window, Sam and Mac were working side by side. I was transfixed when Mac lifted his shirt to wipe the sweat from his brow. His abs were defined. My fingers itched to touch him, to erase the pain I'd seen in his eyes earlier today when he'd found me sitting with Carter.

What Mac didn't understand was he was the man I wanted for my future. He was strong and confident when it came to business, and he'd been knocked down in relationships, but I was hopeful that he'd regain his footing. I just had to be patient and show him I had no intention of getting back with Carter. Surely, he'd see that.

Needing a break from the work going on outside, I headed to the front counter just as Alice came in with a box.

Hurrying over to her, I asked, "Do you need help?"

She kicked the door closed with her foot. "I've got it."

"Let me open your door for you." I had the key to her store in my pocket, so I pulled it out and fitted it into the lock.

Alice moved past me and dropped the heavy box on the table.

"More mosaics?" I asked her.

"These are the shapes I'm using for my next workshop." Alice made these beautiful glass mosaics and loved teaching others how to make their own. They usually didn't come out as amazing as hers, but she said art was about the process, not the end result.

"How are things going with the B&B?" Alice asked as she started taking the various shapes out and displayed them on the table.

"Sam just started on the outside."

Alice paused to smile at me. "It's going to be amazing when it's done. You should go on a vacation before you open. It'll probably be your last chance for a while."

I laughed. "How could I go on vacation with the renovation incomplete?"

"You said yourself they're almost done. Do you really need to be around for that? I think it's the perfect time to take a break."

"Where would I even go?" I asked, my mind racing with possibilities.

"Does Delaney have any time off school soon?"

"They have a three-day weekend next week. It's the end of the marking period."

"Perfect. Because I know just the thing." She pulled her phone out of her pocket and pulled up a site. She tipped the screen toward me.

"Juliana's B&B? But this is in Annapolis, Maryland," I said, reading the information on the page.

"You know I sell my crab mosaics to a store there, right?"

"I remember," I said, handing her phone back to her.

"I visited Annapolis to meet the owner and to get a feel for the area. It allowed me to come up with more shapes that fit the town. Like anchors." Then she shook her head. "Sorry, we were talking about you, not my endless ideas for mosaics."

"It's okay. I love hearing where you come up with your ideas." I sat in one of the chairs at the table as she slowly pulled out new shapes and set them on the table.

"We stayed at that B&B." She nodded at her phone, which was resting on the table. "The owner is so amazing and sweet. Juliana could give you advice on opening your B&B. She never lived on-site, so she could give you some pointers."

"I live on-site, though."

Alice frowned. "I thought you were worried about having a life being so close to the guests."

"It's a concern, but I can't back out of my plan now."

"Go and talk to Juliana. See how she runs her place. Get some inspiration and take some time off. You'll love Annapolis. If you stop by Lavender, tell Savanah I said hello."

"It sounds great." I flipped through the pictures on the website. There were only a few rooms, but they were luxurious. She even held weddings and receptions in the backyard. I hadn't even thought about holding events, but with Sam's addition, it would be a possibility.

"I'll call and see if you can get a discount for a room."

I handed her the phone. "Oh, I couldn't ask you to do that."

"At least write it off as a business expense. It's research, after all."

It was a great idea. I already had so many questions. How did she handle the business? Did she have any time for herself?

"Juliana has two little girls. She divorced before she renovated the B&B and married her contractor."

"What?" I asked.

Alice laughed. "I'll never forget it. She said he fell in love with her little girls, even though he swore he didn't want a family. It stuck with me because I fell in love with Maggie before Sam."

"That is a nice story." I couldn't believe Juliana's journey was so similar to mine. "I'll definitely reach out to her."

"Tell her I sent you. I'd love to visit again."

"You'll have to tell me all the good places to visit."

Alice brushed a strand of hair out of her face. "Just walk out the front door and start walking. The B&B is downtown, next to the Naval Academy, and within easy walking distance to the shops, restaurants, and the harbor."

It sounded like the perfect vacation. Was it awful that I wanted to leave town when Carter was here? Would Mac be able to take time away from work to go with me? Why was I even thinking about that?

Saying good-bye to Alice, I returned to the front counter area, where I sent an email to Juliana, the owner of the B&B. I wasn't expecting a quick response, but later that afternoon, she replied, telling me she had a cancelation for the next weekend, and I was welcome to take it.

I immediately accepted, excited that I was doing something for myself and the business. On Wednesday evening, Carter asked to take Delaney to dinner. I said yes because Delaney wanted to see him. I just hoped I wasn't making a huge mistake.

He picked her up shortly after she got home from school, and I was at a loss for what I should do. I hadn't bothered to make dinner since it was just me.

When there was a knock on the door, I worried that there was something wrong. My heart pounded in my chest as I pulled the door open. I let out the breath I'd been holding when I saw it was Mac.

He held a carryout bag of food, a wine bottle, and a bouquet of flowers.

"Is this all for me?" I stepped back so he could enter, blinking back tears that he'd shown up for me.

He paused to kiss me before heading inside. "I thought you could use the distraction."

I closed the door behind him. "I didn't think it would be this hard to let her go with him. He's her father."

Mac pulled take-out containers out of the bags and grabbed plates and silverware before reaching for the bottle of wine. The knot in my stomach slowly unraveled as Mac uncorked the bottle of wine and poured me a glass. I took a large sip.

We sat next to each other at the island. "Thank you for thinking of me. I didn't even plan anything for dinner."

"I'll always think of you."

My heart couldn't take much more of his thoughtfulness. He made me want forever with him. After we'd eaten most of our food in silence, I said, "I did something a little crazy." Other than moving to Colorado, I wasn't an adventurous person.

Mac chuckled. "What's that?"

"I booked a B&B in Annapolis, Maryland. Alice told me about it, said it was a cute town, and suggested I could pick the owner's brain about her business."

"When are you going?"

"She had a cancelation for next week that coincides with Delaney's three-day weekend."

"That'll be a nice trip for you."

I wanted to ask him to join us, but I wasn't sure if he would be interested in going, or even able to.

"Carter's still here. Do you know if he's planning to stick around?"

He hadn't mentioned Carter since Monday, and I wasn't sure how he felt about him hanging around. "I don't know his plans. The not knowing is making me a little crazy."

"Sam used to go through this. He'd let Felicia uproot his life whenever she showed up. But when he took control of the situation, that's when things got easier."

"You're saying that Carter should work around my schedule?" I turned the idea over in my brain.

"Something like that. He put himself in this situation. You and Delaney shouldn't have to accommodate him."

I rested a hand over his. "I don't feel like I have changed my schedule for him."

The muscles in his hand tensed under mine.

"You let him get to you."

"It's hard not to be worried about what he could do. Will he fight for custody or visitation? Will he move here?" I couldn't suppress the shudder that ran through my body.

"I think you have to try not to let his plans, or lack thereof, affect you."

I appreciated that Mac was attempting to offer advice and wasn't stuck on the fear of me getting back with Carter. I hoped this meant he'd worked through his past issues. "That's easier said than done."

"Planning a trip out of town was a good idea. It will give you a break from it."

"I think so too." I wondered if I should invite him. If he'd be able to go if I did. "Would you like to come with us? Alice said there were a lot of things to see and do there. It's near Washington DC, if you'd like to go there."

Mac shifted closer to me and smiled. "I'd love to go with you."

"Can you get away from this place?"

He winked. "I don't know. My boss is a slave driver."

"I'm being serious."

"We're just putting the finishing touches on the inside. Sam's doing the heavy lifting at this point. When we return, you can furnish the place and take your photographs."

"Reservations should pick up then."

"I think so too. You're going to be so busy soon that you won't have time for anything else." Mac said it flippantly, but that was what I was most worried about.

"What have I gotten myself into?" I asked him.

"Hey, you've got this. You'll get some tips from this other B&B owner, and you'll return from this getaway refreshed and energized."

"I hope so." And maybe Carter would take the hint and go back to Texas or South Carolina. As much as I thought I wanted him in Delaney's life, I wasn't sure it was healthy for me.

We finished eating and cleaned up.

"I can think of a way to distract you," Mac said after he put the last dish in the washer and turned it on.

Men doing dishes was sexy. How did I not know that before?

He stalked toward me, cupping my jaw with his large hands as he kissed me slowly, reverently, like we had all the time in the world.

He pulled away slightly to ask, "When will she be back?"

Glancing at the clock, I said, "We have an hour."

"Perfect." He lifted me in his arms, my legs wrapping around his waist as he carried me down the hall into my room. He kicked the door shut behind us and lowered me to the bed. He followed me down, kissing me as his hands ran over my body. He pulled my shirt up, and his palm coasted under, touching my bare skin. My stomach muscles quivered in response.

He lifted his mouth from mine and moved down, pushing my shirt farther up and the cups of my bra down. I'd never get enough of being with him.

There was a sense of desperation as I lifted up and pulled my shirt over my head, and he tugged my jeans over my hips and off.

I went up on my elbows as he stood at the end of the bed to rip off his shirt and push down his jeans, leaving himself in tight-fitting briefs. There was a significant bulge, and I couldn't resist moving to my knees and cupping him. I felt the heat of him through the soft material, but I wanted more. When I removed his briefs, his cock bobbed out.

He groaned as I wrapped my hand around it. I wanted him. I

wanted this. I licked the crown, squeezing the base of his cock as I sucked him inside.

I felt powerful on my knees in front of him.

He cupped my breast. "I want to see you."

I reached around and unhooked my bra, letting it fall down my shoulders before gripping him again.

He tapped my ass. "These too."

I glared at him for the interruptions, and he chuckled in response. When I was naked, I got back into position, sucking him deep.

I wanted to erase the amusement from his expression and make him desperate for me. I wanted him to never forget what we had, to get lost in us.

His hand rested loosely in my hair, not guiding me.

I worked him harder, twisting my hand and squeezing him as I licked him and sucked him into my mouth, hollowing my cheeks to take him deep.

His head tipped back as he groaned. "As much as I want to come in your mouth, I want to be inside you when I blow."

My head was spinning as he pulled me off him and tugged me to stand. He turned me and, with a hand on my back, gently pushed me into position, my palms flat on the bed and my feet on the floor. He pulled my hips back, separating my feet, and his fingers dipped between my legs. "You got that wet from sucking me?"

I nodded, feeling a little wild in this position. I wanted to make him desperate, but it was affecting me.

He moved to grab a condom, and I heard the rip of the wrapper. Then he was behind me, his cock teasing my entrance. I tipped my hips back, enticing him.

"You're gorgeous like this."

I could only imagine how I looked with my ass in the air, my back arched. I was dripping by the time he nudged my entrance and pushed inside. His hands gripped my hips as he pulled out to the tip and stroked inside. It felt deeper this way, and he was hitting a spot that made me burn for him.

"You need me, baby?" he asked, his voice a low rumble.

I nodded, looking behind me to see the dark promise in his eyes. He reached around to pinch my nipple, cupping my breasts before moving one hand to my clit. When he circled it and then pressed down, I spasmed around his cock, somehow intensifying my orgasm.

He thrust deep one more time, nipping my shoulder as he let go.

I hung my head as the aftershocks went through my body.

"Baby," he said, and I couldn't resist moving so he could kiss me. He broke it off to pull out and take care of the condom.

I dropped onto the bed like I didn't have any energy to hold myself up anymore. I curled onto my side.

He chuckled when he returned to the room, his strong arm coming around me to lift me higher on the bed. I brushed my hair out of my face. "You move me like it's nothing."

"Because it is. I like moving you around where I want you."

There was something to be said for a man who was strong and good with tools. Not only was it sexy, but it equaled stamina in the bedroom. But I liked Mac for so much more than his skill and muscles. He was sweet. I couldn't believe other women had shut him out when he had the biggest heart.

I nestled into his chest, content to be in his arms.

He kissed my head. "We need to get ready soon."

It wouldn't be good for Carter to see me with just-been-fucked hair. I groaned as I moved and stretched. "You're probably right."

"Does that B&B we're going to have two rooms?"

"Mmm. I don't think so, but there might be a separate area I can put a cot in for Delaney."

"It's not exactly private, but it's something."

I rolled so I could see him. "We're not always going to have privacy with a kid at home."

His lips twitched. "I'm adventurous. I can figure it out."

Pleasure hummed in my body, my skin tingling with the aftermath of our lovemaking. I'd never get enough of this man. I just hoped he was strong enough to stay present with me. I didn't need him by my side, but I sure as hell liked it.

After a few more minutes of snuggling, I sat up. "We should get ready."

We heard a knock on the door.

Mac swore as he got up and pulled on his briefs.

"He's early. I'm sorry."

"I should have known."

I stood behind him, wrapping my arms around his middle and kissing his shoulder blade. "It was worth it."

He turned in my arms and kissed me hard. "I think so too. I'll grab the door."

Any moment we got together was worth whatever trouble we went through to get it. We rushed to throw on our clothes. I ran a brush through my hair and heard the door open and male voices. It wouldn't be good for those two to get into a confrontation with Delaney present. I hurried to the front of the apartment.

Mac had leaned down to hug Delaney, and she looked up at him. "You're here."

"Yeah, I kept your mom company while you were with your dad. We had dinner too."

Carter raised a brow as he looked from Mac to me. He knew exactly what we'd been doing, and when a muscle ticked over his jaw, I knew he didn't like it. Was it that I'd moved on with someone?

I couldn't tell with Carter. Sometimes he treated women as if they were a new toy he wanted to show off, but they eventually lost their shine and his interest. I was fairly positive he didn't want me or our marriage. It might be a pride thing that I'd moved on when his life was imploding. But whatever he was thinking or feeling didn't mean anything to me anymore.

"Did you have a good time at dinner?" I asked Delaney.

"We ate pizza."

"The brick-oven place?" I asked Carter.

"I'm sure there's only one place. This town is small." His voice was tinged with barely disguised irritation.

If he didn't like Telluride, I could only hope he'd leave.

"Can I see her on Saturday?" Carter asked me.

"Can we talk outside?" I moved without waiting for him to respond. Outside, with the door carefully shut behind us, I said, "I don't want to discuss visitation in front of Delaney."

He rolled his eyes. "Not everything is a legal thing. I just want to see my daughter."

I crossed my arms over my chest. "I make those decisions. That's what you agreed to when you wanted the divorce. It's not healthy for us to discuss this in front of her."

He gestured between us. "You're making this adversarial."

"I'm protecting my daughter. You can't show up here after all these months and think you can slip back into our lives again. We have things to do." I looked away and sighed. "Maybe we should come up with a schedule."

He kicked his toe in the dirt. "I won't be sticking around long enough for that."

"You're leaving?" I asked, tipping my head to consider him.

"I don't know when, but I can't commit to a schedule. I don't live here. You're the one who moved across the country, taking my daughter from me."

I laughed. "That's funny when you're the one moved to Texas, putting this whole thing into motion." I wasn't sure if I would have left him if he hadn't, but I wasn't the one who moved away first. "I'll let you know about Saturday. I'm not sure what our plans are." Or what Delaney wanted. I needed to check in with her first. It was my job to protect her.

I turned to go back into the house without waiting for his response.

"Are you fucking him?" he asked, sounding pissed.

Disgusted by his tone, I said, "That's none of your business."

"It is if he's around my daughter."

"He's a good man. A better one than you." Then I opened the door, shutting him out.

"Everything okay?" Mac asked when he saw my face.

"Uh-huh." I was shaking. I was proud that I stood up for myself and hadn't let him turn things around on me.

Mac wrapped an arm around me. "We were just watching a quick show. Is that okay?"

"Yeah, thank you." I was so grateful he was here for us.

"Do I need to punch him?" he asked, his voice soft so Delaney wouldn't overhear.

"I handled it. We can talk about it later, after she goes to bed."

"Do you mind if I take a shower? I brought a change of clothes."

"Of course not."

He went outside to grab his bag from his truck, and when I heard the water turn on, I asked, "How was it?" I asked Delaney again, knowing she might be more honest when her father wasn't in the room.

She grimaced. "It was okay. It was a little weird."

"Why's that?"

"He was gone for so long, and now he's back."

"That is a hard adjustment."

Her nose scrunched. "It's confusing."

"I'm sorry. But whatever you're feeling is perfectly normal. Do you want to see him again?"

She shrugged. "I should, right?"

"We'll do whatever you want to do."

"Can I think about it?" Delaney asked.

I put my arm around her and pulled her in to my side. "Of course, you can."

I rested my cheek on her head, reveling in the feel of her in my arms. She rarely let me cuddle with her like this anymore. She was getting older, and soon, she wouldn't want to spend time with me.

Carter was missing out, but he'd made his choices.

CHAPTER 20

MAC

For the next week, we stayed at Natalie's on weeknights and at my place on the weekend. We attended family dinner at my parents' as a unit. It was nice, and everyone adored Rocky. Sometimes, I think they liked him better than me.

But I was ecstatic to get a weekend away from everything. Carter was still hovering, asking when he could see Delaney, but so far, she wasn't interested. She was confused about the situation, and I couldn't blame her. I would be too.

Sam and Alice offered to watch Rocky while I was gone, so I didn't need to worry about him. I was fairly sure that either Maggie wouldn't want to give him back or she'd convince Sam to get her a puppy too. I was secretly hoping for the latter so Rocky would have a playmate.

On the plane ride, Delaney sat between us, and it felt like we were a family. Everyone assumed we were, and even though Delaney wasn't technically mine, I wanted her to be. Being with the two of them was everything I'd ever wanted.

In Baltimore we rented a car and drove to Annapolis. As we

rode through the historic area of the town, Natalie and Delaney exclaimed over the cute shops and historic buildings.

"This place is adorable," Natalie said when we pulled up in front of Juliana's B&B.

It was fairly similar to her place in that it was within walking distance of the restaurants and shops. We got out, and I pulled out our carry-on luggage.

When we checked in, the woman at the front desk promised to get Juliana for us. Then she took our luggage and directed us to the living room, where there were drinks and pastries.

"This is a nice touch," Natalie said as she filled a plate for Delaney.

"You're here," a blonde woman said as she came into the room and hugged Natalie. "I'm Juliana."

"It's so nice to meet you. I'm Natalie. This is my daughter, Delaney, and my friend, Mac."

We'd never discussed any labels, but we were more than friends at this point. I'd have to discuss that with her later.

"My daughters are a little younger than Delaney. Maybe they can get together while you're here. There's a nice playground across town."

"That would be great." Natalie beamed at her.

"Eat a snack, and then I'll give you a tour. I can tell you my story while you relax. I'm a realtor, but I always wanted to own a B&B. My divorce was the push I needed to take that first step. How about you?"

Natalie waved a hand at her. "Oh, it's nothing like that. After my divorce, my friend, Kylie, sent me a picture of this old Victorian for sale in my hometown and told me I should buy it, move home, and renovate it. It's been a crazy few months."

"When do you plan to open?" Juliana asked.

"In a couple of months if everything stays on schedule."

"It should be earlier than that. We're just doing the finishing touches, and my brother is designing the outdoor space."

"Can I see pictures?" Juliana asked, sipping her tea.

Natalie moved to sit next to Juliana on the coach and pulled out her laptop so they could flip through them. They oohed and ahhed over the pictures documenting the renovation while I kept Delaney entertained with my phone.

Juliana looked up from Natalie's computer. "You do amazing work, Mac."

"Thank you."

The door opened, and Juliana said, "That should be my husband, Nolan, and our girls."

Two identical girls flew into the room, blonde hair flying. One was in a dress and the other in leggings and a sweater. Juliana greeted them with a hug and introduced them to Delaney. They ran off to play in the backyard while Nolan greeted me. "Nolan. Nice to meet you."

I stood to shake his hand. "Mac. Thanks for bringing them."

"They were excited to meet someone new," Nolan said warmly.

Juliana raised a brow as we took our seats. "Mac is the contractor renovating Natalie's B&B."

"Huh. That's how we met," Nolan said, his voice full of affection.

"Oh, I think they're just friends—" Juliana began.

Natalie blushed, and I jumped in. "We're together, but it's complicated. Natalie has her daughter, Delaney, and Delaney's dad is in town."

"We have two kids, so I get it. But I'm confident you'll figure it out."

"Now, what questions do you have for me?" Juliana asked.

"I'm living in the owner's suite, and it's small, and I'm a little worried about how it will be when guests are checking in and out. Will I have a life?"

Juliana frowned. "I've never lived on-site. At first, my sister, Ava, managed the place for me, and then I hired McKenzie. I think it's important to have someone you trust on-site, but I don't think it needs to be you. Especially if you have a family. You'll want separation between work and home."

Natalie chewed on her lower lip. "That's what I'm worried about. But I'm not sure I'll be able to afford it at first."

"I researched Telluride, and I've seen the pictures. It's adorable, and it's the perfect location. As soon as it's finished, you'll be booked," Juliana said with all the confidence of an experienced realtor.

"How can you be so sure?" Natalie asked her.

"From what I've read, you get tourists year-round there. Figure out how much you'll need to bring in to hire someone. You can offer them free room and board."

Natalie's eyes were filled with concern. "Anyone I hire will be on call twenty-four seven."

"Listen, it's your business, and you can run it how you want. But I don't allow my manager to be on-call twenty-four seven. From eleven to six a.m., the only calls that should come through are emergencies, plumbing, that kind of thing. If a guest forgot an item or needs a towel, that request should come in earlier. It helps if you think of things they might forget and put them in the bathroom with a note as to what's there. That will cut down on a lot of calls. I have a folder that shows them the closest restaurants and bars, things to do, hours, et cetera."

Natalie nodded. "That's smart."

"You want things to be as automated as possible. We're working on an app so that requests are automated, and they can check in without stopping at the desk."

"That would be amazing," Natalie said.

"I can show you what we're doing so you could implement it in the future."

Natalie relaxed slightly. "I'd love that. Thank you."

"Let's do that tour now that the girls are occupied." They left the room, and I was alone with Nolan.

Nolan leaned forward, resting his elbows on his knees. "Juliana said you own a construction company?"

"My family does. It's my dad, me, and my brothers."

Nolan nodded. "Same here, except it's just me and my brother. Owning a business keeps you busy."

"It does, but for the first time, I'm getting the urge to slow down and have a life outside of work."

Nolan smiled. "Does Natalie have anything to do with that?"

"Natalie and Delaney." I wasn't sure why I was comfortable sharing with Nolan. Maybe it was how similar we were, dating single moms and running construction companies.

Nolan shook his head. "I didn't want kids when I met Juliana and her girls, but I didn't stand a chance."

I chuckled at his honesty. I wondered if he'd struggled with the decision of not being good enough or the right man for Juliana and her girls. "I've always wanted a family. I just haven't had much luck in that department."

Nolan straightened. "Hopefully, this time is different. The kids make it extra special. There's nothing I wouldn't do for those girls."

"Is their father in the picture?" I couldn't help but ask.

Nolan grimaced. "He was difficult in the beginning, but we've gotten into a good schedule and rhythm. I think it helps that I'm here. He won't mess with her or the girls because I won't let him. Don't tell Juliana that."

I chuckled, admiring his confidence. "I won't."

"I'm not saying everything was smooth. I fought the attraction at first, but in the end, I couldn't resist. I messed up a time or two—went back to my old ways, thinking I didn't need them in my life, but I was wrong. There's nothing like loving them, you know?"

I nodded, my throat tight with emotion.

Juliana returned with Natalie. "Let's have an early dinner at Max's. I'll arrange for a sitter for the girls."

"That would be great," Natalie said.

I was glad they'd connected. Juliana would be a great resource for Natalie. She'd been running her B&B for a few years and already knew the ups and downs. Hopefully, she'd help Natalie avoid the common pitfalls. I wanted Natalie to have success, but I was worried she was overextending herself. Selfishly, I wanted her to hire a manager so she could move in with me. But we weren't there yet.

* * *

WE'D WANDERED Annapolis that afternoon, doing all the touristy things. There was so much to see, and Delaney and Natalie wanted to stop at every shop and historical site. They even went down side streets, marveling at the 1800s architecture.

That evening, we returned to Juliana's B&B to freshen up and rest before leaving Delaney and the twins with the sitter Juliana hired. After Natalie met the sitter and felt comfortable leaving Delaney, we headed to Max's with Nolan and Juliana.

As we walked, Juliana chatted about the area and the tourism. It sounded like it was mainly spring through fall, and the winter was more locals. It was an interesting area, close to Baltimore and DC, yet it was its own tourist destination. It wasn't hidden in a canyon of mountains like Telluride.

We walked into Max's, with Nolan mentioning he'd like to bring his family to visit Telluride for some skiing. I told him about Wilde Ski Resort and the various accommodations.

"You're welcome to stay at my B&B if you'd like. Although I'm sure the ski resort would be more convenient if you're there for winter sports," Natalie said after the hostess seated us in the dining room.

The restaurant was packed, even though it was early. There was a dining room on one side of the staircase and a bar on the other. The street out front had been shut down to accommodate outdoor dining for the various restaurants facing the harbor.

We ate crab cakes since those were the local specialty.

"I love that we're getting the traditional Maryland fare while we're here," Natalie said.

"You have to try it once. So many of my friends have lived here their entire lives and hate seafood," Juliana said, sipping her white wine.

Nolan shuddered. "I don't even know how that's possible."

"Right?" Juliana said with a smile.

Juliana and Natalie talked about their girls and what it was like raising them after a divorce while I chatted business with Nolan. It was good to hear someone else's perspective. I was impressed that he and his brother, Cade, were so involved in local charities. They even ran one themselves, making homes more accessible for those with disabilities.

It had me wondering if we could do something similar in Telluride.

We talked and laughed until we needed to relieve the sitter, and I couldn't help but think we'd made lifelong friends. Hopefully, they'd visit Telluride this winter, and we'd return to Annapolis. We were similar in so many ways.

We paid the sitter, said good-bye to Juliana's family, and tucked Delaney into bed. Juliana had provided a cot that fit nicely into an alcove, so we had some privacy in the bedroom.

"What did you think?" Natalie asked as we got into bed.

"I enjoyed talking to Nolan about his business. They're doing some things I'd like to talk to my dad and brothers about. Did Juliana answer your questions?"

"She had some good tips, so I'm off to a great start. But she highly recommended I hire a manager as soon as I can."

"I have to agree."

Natalie's face pinched. "I'm just not in a position where it makes sense financially. I don't know when I will be."

I touched her hand, soothing her. "You'll get there."

Hopefully, sooner rather than later. "We have a few more weeks of work and then you can open."

"I'm eager to get home, take the pictures, and start marketing. I'll relax when the bookings start coming in."

I pulled her into my arms. "Once everyone knows about the B&B, you'll be booked."

"I hope you're right."

There was a crease between her eyes. I knew she was worried about not having any guests, but I was concerned about the opposite. That she'd be so busy she wouldn't have time to see me. But that's how the early days of a business were. At least that's what my dad always said. My brothers and I were lucky to take over an established one. We never had to struggle. It had been easy for us.

But being in the business world, I'd heard lots of horror stories. And I knew firsthand how owning a business meant you worked harder, not less.

A sense of dread filled me. I didn't want to let old securities creep in, but I couldn't help but worry about our future. Would we be strong enough to survive the opening of the business? Would Natalie have any time for me? Or would she be working nonstop?

She was determined to be successful and independent. I admired that, but I also worried she'd be one of those business owners who worked too hard. I'd have to remind her to work smarter, not harder. But it wasn't the time to talk more about business.

Instead, I tipped her face toward me to kiss her. I wanted to enjoy our time here and forget about what awaited us at home.

I took my time, kissing and touching before we removed each other's clothes. The effort to stay quiet only fueled my desire. I rolled on top of her, my cock nudging her entrance. Her fingers tangled in the hair at the base of my neck.

It would be so easy to slide inside and forget about responsibilities, but I lifted up to grab a condom. Natalie stopped me with a hand on my wrist. "Do we need one?"

My brow furrowed. "I figured you'd want to be protected."

"I'm on birth control, and I want to feel you inside me," she said.

I dropped the wrapper, hoping that meant she was all in with me. This time, I rolled her onto her side and lifted one leg so I could slide inside. I wasn't prepared for how good it felt to be inside her without the barrier. She was all warm heat, her muscles clamping around me. I was going to come too soon.

I kissed her shoulder as I tried to think of anything but the way her walls rippled around me. But when she reached down to touch herself, it was like she'd pushed a button in my brain. I thrust inside harder, needing to get her there before I blew my load.

She bit her lip against the moan as she spasmed around me, milking my orgasm from me. Afterward, I got up to grab a warm washcloth to clean her. I'd never gone without a condom before. I didn't think I'd ever trusted a woman to go without.

I held Natalie in my arms as her breathing deepened. I couldn't sleep for a while, the what-ifs running through my head on repeat. I couldn't stop myself from conjuring up every worst-case scenario for the next few weeks—Carter moving to Telluride, the B&B perpetually booked, and never having time to see Natalie and Delaney.

By the time I finally fell asleep, my eyes were gritty with exhaustion. Delaney jumped on our bed at six a.m., excited to start the day, but I'd only gotten a couple of hours of sleep.

Natalie kissed me. "I'll get her breakfast. Why don't you sleep for a few more hours? You look tired."

I rubbed my eyes. "I had trouble sleeping."

Natalie smiled, but there was concern etched on her brow. "I get it. It's a new place."

I didn't bother correcting her; I just lay there while they got ready for breakfast and left.

I rolled over but couldn't find a comfortable position to fall back asleep. My eyes hurt, and a full-on headache was threatening. We had two more days in Annapolis, and I wanted to enjoy every minute, so I got up and showered, hoping I'd feel refreshed afterward. Then I wandered downstairs for coffee.

I found Natalie rocking in a chair on the back porch, the air crisp but not so cold we couldn't enjoy the outdoors. I sat next to her. "This is nice."

There were others eating in the dining room, but no one was back here yet.

Natalie smiled at me. "I wonder if my place will be this inviting once Sam is done."

"It will be. He creates amazing spaces, and I'm fairly sure he's going overboard with yours. He wants it to be impressive."

"I moved to Telluride for a fresh start. I didn't anticipate meeting you or your family, but you've been so good to us. It's almost like it was meant to be."

"I think so too." Or, at least, I wanted to believe that. I felt a little like we'd built a straw house of a relationship and a strong wind could tear it down. I needed to build a brick house that was indestructible, but was it too late? Then I wondered if I just needed to change my beliefs about the relationship.

Before I could spend much time thinking about it, Delaney ran from the gazebo, in the center of the yard, to us. "What are we doing today?"

"I thought we'd take the boat tour. Juliana said it has a nice view of the Naval Academy."

"We can tour the Naval Academy grounds if you'd like," I added, trying to remember everything Nolan and Juliana suggested last night.

"Is that what you want to do?" Natalie asked me.

"This is your trip. I'm happy to do whatever you want."

Natalie and Delaney listed off the things they still wanted to see, and I listened, content to just be here. I knew reality would settle in soon, but I had two more days where I could put it out of my mind.

CHAPTER 21

NATALIE

I returned from Annapolis only to hit the ground running with getting pictures for the website and interviews with local news outlets and the paper about the opening. When Carter called to say he needed to go on a business trip to Texas, I was relieved. I couldn't handle him on top of everything else.

Piper suggested we hold some kind of ribbon-cutting ceremony, and even though I thought it was over the top, Kylie and Alice disagreed.

They thought it would be good publicity, so suddenly, I was planning that along with a party so that locals could tour the inn and tell others about it.

Each new suggestion sounded amazing, but preparing for them was something else. I was overwhelmed with the details of finishing the renovation and preparing for the upcoming opening. I was up late one night, approving the photographs for the website, when my phone buzzed with an incoming text.

Mac: Can you talk?

I couldn't, but I'd been too busy to do much more than see

Mac in passing in the few weeks since we'd returned from Annapolis.

Instead of answering, I called him.

"You're still up?" he asked.

"Just approving the photographs for the website." My voice felt gritty with disuse. It was later than I thought.

"I bet they're all great."

"I'm not sure about that. I'm worried if I pick the wrong one, it will make a difference. What if I screw this up and make the wrong decisions?" I dropped my head onto the counter.

"You're working too hard. You need to get some rest, make sure you eat, and take more breaks."

"I can't." The counter was covered with Post-it Notes of lists. There was a list for the opening, one for the website, marketing, the rooms, and food. My to-do list was endless, and I was the only one who could cross off the tasks.

"You need help," Mac said simply.

I ran a hand through my hair. "I've got this."

"I'm not saying you don't, but you're working around the clock. It's not healthy." His tone was filled with concern for me.

"It's just for a few more weeks, and then things will slow down."

He grunted in response, and I knew he didn't believe me.

"I just need to get through the opening. Then things will slow down. You'll see."

"You have to work smarter, not harder." This was something Mac said to me almost daily these days.

"That's when your business is established, not when you first start out."

"The quicker you embody that theory, the better things will be. You don't have to do everything on your list. You can get help."

"We've been through this. I can't afford to hire anyone." I was tired of this conversation. We talked in circles and never agreed.

"You have friends and family willing to help."

"Are you offering yourself up?" I asked him.

He'd finished the B&B and moved on to another project, one that was outside of town. I no longer saw him during the day, and it wasn't as convenient for him to stay the night. Sam was still working on the backyard and landscaping, but we were nearing the finish line.

My friends had these amazing suggestions that I needed to implement on my tiny budget. I'd gotten bookings but nothing earth-shattering. It was like people were waiting for word-of-mouth referrals or reviews. Piper said they wanted social proof, evidence that the place was amazing, and I could only get that with people staying at the inn and voluntarily reviewing it.

It was too much pressure.

Mac interrupted my train of thought. "You need to rest."

I sighed. "You don't understand. You've never had to build a business from scratch."

"That's true, but I've seen enough people do it to recognize you're racing toward burnout."

I grimaced. "I don't believe in that word. I have to believe I'll succeed if I put in the work." But my biggest fear was that all my work would lead to nothing. That no one would book the hotel. That I'd struggle to bring in business. It was the fear that kept me awake all hours of the night, making more lists.

I felt like I was drowning. For every one thing I crossed off the list, I added five more. It was never-ending, and I didn't know if what I was doing would amount to anything.

"What did Juliana say?" Mac finally asked.

"I haven't had a chance to talk to her since we've been back."

"You should. She's been through the same thing."

"She had her sister to help. It wasn't the same." She was a realtor, so she had a good grasp of the business world already.

"She might still be helpful."

"I'll ask her," I said to appease him, knowing I didn't have time to chat about my problems. I just needed to put my head down and get to work.

"Will you go to sleep now?"

"I will." Soon. I just had a few more things to do.

"I just wanted to check in, but I don't want to be the reason you're not going to sleep."

"You're not," I quickly added, because I'd barely seen or talked to him in weeks. Delaney was asking for him, so I let him take her to Rocky's obedience classes on Saturdays, and we still attended family dinner on Sundays, but otherwise, my time was limited.

It sucked because I missed him, but at the same time, he was the one who'd tell me to take a break when I didn't have the time. I needed to do this my way.

"Don't be up too late."

"I won't."

"Night, Natalie."

"Good night," I said softly, missing Mac in my space, working and coming to my apartment at night. I just needed to get through the opening and then things should slow down, and I could spend more time with him. Surely, he understood how busy it was for me.

I stayed up for another hour, approving the photographs for the marketing and website. When I was finished, my head hurt, and I was exhausted. Maybe Mac was right about not making the best decisions when you were tired. But I just needed to keep moving.

When I fell into bed, I struggled to fall asleep. My mind was still turning with ideas and unfinished to-dos.

* * *

I BARELY HAD a second to breathe the last week before opening. My list grew to insurmountable levels. With the website finished and ads running, I'd seen an uptick in bookings, but we weren't sold out by any means. Hopefully, the hoopla surrounding the opening itself would push it over the edge. The fear of any other outcome kept me up at night.

On the morning of the ribbon-cutting ceremony, I let Delaney stay home from school so she could be involved. Kylie and Alice came over early with possibilities for dresses. I was grateful because I'd been so busy, I hadn't even thought about what I should wear or what I'd look like.

But the B&B itself was cleaned, decorated, and shined. A lot of people would be walking through today, and I wanted it to look its best. Maybe locals would book the rooms for a weekend away from the kids.

Thinking it was another marketing angle, I paused to write the idea in the notes section of my phone, but Kylie lifted it right out of my hands.

"Hey," I protested.

"Stop working so we can get you dressed and put some makeup on your face."

I pouted. "I'm going to forget my idea."

"You're going to forget to brush your hair if you don't stop already," Kylie said, frustrated with me. She didn't understand why I worked so hard. She was born into money; she could take months off to figure out what she wanted to do with her life. I didn't have the same luxury. I needed to support myself in this business. Because if it didn't work out, I had nothing. My entire savings had gone into this building. I needed it to generate money.

I stood while Kylie drew the first dress over my head.

"We understand how important the B&B is to you, but you need to take care of yourself and Delaney."

"I am."

"You're not. The dress is loose. Did you lose weight?"

I looked down at myself. "Probably. I don't always remember to eat."

Alice exchanged a concerned look with Kylie.

I held up my hands. "Okay, okay. I get it. I need to slow down. And I will, after today." Just as soon as I got into a good routine.

"You hired house cleaners, right?" Kylie said as she rejected the black dress and drew a red one over my head.

My face flushed. "I figured I could do it myself."

"How will you have time to do the front desk and answer the phone—" Kylie broke off, clearly shocked.

"And do the million other administrative tasks around here?" Alice added.

I shrugged. "Why would I hire someone when I can easily do the work myself?"

"Because it's time-consuming," Alice said.

"But I won't have to do every room every day." I'd thought about it, but it saved me money by not hiring someone else.

"I think that's a bad idea," Alice said, clearly worried about me.

"I'll be fine. Besides, once the money's there, I can hire someone."

"You're doing too much," Alice murmured as she shook her head at the red dress. "Let's do the blue one. It matches her eyes."

I felt like a doll, but I was too exhausted to be much help. I didn't really care what I wore or how I looked. I just needed to get through this day, then I could sleep tonight.

I tried not to think about how my first guest would be checking in tomorrow. I wasn't ready for that, and panic streaked through my body.

I lifted my hands as they pulled off the red dress and then dropped the blue one over my head. "This is it," Alice said triumphantly.

"It's pretty," I acknowledged, looking at myself in the mirror.

"Now sit. I need to do your hair and makeup," Alice ordered.

"I don't think this is necessary." I had a million little things to do before the first person walked through the doors.

Alice leaned over to curl my lashes. "So, you would have shown up in sweats and a tee?"

"That's a definite possibility." I probably would have done a last-minute wipe-down of the kitchen counters and dusted the mantle. I still felt this niggling in the back of my brain that I'd forgotten to do something.

"Remember why you're doing this," Kylie said, pulling up a chair to sit next to me.

My face screwed up in the mirror. "To earn a living."

Alice paused to look at me. "You're doing this to create an inviting house for people to stay. To create memories."

"That too," I said, sighing as Alice brushed over my face with blush.

"You're too wrapped up in the end result. You need to relax and imagine the B&B filled with guests, tired from a day of walking in Telluride and enjoying the backyard. You're going to make people happy."

The muscles in my back slowly relaxed one by one. "That sounds nice."

"It's what you're going to tell the reporter today when she asks. But you need to believe it and stop brushing it off. That's your why. It's not just to support you and Delaney."

"Yeah, I get that."

"Do you? Because if you get too wrapped up in bookings and money, you're going to drive yourself crazy. You're not going to be fulfilled or happy. You're going to be stressed out."

I smiled at her in the mirror. "Like I am now."

"Yes."

"Okay. I'll try to relax and remember why I'm doing this."

We were quiet for a minute while Alice worked, then she

said, "I'm excited about the B&B opening. I'll get more traffic for my store, and we can offer weekly workshops for the new guests."

"I'm excited for you." I hugged Alice.

"You've got this. Just don't forget your why."

"I won't. Thank you, guys, for being here to support me. I couldn't have done this today without you."

"And accept more help. You have Mac and his family too."

"I don't want to assume or lean too hard on them. I want to be independent."

"You have nothing to prove. You are doing it, and a smart business owner delegates. My old boss was great at that." Kylie made a face, and I wondered if she bore the brunt of the work while her manager reaped the rewards.

I wished she'd talk to me about what happened in Paris. But today wasn't the day to delve into her past. I had a ribbon to cut and a party to hold.

I just wished I'd gotten more sleep. I should have listened to everyone around me who was just worried about my well-being. When I stood, I felt light-headed.

Alice grabbed my arm. "Have you eaten?"

"I don't think so." I swallowed, suddenly feeling nauseous. It was probably my empty stomach and nerves.

"I'll make you a sandwich," Alice said, hurrying out of the room.

Kylie sat on my bed. "Are you okay?"

"I will be." As soon as I got through this. Just thinking about cameras and reporters made my stomach situation worse.

"We'll be by your side all day."

"Thank you for that. I couldn't do this without you." But after today, I'd need to. I'd be responsible for everything: checking in and out guests, taking care of any issues or problems, cleaning the rooms, and the list went on and on.

"That's what friends are for. Besides, I was the one who convinced you this was a great idea."

"It's still a good idea." I smiled to reassure her, but it felt weak.

"Is it?" Kylie leveled me with a concerned gaze. "You seem overwhelmed."

"I've got this." My pulse fluttered in my neck, and I felt perilously close to a panic attack.

"You don't have to do everything yourself."

"I know. I've got you." I hugged Kylie, and we made our way to the kitchen, where Alice had a sandwich waiting for me. I ate, the food tasting like dust in my mouth, and drank the cold iced tea I'd made, thinking B&Bs always needed to have lemonade and tea on hand. Did guests expect afternoon pastries and dinner too? What kind of breakfast should I make?

Then I reminded myself I'd handle the ribbon-cutting ceremony first. There was no need to think beyond that. As long as I kept the to-do list out of my mind, I was able to slightly relax.

We went outside to make sure everything was set up as people started arriving. I talked with a couple of reporters and posed for pictures before the official ceremony. A small crowd gathered to watch. When it was time for me to cut the ribbon, Delaney stood next to me, but I felt very alone in front of my dream house.

Right before I closed the blades of the large scissors, I caught Mac in the crowd. I wished he was the one comforting me this morning, but he had work to do, and this was my thing. I wondered if he would have come earlier if I'd asked him, but it was too late. I cut the ribbon, the crowd cheering afterward, and led everyone inside to view the finished B&B.

My heart thumped in my chest as I acted as a guide, showing them each guest room and connected bathroom. It was scary letting everyone in. This project was personal to me. I did it because I wanted something that was mine after the divorce, but it became so much more—a way to prove to everyone I was strong and independent. That I could handle being on my own. But as I smiled and shook hands, answering questions about capacity and amenities, I felt like I was going to crack.

What was I thinking that I could do everything myself? When everyone had toured the inside, they wandered outside to enjoy the backyard space. Sam had done an amazing job but wasn't here today to hear everyone's comments.

I'd need to tell him that it was everyone's favorite spot in the house with the outdoor kitchen, pizza oven, two firepits, and private areas in the yard.

Eventually, people trickled out, promising to return for the celebration tonight. I still needed to hang the twinkly lights in the backyard, pick up more fresh flowers to brighten the space, and ensure the caterer was here on time.

"I think hosting a party was too ambitious," I said to Kylie and Alice once the ribbon-cutting guests left.

Kylie grasped her hands together. "Trust me, you're creating the perfect buzz. You're satisfying the locals' curiosity, and when someone asks them for a recommendation, they'll be able to say your B&B without hesitation."

"I hope you're right." My fingers trembled as I accepted the glass of iced tea Alice handed me before setting another plate of sandwiches and cookies in front of me.

"I have to say, Sam went above and beyond what he'd initially promised with the backyard. I love how he created multiple secluded areas for guests to congregate or even private alcoves for couples."

There was the main social area, where we were seated, but he'd worked with the landscapers to create several other smaller social areas for those who wanted a private space. "I'm so grateful."

Sam had done it for free, but I'd already given him credit on the website and intended to recommend him to anyone who asked. Not only was the quality top-notch, but he was also a dream to work with. He was passionate about his work and eager to create inviting spaces.

Alice poured each of us a glass of champagne. "To the success of your B&B, my store, and more importantly, our friendship."

We clinked glasses and said cheers, and I limited myself to one sip. The last thing I needed was to feel tipsy on top of everything else.

The doorbell rang, and Alice jumped up. "That's Elle and Piper. They wanted to see the place."

Piper was the one who'd created my logo and website. I'd never met her in person, but we'd done several video calls in an effort to narrow down my style and the feel I wanted for my branding.

Alice greeted them at the door and led them outside to the patio.

I hugged Piper. "It's so nice to finally meet you in person."

"This place is gorgeous," Piper said when I let her go.

I held my hands out. "This is Sam's doing."

"He's amazing. I'll need to hire him to work on the new house we're building," Piper said.

Alice told me she was married to a professional baseball player and traveled with him when he went to games.

Kylie came out with a charcuterie board of fruit, meat slices, cheese, and crackers. "I let the caterers in. I'd asked them to prepare a few of these for us. It's important for us to eat today."

I stood. "Do they need my help?"

Kylie held up a hand to stop me. "They're setting up in the kitchen. Relax."

I sat on the couch and popped a grape into my mouth. I'd already learned my lesson from this morning. I knew I needed to eat to make it through this day.

"The pictures didn't do this place justice," Elle said.

"Thank you. I hope my guests think so too."

"Once the reviews start coming in from your first guests, you're going to be busy," Alice reassured me for the millionth time.

My heart fluttered. It was exactly what I'd hoped for, yet I was scared about the possibility too. I worried I'd be too busy to be there for Delaney. That I'd be working late nights for months to come when I already felt like the pace was unsustainable. I thought I could rest after today, but that was unlikely. The pressure continued to build because there were so many expectations I needed to meet.

CHAPTER 22

MAC

I'd taken a break from my current project, a new build in the suburbs, to catch the ribbon-cutting ceremony. I wished I could have been there for the day, but it was early in the project, and Natalie hadn't asked for my help.

I kept waiting for her to reach out, but she didn't. I worried about her doing too much, but I could only do so much when she wouldn't listen.

She'd neglected our relationship, and I understood why, but it still worried me. She'd let me take Delaney to obedience training, but it wasn't enough. I wanted to be there for her.

I'd gotten an invitation to the party, but everyone in town had. People were invited to tour the B&B during the day and return in the evening for a cocktail party. It wasn't personalized. She hadn't asked me to go as her date.

I'd go to support her and get a glimpse of her and Delaney. Besides, my family was going to support Natalie and represent the work we'd done for the B&B. It would be good publicity for the business.

I straightened my tie in the mirror. I was alone this time. I wished Natalie and Delaney lived with me, and we were getting ready together. But then I hadn't asked for what I wanted. I was giving Natalie time, cognizant that she was overwhelmed with the opening.

But after, I'd need to talk to her, tell her what I wanted out of a relationship, and if she didn't want the same things, I'd need to deal with it.

I took Rocky outside one more time. He was growing each day and was already bigger than he was last week. I felt a pang, thinking that Delaney hadn't seen him much.

I missed being in their space every day. The distance between us was more than physical, and I could blame it on Natalie's business, but she'd pulled away from me emotionally as well.

She didn't call to confide in me or share her concerns. I understood she was busy, but I was worried it was something more. That she was going to pull away entirely. That I wasn't the man for her.

That thought made it painful to breathe, so I tried to put my worries out of my mind.

I drove downtown and parked, wishing we were together. We should be a team. Instead, we were farther apart than ever.

I got out, straightened my tie, and headed in the direction of the B&B.

"Uncle Mac," Maggie called from somewhere behind me.

I smiled and turned, pleased to see her. Alice and Sam followed at a distance. Maggie jumped into my arms, and I hugged her tight. "I missed you."

"Where've you been?" Maggie said, her breath hot on my chin.

"I just saw you at Sunday dinner."

Her lower lip popped out. "It's not enough."

"I know it's not. I'm sorry."

"She's really working it, huh?" Alice said with an amused smile.

"I'm putty in her hands, and she knows it."

Maggie giggled. "What's putty?"

"Like slime," Sam said when I let her down.

"I don't get it," she said with a frown.

"It means he'll do anything for you," Sam murmured into her ear as he picked her up and put her on his hip.

Her eyes widened. "Oh?"

"You shouldn't tell her that," I said as we started walking again.

"I just speak the truth," Sam said, nuzzling Maggie's neck with his beard until she giggled and squirmed to get down. She skipped ahead of us when she saw the lights from the B&B illuminating the sidewalk. As we approached, we could hear the crowd inside, talking and laughing.

"This is a great turnout," Sam said.

"Natalie did well." Not that I had anything to do with it.

Alice stood between us, touching my shoulder and Sam's. "It's your renovation."

"That's true, but it was her idea."

"And Kylie's. She's the one who saw the listing and suggested Natalie move here."

I was grateful for Kylie's suggestion, but I wondered if Natalie wasn't just another person on the long list of people who would reject me in the end.

"Kylie? You're not talking about Kylie Wilde, are you?" Tyler asked as he approached us with his hands stuffed into his jeans. He hadn't gotten dressed up.

"The one and the same," Alice said in greeting before she hugged him.

"You ready for this?" Sam asked me.

"As ready as I'll ever be." I didn't think I'd get any answers tonight, and I wouldn't press Natalie for any, but we needed to have a conversation soon.

When we approached the front door, Kylie pulled it open.

"The Fletcher brothers are here," she called out. Then her eyes widened when she saw Tyler. "I stand corrected. *All* the Fletcher brothers are here."

We greeted Kylie as we walked inside. I moved off to the side so that Maggie could go in ahead of me, and Tyler was the last to enter.

Tyler tugged on a strand of Kylie's hair. "Baby Wilde. Never thought I'd see the day when you came back to town."

Kylie moved away from his touch, crossing her arms over her chest. "My family lives here."

"You were never much for family."

Kylie scowled. "You don't know anything about me. You were always too busy running with my brothers to notice me."

I chuckled, throwing an arm around Tyler's shoulder and squeezing. "Come on, man. Leave Kylie alone. Where can we find Natalie?" I asked Kylie.

"She was in the kitchen the last time I saw her. Good luck getting her alone." But Kylie's gaze was on Tyler.

I nodded my thanks and pulled Tyler away from the front door.

When I let him go, I said, "What was that?"

Tyler rubbed his shoulder where I gripped him tight in warning. "What was that for? I was just saying hi."

"That's not what you were doing. You were treating her like a little kid." Even I could see Kylie hadn't appreciated the "Baby Wilde" comment or the dig about coming home.

Tyler shrugged. "That's just how it is when we're together."

"You mean you act like a shitty teenager again?"

Tyler chuckled. "Something like that." Then he sobered, a look of vulnerability washing over his expression. "I was just surprised to see her. I'd heard she was back, but I figured she'd be gone before I saw her."

"I don't know what's going on with her. She left her job in

Paris and is home for the foreseeable future. Natalie said she's trying to figure out what to do next."

"Interesting," Tyler said, and I wasn't sure what to make of it. Growing up, we'd hung out with the Wilde brothers. They were fun, and their ski resort was the perfect playground for rough-and-tumble boys, but we didn't pay much attention to Kylie. We avoided her and her friends as much as possible.

When I caught a glimpse of Natalie smiling and the exhaustion in the lines around her eyes, I clasped Tyler's shoulder. "I'll see you around."

Then I walked away without another word. I needed to see Natalie. I'd texted her *good luck* this morning, but it wasn't enough.

Her gaze snagged on mine as I approached, and she turned her body to welcome me. I leaned over to kiss her cheek, lingering to whisper in her ear, "Congratulations, sweetheart."

Her cheeks flushed from either the champagne in her glass or my proximity—I wasn't sure which.

"Thank you. I was just socializing with everyone." Her eyes were a little wild.

I maneuvered us down the hall to a quiet corner. "How are you holding up?"

"I only have a few more hours, right?" Her shoulders seemed to sag under the weight of that proclamation.

"You want me to stand guard and give you a few minutes' peace?"

Natalie rolled her shoulders back, steeling her gaze. "This is what I signed up for. It's great publicity. This is good for me and my business."

"If you say so." As much as I admired her resolve and perseverance, I was worried about her. "Where's Delaney?"

"She's watching TV in the suite."

"By herself?" I asked, surprised.

"I'm checking in on her every twenty minutes or so."

"I'll hang out with her if you don't need me here."

Natalie's expression softened. "That would be great. Thank you."

I leaned over to kiss her softly, wishing I could tell her I loved her, but it wasn't the time or place. "That's what I'm here for."

Maybe we'd get a chance to talk tonight.

I headed toward the owner's suite, excited to see Delaney. I knocked on the door, announcing it was me, in case she'd been instructed not to answer it. She opened the door and hugged me tight.

"I missed you," she said as she moved back so I could enter.

"I missed you too. What are you up to?"

"Watching TV and eating snacks."

There was a cartoon playing on the TV, and goldfish were scattered on the coffee table and floor. I tidied up while she started the show again.

"Are you hungry?"

Delaney's face scrunched. "Whoever Mom hired gave me a sandwich."

"The caterers?" I asked, putting the dishes from the sink into the dishwasher and starting it. I could make Natalie's life easier in some ways.

"When will it be over?" Delaney asked.

"Hopefully, in a couple of hours." I loosened my tie as I sat next to her, toed off my shoes, and rested my heels on the table. "Let's find a movie to watch."

We scrolled for a while before finding something we were both interested in. Delaney snuggled into my side. My heart expanded, and warmth spread through my body. This was what I wanted. Quiet nights at home, cuddling on the couch while watching a movie.

I didn't want to think about what would happen if Natalie

didn't want me. But the thought always hovered at the edges of my consciousness.

I should have carried Delaney to bed, but I must have fallen asleep before I could. I woke when the door opened. It was dark outside, and I rubbed my eyes. Delaney's head rested on my shoulder.

"I can carry her to bed," I whispered to Natalie.

I lifted her easily and carried her to her bed. When Natalie tucked her in, she followed me to the living room. I turned off the TV and cleaned up the remaining snacks and glasses.

"Thanks for watching her."

"You could have asked for my help." My tone was a little testy.

"I didn't even think of it. I thought she'd enjoy the party, but she wasn't interested. I think she's tired of all the hoopla."

"I bet." I was tired of it too, and I didn't live it.

"You want to head home?" Natalie asked, picking up on my irritation. "We don't have the privacy here that we do at your house."

"I can just sleep with you here. We don't have to do anything. We're both tired."

"Okay."

I moved closer to massage her shoulders.

Her head fell back on my chest. "That feels good."

"Let's get you to bed. You must be exhausted."

"I am."

"Was it successful?" *Was it worth it?*

She moved so she could see my face. "We had a great turnout. I think Sam and your company got a lot of attention with the backyard space."

"That was the idea." I was pleased Sam's hard work paid off.

I guided her to bed, waiting while she brushed her teeth and got dressed. When she slid into bed next to me, I held her, wondering if it was the last time I'd get to be this close to her. It didn't escape my notice that she hadn't invited me to stay the night. I'd insisted. We needed to have a conversation soon. I couldn't handle much more of this uncertainty. It brought out all my insecurities.

* * *

THE NEXT MORNING, I woke to an empty bed and a buzzing phone. When I answered it, my father said a pipe had busted at the new build, and I needed to get there. I dressed quickly and headed out to the kitchen where Natalie was making pancakes.

I kissed her temple. "I'm sorry. I have to go. There's an emergency at the house we're working on."

"On a Sunday?" Delaney asked, her lower lip protruding, similar to Maggie's.

"A pipe burst. I'm sorry. I was hoping we could spend the day together."

"Maybe we can come over later to see Rocky," Delaney said.

"That's up to your mom."

"We'll see, sweetie," Natalie said as she slid a plate with two pancakes in front of her.

"I'll call you later," I said to her.

"Sure," Natalie said, sitting across from Delaney. But her smile was brittle.

Did she regret allowing me to stay last night? Was she biding her time until she could cut me loose? I hated thinking like that, but I couldn't help it.

I kissed Delaney's head and said good-bye. My mind should have been on the issue at the build, but for once, I was distracted. I resolved to talk with Natalie about it, once and for all. I couldn't live like this anymore. Either Natalie let me in, or we were done. I didn't think I was being unreasonable by demanding an answer.

When I got to the house, Dad was already there. The water was turned off, and he'd set up fans to dry out the floors.

"Where were you? It shouldn't have taken you that long to get here from your house."

"I fell asleep at Natalie's last night. It took me a while to fall asleep, so I didn't hear it the first time you called."

Dad gave me a look. "I'd lecture you on your priorities—"

"I know I've been distracted lately. It's my fault."

"I'm just worried about you. Things good with Natalie?"

"She's so busy with the opening of the B&B, I haven't seen her much. I'm not sure where we stand."

"What are you going to do?" Dad crossed his arms.

"I think we need to talk. I was waiting for the opening to be over and for things to slow down."

Dad dipped his chin. "A new business is stressful. Things might not slow down for a while."

"That's what I'm worried about. She won't ask for help. At least not from me."

"She's trying to do too much." Dad was speaking from a place of experience.

"I agree, but she won't listen to reason. She said she can't afford to hire anyone."

Dad shook his head. "The way I see it, she needs to run the numbers and make it work. She can't do the cleaning. That could take hours out of her day."

"And Delaney is home by four. I know she wants to spend time with her."

"Talk to her. See if she'll consider other options. Otherwise, she's going to burn out. She won't be able to be a good hostess if she's cleaning toilets when a guest needs something."

I chuckled without any humor. "I agree."

"But at the end of the day, it's her business. She can run it the way she wants to."

"Even if she runs herself into the ground?"

"Even then. You might have to let her go if she's not focused on your relationship."

"That's what I'm afraid of." In the past, women had always walked away from me. Natalie hadn't done that, but she'd distanced herself. I was afraid to ask why.

"I'd talk to her. Get things settled."

"I will."

"You love her, don't you?"

I nodded, feeling miserable. I'd let myself fall for her when I wasn't sure if she felt the same.

"Lay it all on the line. Let her know how you feel and what your boundaries are. If you want more time, ask for it. If she says no, then you have your answer. No more wondering."

"I wish it were easier."

"Women don't always tell us what they want or what they're thinking, and we're left wondering. It's always best to be direct with them."

"I will." Maybe that was the issue with my past relationships. I hadn't asked for what I wanted. I just assumed they knew how I felt. I wouldn't make that mistake again.

"Let's finish this up and let the owner know what's going on."

I hated telling the owners when there was an unexpected delay, but it was part of the job. Maybe Natalie would come over tonight and we could have that talk. I felt light-headed thinking I might have the answer, but it might not be what I wanted to hear.

CHAPTER 23

NATALIE

I wanted to relax, but my first guests were checking in today, and I needed to finish cleaning up after the party. I could have hired someone for that, but my budget was blown on the caterer.

As soon as we finished breakfast, I asked Delaney to help me throw out the trash, tidy up, vacuum, and scrub the place again. I barely finished before the first guests arrived.

I greeted them with a smile, despite how grimy I felt. Hoping they didn't notice, I gave them the key, told them where the information was inside the room, and invited them to contact me should they have any questions or issues.

I was already regretting telling guests I'd be available twenty-four seven for any issues that came up. Juliana warned me about spreading myself too thin when I talked to her, but I hadn't listened, thinking I knew better.

When the happy couple went up to their room, I finished cleaning, made some cookies, and set them on the kitchen counter with a cake cover and a note to take as many as they'd like. I also set out fruit and drinks.

I wasn't sure if I was supposed to hang out in the kitchen in the event a guest wandered down. Instead, I returned to my apartment to find Delaney watching TV. I couldn't fault her because what was she supposed to do while I managed the B&B? I was already feeling resentful of the guests. This was the time I should have been spending with my daughter.

I plopped down next to her on the couch. "Everything okay?"

"Why do you have to work on the weekend?" she whined.

"Remember? This is why we moved here. So I could open the B&B. I need to tend to the guests." But this was what *I* signed up for, not Delaney. She didn't want or ask for any of this.

Her expression fell. "I miss Mac."

"He had an emergency this morning, remember?"

Delaney's face screwed up. "I want to see him."

"Maybe he could pick you up. But I can't leave the B&B. Not on opening weekend."

"I don't want to be stuck here all the time."

My stomach sank. "It's just the first weekend. It's important we make a good impression."

"We?"

"I mean, it's important that *I* make a good impression." I was the sole owner, and everything rested on me. The weight on my chest increased, making it difficult to draw in a deep breath.

"I don't want to own a hotel."

"It's a B&B," I said tiredly, "and I'm doing my best." I felt like everyone was pulling me in different directions. Delaney and the guests wanted my attention, and I'd felt something coming off Mac last night. Disapproval or disappointment. He wanted something I wasn't giving him, and it wasn't surprising. I'd put everything into the B&B the last few weeks. I barely had the energy to return his texts.

I kept putting him off, telling him it would get better, but I wasn't so sure. With people staying at the B&B, it would only get worse. The business number was forwarded to my cell, but I still felt uneasy at home. Shouldn't I be at the front counter?

My phone buzzed. I'd installed a camera at the front door so I could see when guests were arriving. "The next guests are checking in. Let me greet them."

Delaney growled.

"Watch TV, and I'll be back soon to make dinner."

I didn't like walking away from Delaney, but I didn't have a choice. There was no way I could be at Mac's and be a good hospitality worker.

Everything I'd read online suggested that someone needed to be on-site, and, for now, that person was me.

I pasted on a smile and greeted the older couple in the lobby. I checked them in and invited them to enjoy the snacks and beverages in the kitchen.

I snuck away as soon as I could. When I opened the door, something smelled burnt, and Delaney was in the kitchen. Looking around for signs of smoke, I asked, "What are you doing?"

"I was hungry. I tried to cook mac and cheese," she said defensively.

She'd used the quick-serve cups, but the noodles were burned on the bottom.

"I think I forgot the water."

"You did."

"I was hungry, and you weren't here." Her tone was accusatory, and I couldn't blame her. This was my fault.

Tears pricked my eyes as a knock sounded on the door. Frustrated, I opened the door to find Mac standing there with a smile. "How is everything?"

"Not great," I said, letting him in and returning to the kitchen so I could clean up the mess. Delaney was lucky the fire alarm hadn't sounded. I opened the window and turned on the ceiling fan to dissipate the smell of burnt noodles.

"What happened?" Mac asked cautiously.

"I was hungry," Delaney whined before she dissolved into tears.

The guilt was a band around my chest, tightening with each sob.

"Let's get you some dinner," Mac said practically as he wrapped an arm around her shoulders.

"Mommy's never here anymore. She's always over there cleaning and talking to customers." Delaney pointed at the door to the B&B.

"It's the first day we've been open. I wouldn't say I'm never here," I said defensively.

"Ever since we came here, you've been busy with the B&B, and it's only going to get worse. You say it will get better, but it won't."

"You don't know that," I said, feeling defeated.

Delaney threw off Mac's arm, ran down the hall, and slammed her door.

I couldn't look at Mac while I cleaned the mess with jerky hands.

"Hey, it's okay. It will get better."

"Will it? You heard Delaney; it's only going to get worse." I threw a hand in the direction of Delaney's bedroom.

Mac drew me into his arms. "It's the first day."

"I know." I buried my head in his chest. Delaney was right. Things were only going to get busier. More guests meant the less time I had to give to Delaney. The more rooms I'd need to clean. "I wasn't thinking about the mess the party would create, and the first guests arrived today."

Mac drew back to see my face. "You didn't hire a cleaning crew for the party?"

"I stupidly didn't think it would be that big of a deal."

He rubbed a hand on my back. "You're not stupid."

I stepped back from him, feeling like I was going to jump out of my skin. "You should probably go. We're a bit of a mess."

"I can get dinner. I bet you're exhausted after last night. I thought we could celebrate."

"Delaney's mad. I'm exhausted. What is there to celebrate?" I knew I was being stubborn in the face of Mac's kindness, but I couldn't help it.

"You're the owner of a B&B. Your dream came true. Money is coming in." But his tone was flat.

"It is nice to swipe their credit cards. I like to think I'm getting paid, but really, I'll be paying back the credit cards. I'm in this hole I'll never dig my way out of."

"You can't look at it that way."

I felt defeated. Like I'd come all this way and created something I couldn't sustain. I sat at the kitchen table and dropped my head in my hands. "I think I screwed up. I thought I could handle this, but I can't."

Mac rubbed my back for a few seconds and then sighed. "This probably isn't the best time, but I was wondering where I fit into all of this."

He'd stood patiently by while I sorted out the new B&B, and now he wanted answers. Answers I couldn't give him. "I don't know what to say. I can't be there for everyone when I need to be there for my guests. Out of anyone, you should understand."

He looked away from me. "I want to be there for you, but I need to know that there's a place for me somewhere."

"I can barely take care of Delaney right now." My shoulders lowered.

"She deserves better."

"Don't you think I know that?"

"It doesn't look like it from where I'm standing. You're not hiring any help. You're taking on everything yourself, and I can't stand by while you do that."

Anger churned in my gut. "I didn't ask you to."

"I'm going to go."

I bit my lip. "I don't want you to."

"You have some things to figure out. I don't think I should be here while you do."

"Is this you just walking away from a relationship because you're afraid?" I was racking my brain for what he'd said about his exes. Maybe this wasn't about me at all.

"For the first time, I'm asking for what I want. I love you. I want to be with you, but not like this. I want all of you."

"That's not even possible," I murmured, still not processing that he loved me and was walking away from me.

"You're taking on too much. You're worn down, exhausted. You can't do everything you need to because you're doing too much."

I shook my head, trying to process everything he was saying. "That doesn't even make sense."

Mac shook his head. "You need to figure things out, and I can't stand by while you self-destruct."

That wasn't what was happening. He was wrong.

He moved toward the door, and I couldn't do anything but watch him go as my stomach dropped to the floor. He was leaving. He was walking away from me and Delaney. "What about Delaney?" I finally asked.

"I'm not walking away from her. If she wants to see Rocky or hang out at the playground, call me."

I wouldn't. If he was breaking up with me, then I'd sever the connection. I wouldn't let him stick around like Carter had. He wasn't her father, and I ignored the tiny voice that said he was more of a father to her than Carter ever was.

I couldn't believe I'd been on a high yesterday from the ribbon-cutting ceremony and the party, while today, it felt like I had crashed.

I'd lost Mac. Delaney was angry with me. I was failing in my personal life, and I hadn't even gotten off the ground with my business. I wasn't doing anything right.

But I still needed to make dinner and check in with the guests. I couldn't find a soft place to roll into a ball and give in to the despair creeping through my body.

Why did it feel like the guests got more of me than my loved ones?

While I made boxed mac and cheese, I paused when I remembered Mac had said he loved me. When had that happened? Did I feel the same? I felt too overwhelmed with the inn to think of anything else.

Why couldn't Mac just give me more time? Everything would have gotten better with time.

Delaney ate very little for dinner and asked to go to her room afterward. I didn't have the heart to argue with her. I left her with the phone and said I needed to check in the new guests, who would be arriving any minute.

I smiled and greeted them, making sure the other guests were comfortable and didn't need anything. Even if I wanted to talk to Mac tonight, I couldn't.

I thought I'd feel accomplished once the B&B was open, but instead, I felt trapped under a crushing weight. The worst part was, I couldn't be there for Delaney when she was home. The B&B would always be beckoning.

Even if I thought it was a mistake to open the B&B, it was too late to do anything now. I couldn't sell it. Not when I'd put all my savings into it. I had to recoup my costs.

But as upsetting as the reality of business ownership was, I didn't want to sell. I wanted it to be a success. I didn't want to be as hands-on as I thought. Everything I read said you needed to learn from your mistakes and pivot. But I had no idea what I could do, not with the lack of funds I was faced with.

I'd hoped the attention from opening day would fill the remaining vacancies, but when I checked the reservations, my stomach dropped. There were none. How was that even possible?

I'd need to wait for the news article to hit the papers. The media attention was local, and I probably needed people from around the world to see it.

How could I get more reach? Everyone said I'd rely on the reviews of the first guests to spread the word on travel sites. I'd need to hope these guests left reviews. What if they didn't?

So, I'd need to be very accommodating and available to guests. At a time when I suspected I needed to give more attention to those in my personal life, it wasn't possible. I felt so torn. So utterly hopeless.

I pulled out my phone and scrolled to the text chain with Mac. There was nothing else to say except I was sorry. What was the point in apologizing when nothing was going to change. Not yet anyway. I put my phone away without sending a message. Maybe if I slept on it, a solution would come to me.

I couldn't approach Mac unless I altered how I was operating the business. I needed to make some changes and prove to him and Delaney that I could handle the business and my personal life. And until I figured it out, there was no point in having a conversation with Mac about our relationship. It wasn't fair to him.

Even if the way he left was ripping me apart inside, I wanted to fix it, but I couldn't. Not yet. I stupidly waited for a response to my text, but there wasn't one.

All the guests were inside for the night and had a keycard that gave them access to the front door as well as their rooms. They were free to come and go as they pleased. As I made my way back to my apartment, I wondered if I should hire someone to man the desk twenty-four seven.

If I hired someone, it would save money if I could offer them free room and board. But then, I'd need to find a place to live with Delaney. I couldn't ask to move in with Mac. Not when he'd walked out.

Delaney stayed cooped up in her room for the rest of the night, which gave me too much time to ruminate. By the time I tucked her into bed, my head was throbbing.

There was a knock on my door around nine just as I was about to head to bed for a sleepless night. It was Alice and Kylie.

"What are you guys doing here?" I asked, pushing the door open wider so they could come inside.

"Mac said you might need us."

I waved a hand. "He didn't have to do that. I'm fine."

"Are you sure? Because you don't look fine," Alice said as she set the grocery bag on the counter and pulled out a pint of ice cream and plastic spoons. She lifted the lid and handed me a spoon.

I didn't hesitate to dig in. I couldn't taste the flavor, but it was cool on my tongue. "Don't I look fine?"

"I mean, you're standing," Kylie said with a grimace, as she scanned me from head to toe.

"I look that bad?" I asked as I sat on the stool.

Alice grimaced. "You don't look good."

"Did Mac tell you he left? We're broken up. At least, I think we are." I stuck a spoonful of ice cream into my mouth, feeling a little hysterical admitting it out loud. I'd finally found myself a good man, but I couldn't get my shit together to be the woman he needed.

After his past, I should have made more of an effort to reassure him everything was fine. But there was a part of me that was a little irritated he couldn't see that I needed time.

"You've been working a lot. He's worried about you," Alice finally said.

Both of my friends seemed a little afraid of what to say to me. I wondered if they were even on my side. "I just opened the

B&B. It's stressful and busy, and I have no idea what I'm doing. I'm so scared that whatever I do won't be enough."

"Did you tell Mac this?" Alice asked carefully.

"Well, yeah." I mean, hadn't we talked about it a million times? Or maybe I'd just said I was tired and needed to work more without explaining to him what was going on in my head. "I think so."

Alice sighed. "He feels like you shut him out."

I paused spoon midair. "*I* shut him out?"

Alice nodded. "That's what he said to Sam."

I tried to remember the last few weeks, but it was a blur of work, preparations, and to-do lists.

"Did you let him in? Did you tell him what was going on? Did you give him a chance to help?" Kylie asked.

"I mean, I thought he knew."

"You can't assume he knew what was going on inside here." Kylie tapped my head.

"You feel like you need to do everything yourself, and it's taking a toll on your relationships," Alice said.

"Delaney's unhappy with me too. But I don't see how I can fix it unless I sell the business. I can't even afford to do that right now without losing everything." Who was going to buy an untested business? They'd want to see the books, and there weren't any.

"Did you ever think about discussing these issues with Mac? Letting him in and asking for his advice?"

"The B&B is my problem. I need to do this on my own."

Alice sighed. "You know, when I was unsure where to go next with my business, Sam talked to you about leasing me the front room. He knew I was struggling. I couldn't find a space or someone who wanted to sell my mosaics here in town, and when an opportunity came up, he seized it. He was the one who negotiated the deal. Do you remember what that was?"

"I gave you a discounted lease in exchange for..." My voice trailed off. "You helping me with the front desk."

"Have you asked for my help?" Alice asked gently.

"I didn't want to ask. You have a family."

"Or do *you* have to be the one who greets the guests, answers the phones, and cleans the rooms?" Kylie asked.

Guilt spread through me. "Both. It's my baby, and I felt badly taking you away from Sam and Maggie."

"But it's what we agreed to, and I've been benefitting from the reduced rent for months without you asking for anything in return."

"So, you'd work the desk in the evening so I could be with Delaney?" I asked her, feeling like my brain was working again.

"Or with Mac. Whatever you need. You don't need to be tied to this place," Alice said pointedly.

"That's how I've been feeling. Like I'm stuck."

"You've got me, and you could hire someone who's retired and only wants to work a few hours or days a week. Someone who loves to socialize and will talk up the guests."

"That's a nice idea. Do you know anyone?" I asked, licking the spoon clean. The ice cream carton was mostly empty at this point. I should have felt sick, but I didn't. Instead, I felt energized, as if this was a problem that could be solved.

"I can ask around," Kylie said.

"That would be amazing." I didn't need to pay Alice a salary for her work, so it was possible I could swing another part-time worker.

"Now, what about a cleaning service?" Kylie asked.

"When I looked into it, cleaning companies were crazy expensive," I said, throwing the carton into the recycling bin by the back door.

"What if you hired someone to clean, but it wasn't a service?"

"I hadn't even considered that."

Kylie's eyes brightened. "Maybe someone who has kids in

school and just wants a daytime gig. No work to bring home."

"Do you know anyone?"

"I can ask Elle if she has any ideas. She meets so many people at the barbershop. She can put some feelers out, see if anyone knows someone."

"That would be amazing. I'm so lucky to have you two." My eyes stung. "But what about Mac? What if he's done with me?"

"What happened exactly?" Alice asked.

I tried to remember his exact words, but I felt like I was in a fog. I was exhausted and stressed out. "He was rambling about a lot of stuff, but somewhere in the middle, he said he loved me."

Kylie pointed a finger at me. "That doesn't sound like a man who's uninterested. What did you say?"

"He made this speech and walked out." There wasn't any time to express myself, but if I was being honest, I was a little shocked by his declaration.

"Do you love him?" Alice asked gently.

I thought about how I felt when he wasn't here. How hard things had been when I tried to do everything for the B&B myself. It had been lonely. Then I remembered how I felt when we were together. I felt cherished and loved and appreciated. "I think I do. But it's too late. I'm not any different from his exes."

Kylie frowned. "How so?"

"I was too busy to give him the attention he deserved and needed in the relationship. I shut him out."

"I think you can work this out. But we need to get the B&B sorted first," Alice said.

We got out a notebook and made another list. Except this one felt lighter. I was paving the way to building a sustainable future. And maybe at the end of it, Mac would take me back.

The girls stayed a little longer, and I felt better when I finally got into bed. We'd solved a few of my problems at the B&B. I had a plan of action. But I still hadn't figured things out with Mac.

CHAPTER 24

MAC

$\mathcal{I}$ was in the zone, carefully placing the tiles in the bathroom of the new build we were still working on. It was the weekend, so it was just me on-site. I hadn't heard from Natalie. Not that I expected her to reach out after my little speech. I'd told her I loved her and walked out. What idiot did that?

I was working late nights and weekends on the new project because why not? I had nothing else to fill my time. I still went to Sunday dinners with my family and doted on Maggie, but my life felt empty.

The only thing that lifted my mood was Rocky. I brought him to work with me when the crew went home so that he didn't have to be home all day alone. But I think he missed Delaney and Natalie. I know I did.

If I hadn't been so stubborn, maybe I'd still be with them. Sure, I hadn't seen much of them lately because they were busy, but the possibility was still there. But I'd severed the connection. Telling people what you wanted only hurt you in the end.

I should have covered it up. Buried it. Shoved it down deep.

Instead, I'd put everything on the line, and the ball was in Natalie's court.

"What are you doing?" Sam asked me.

I startled. "I didn't hear you come in."

Tyler walked in behind him. It was the master bathroom, so the space was large.

"Obviously," Tyler said, crossing his arms over his chest.

"Why are you working all the time?" Sam asked me. "Dad's worried."

I clenched my jaw. "We'll be done ahead of schedule. There's nothing to worry about."

"We're worried about *you*, dumbass." Sam sat on the edge of the standalone tub.

I unclenched my teeth long enough to bite out, "I'm fine."

Sam tipped his head to the side. "Are you? Alice said you broke things off with Natalie."

I waved a hand. "She was all wrapped up in the business."

"Isn't that what you'd expect of a new business owner?" Tyler asked, genuinely curious.

"She was doing too much and not asking for any help."

Sam cleared his throat. "Sounds like every new business owner ever. Why didn't you try to help instead of giving her an ultimatum?"

"I did. She wasn't listening." Had I done the right thing? Tyler and Sam were making it seem like I hadn't. I stood, stretching my neck and back from sitting in the cramped position for so long. "I told her how I felt. Isn't that what I'm supposed to do?"

Sam dipped his chin. "You told her you loved her and then walked out."

I gripped the back of my neck. "You should be proud of me for saying my piece."

"Why would you tell a woman you loved her and then break

up with her?" Tyler asked, genuinely confused, but then he'd never been in a serious relationship.

"That's rich, coming from you." He prided himself on dating women and keeping things casual. He claimed to leave them satisfied, but I wasn't so sure.

"Sure, throw stones, but I'm not the one who broke up with the love of my life," Tyler muttered.

"How do you know that's what she is?" Irritation had my shoulders tightening.

"Isn't she?" Sam asked gently. He had more experience with relationships and probably knew what he was talking about. But I wasn't ready to concede I might have screwed up.

"The ball's in her court," I said stubbornly.

"Why did you run after saying how you felt?" Tyler asked.

"I don't know. I was afraid of what she'd say, I guess. I haven't had the best track record in these situations." When I said I'd loved women in the past, it was the beginning of the end. They'd start to pull away.

"What if she felt the same? What if she wanted to work through it?" Sam asked.

"There's nothing stopping her, but she hasn't reached out." I rubbed the ache in my chest. She obviously didn't feel the same way.

"So, you're just going to walk away?"

"According to you, I already did." I wasn't sure what Tyler was getting at. "If she felt the same, she could have told me, but she hasn't."

Sam shook his head. "What if she's doing what you asked? Getting her shit together first?"

"I don't want to get my hopes up." It was better to assume the worst so I wouldn't be disappointed.

"You're still trying to protect yourself. When are you going to learn?" Sam asked.

I leaned against the countertop. "I thought I was being honest about how I felt and what I wanted."

Tyler chuckled. "That was fine, right up until you walked out."

"I thought I'd give her an ultimatum and let her make a decision."

Sam shook his head. "Relationships are about work and compromise. Not threats and ultimatums."

"It wasn't like that—" I broke off, trying to remember how I'd handled the situation.

"Are you sure about that?" Sam asked.

Normally, his tone would have irked me, but I hadn't given Natalie an opportunity to respond. In fact, she'd seemed shocked by my words. I didn't give her time to process anything before I was out the door. I was in survival mode.

"You can still fix this," Tyler said.

"Why do you care?" I asked him, irritation lining my tone.

Tyler let his arms fall to his side as Rocky danced at his feet. "Because as much as we teased you over the years, you deserve this. You deserve to be with a good woman who loves you back. You deserve the house and the white picket fence. A family and a dog."

"You deserve it all," Sam agreed.

Rocky nudged Tyler's hand until he petted him, then dropped to his knees next to him. Rocky was in ecstasy from his attention.

Maybe that was the problem. I didn't think I was worthy of those women. Maybe I sabotaged those relationships, not the other way around. "I should talk to her."

Sam nodded as he stood. "Now you're thinking straight."

What would I say? *I'm sorry I walked out on you, but I still want this thing to work between us. I'm willing to see things differently.* Relationships weren't black and white. We'd go through periods when things were rough, and we'd need each other's support.

Tyler turned as if to leave. "We'll leave you to figure it out."

"Since you're here, you might as well help me out so I'll get this done quicker."

"Seriously?" Tyler asked, over his shoulder.

"That's what you get for showing up at a job site to school me."

Sam stuffed his hands into his pockets. "We'll help, but only if you go to Natalie's after this."

"I will."

After my promise, we worked side by side, making quick work of the tile. We'd always worked great as a team when we weren't competing or trying to one-up each other. I missed working with them since we were usually in charge of separate projects these days.

When we were cleaning up, Tyler said, "I think I'd like to build a house."

He'd always lived in an apartment downtown, saying he liked to be able to walk to the bars and restaurants.

"You thinking about settling down?" Sam asked.

Tyler shook his head. "What? No. I want more space. We spend all day creating beautiful homes for others, and yeah, maybe I'm tired of living like I just graduated from college."

"The bachelor pad not impressing the ladies anymore?" Sam joked.

"Fuck off."

We messed around and gave each other shit, but it was usually good-natured. This time, I sensed that Tyler was hurt by our reaction.

"What do you need from us?" I asked him.

"I'm working with a realtor to find some property that could work. I'd like your advice when I find something."

"You got it," I said.

We often joked that Tyler never grew up. Maybe this was the beginning.

Sam was already in a serious relationship, and I hoped to salvage mine. Tyler was the only one of us that was still happily single. I couldn't see him settling down with a woman, but maybe getting his own place would slow his attendance on the bar scene.

"We're here for you," Sam said.

"I appreciate it. I know you see me as the brother who doesn't take anything seriously, but I'm going to prove you wrong."

I clasped his shoulder. "You don't need to prove anything to us."

"To Dad, then."

Sam had gone through something similar when he met Alice. He wanted Dad to take his business idea seriously. He worked hard on our outdoor spaces and then approached Dad with his plan.

"You want to create a new branch for the business too?" Sam asked him as we headed downstairs.

"Nothing like that. I'm just feeling restless. Like I haven't figured out what I'm supposed to be doing."

My stomach dropped. "You thinking of leaving Fletcher & Sons?"

"I don't think so. I like what we do, but maybe there's something else out there."

We settled in the kitchen where the plans for the house were spread out over the cardboard boxes that contained the new cupboards. "Recently, we visited a B&B in Annapolis. The owner was a single mother. She hired Nolan, a contractor to complete the renovations, and they ended up falling in love."

"Sounds familiar," Sam joked.

I continued without acknowledging his interruption. "I had some time to speak to Nolan about what it was like dating a single mother."

Tyler held up his hands. "I have no plans to date a single

mom or to date anyone seriously. I don't want to have any more one-night stands though. Those are starting to feel a little empty."

I was proud that Tyler had finally figured out that sex without a connection wasn't the best. "The reason I'm telling you this is that he and his brother, Cade, run a nonprofit on the side. They renovate homes to make them handicapped accessible. I think we can do more with what we have. And not just the business side. I think we should do some kind of charity work. Whether that's related to building something for someone in need or donating money to a local sports team to buy gear."

Sam looked at me with newfound respect. "I love that idea."

"It would give us something more. It would elevate our name, but we'd be doing something good."

"I initially thought of baseball, since we'd all played. I don't care if our company name is on the jerseys or if there's a sign in the outfield; I just think we should do something to give back to the community."

"Kylie mentioned something to Alice about starting a nonprofit for girls' teams," Sam said.

"Kylie Wilde?" Tyler asked, his voice incredulous.

"She's trying to figure out what she wants to do. She was talking about skis and boards for kids who can't afford them, but then she mentioned wanting to help female athletes."

"She played softball, didn't she?" I asked.

"She did," Tyler said.

They were closer in age than I was to her, so my memory of her back then was vague. "Maybe you can work on something together. If we pool our money and resources, we can do more."

Tyler grinned. "I didn't come here tonight thinking we'd start a nonprofit, but I love the idea."

"Me too, and I know Dad will be on board," Sam added.

More and more, Dad wanted us to take over the business and make it ours. This was one more way we could do that, and

I loved that I'd gotten the idea from Nolan. "Let me talk to Nolan and get more information. I don't know the tax implications or what we'd need to do."

"I'll handle it," Tyler said. "I want to do something. I'm not sure what, but you two have enough going on."

I took on more responsibility as the eldest, and Sam had recently branched out with the outdoor division of the business, but Tyler was different. We didn't expect much from him. "Are you sure?"

"Let's see what we can figure out over the next few weeks. Mac, you talk to Nolan. Tyler, you figure out the business and tax stuff and talk to Kylie. See if she's interested."

"Do we need to work with her?" Tyler asked.

"I thought we agreed that if we pooled our resources, we'd be able to do more," Sam said.

"I don't know if I want to work with Kylie. She's spoiled. I'll probably end up doing all the work."

"How well do you even know Kylie? We only hung out with her brothers." And listened to whatever shit they spewed about her. They used to refer to her as the princess, but it might have been because she was the only girl and the youngest of her siblings. Not because she was spoiled.

I'd sensed something between Kylie and Tyler the other night at the B&B's opening. Maybe that was his reluctance. But if we wanted Tyler to grow up, we'd have to stop treating him like a kid.

Tyler looked away. "Not at all."

His avoidance made me think he did know her better than he let on. "Get to know her. We're not crazy kids anymore. You can be the adult in this situation. Just because her brothers treated her like a nuisance doesn't mean we should."

"Kylie's friends with Alice and Natalie. She's part of our lives now. You should treat her with respect," Sam said, with no give in his tone.

Tyler's face carefully smoothed over. "I said I'd deal with it, and I will."

Our business was established enough that we could do extras like this. Not only would it help the company's reputation, but we'd enjoy helping others too. Satisfied that one part of my life was working, I said, "I need to talk to Natalie."

Now that we'd discussed what I should do, I was eager to get on it.

"Good luck," Tyler said as he walked out to his truck.

Sam lingered. "You've got this. Just remember to do a lot of groveling."

"I gave her the ultimatum because she was shutting me out. Shouldn't she come to me?"

"You need to be honest with her about your feelings and give her a chance to respond. Weren't you just saying Tyler needed to be more grown-up?"

"I said something like that," I grumbled.

Sam clasped my shoulder. "If she loves you, and I think she does, it will be okay."

Dread pooled in the bottom of my stomach. Sam wasn't intimately familiar with women dumping him. He'd had one serious relationship, and yeah, he'd screwed up at the end, but she'd taken him back. Who could blame him for stumbling when his ex showed up in town to give him trouble? I didn't have that same excuse. I'd messed things up on my own.

"I have faith you'll figure it out." Then he was gone, and I was alone.

Needing to see Natalie, I locked up and headed over to the B&B. Hopefully, she was still awake.

When I knocked softly on the door, it opened slowly.

Natalie wore a tiny sleep outfit as she held the door slightly ajar. "Mac, what are you doing here?"

"I was hoping we could talk."

"I was in bed," she said, not letting me in.

"I'm sorry about the other day when I walked out. I didn't give you a chance to respond. I'd like to talk about it."

Her eyes flickered with interest as she straightened and opened the door so I could walk inside. "Okay."

On the couch, she wrapped a throw around her shoulders as if to protect herself from me.

"What I said must have been a shock." Suddenly, I was worried I'd come over without a plan. Was talking enough? Or should I show her how I felt?

She licked her lips, adjusting the blanket tighter over her shoulders. "You mean when you said you loved me?"

"I was worried you'd say it was one-sided." I could barely look at her; I was so nervous.

She palmed my cheek, forcing me to look at her. "I love you too. I wasn't sure what it was because what I feel for you is so much more than what I ever felt for Carter. And you were right, I was so wrapped up in the B&B's opening, I shut you out. I didn't ask you for help or follow your advice."

I didn't want to talk about her ex or be compared to him. But I was beyond all of that now. I was stronger than I was back then. I could tell this woman how I felt and deal with whatever her response was. "I'm sorry I walked out."

"I understand why you did. But please, don't do it again, and I promise not to shut you out. I'm advertising for a front desk person. I'm hoping to find someone who's retired and wants to work for a few hours a week. Alice has promised to cover most of the evenings until I can find someone."

"That's great news."

"And I'm advertising for a cleaning person. Not a service, because they were too expensive, but someone who'd work directly for me. Maybe a mom who has kids in school and is looking for a few hours a day of work."

"That sounds like a good plan."

"You were right. I tried to do too much by myself. I realized I don't want to live here. I know I said I did—"

"Hey, it's okay to change your mind."

"I don't like being on call for the guests. I want to manage it from afar. But I don't know how long it will take me to find someone or where we'll live when we do. I'd originally planned on living here rent-free until the B&B turned a profit."

"You'll figure it out." Besides, she could always move in with me.

"I hope so. I hope you'll be patient while I get everything into place."

"I'll wait for you." That was the difference between Natalie and my other relationships: I was in love with her. I wanted a future with her, and I wasn't in a hurry to get to the finish line. We'd get there together. Because, for the first time, I was in a committed, loving relationship.

"When I moved here, I swore I wasn't ready for a relationship. Especially not so soon, but I think you were the man who was meant for me all along. I couldn't escape the pull of your love, and I don't want to. I love you, Mac."

"I love you too," I said before I kissed her.

EPILOGUE

NATALIE

I offered the guests thirty percent off their next booking in exchange for filling out surveys about their visit. I used the information gleaned from the results to offer amenities like daily afternoon beverage and snack service and to increase breakfast offerings by ordering from a local bakery. Thankfully, I found two women who were willing to clean the rooms each day. They were both moms who wanted to work part time, so it worked perfectly, and it lessened my load.

Mac talked to me and Miranda about her baking occasionally for breakfast and afternoon snack time. She loved the idea but only wanted to work a few days a week. The bonus was that the guests loved her.

When the first reviews hit the travel blogs, I added them to my website and increased marketing. Slowly, the bookings increased, and with each new one, I reevaluated how I could continue to fill the rooms.

I decided to offer a discount for those guests who booked their next trip before they left. I offered up a weekend trip in a few local charity events in hopes to increase awareness locally of the B&B.

When a popular travel blogger posted about her stay on social media, it filled the B&B for several months and gave me enough money to justify the extra employees and to get something special for me and Mac to celebrate.

I kept Mac apprised of what was going on with the B&B and me. I wasn't afraid of asking for help anymore. We couldn't be in a relationship if we didn't communicate with each other. It only made our relationship stronger.

Tonight was Mac's birthday, and I'd cleared the B&B for the night so we could have a party for close friends and family. I could have done it at Mac's, but it would have been harder to keep it a secret.

It was Sam, Maggie, and Alice's job to get him here while I finished preparations and the guests arrived. I felt almost giddy as I told everyone to hide outside when I got the notice they were on their way.

Delaney huddled next to me, behind the outdoor kitchen, her eyes sparkling with joy. "Will he be surprised?"

"I hope so." We'd put a lot of effort into the party, and I wanted Mac to feel special.

In his past relationships, he was taken for granted, and I never wanted to do that. I wanted him to feel like he was our whole world because he was.

Sam texted they were at the front door, and I motioned for the others to be quiet. When the back door opened, we all jumped out and yelled, "Surprise!"

"What's this?" Mac asked, his eyes wide.

"It's your party, silly," Delaney said as we met them on the patio.

"You did this?" Mac asked me as I walked straight into his arms.

"Happy birthday," I said as he drew Delaney in for a hug too.

"You kept this a secret?" Mac asked Delaney.

"Uh-huh," Delaney said. "Were you surprised?"

Slowly shaking his head, he said, "I had no idea."

His family crowded around next to greet him.

"What about the B&B guests?" Mac asked when people moved on to the food table.

"I blacked it out for your party." It was the first time I'd ever done that, and it was scary but so worth it.

"Are you serious?" he asked, and when I nodded, he kissed me.

"I wanted to celebrate, and I was worried it would be harder to plan at your place," I murmured against his mouth.

"I can't believe you did all of this for me."

I'd been adamant that I wouldn't be able to take any vacations. I wanted to fill as many rooms as possible. But it had been six months, and things were steady going into the fall.

I was in close contact with Juliana, and I discussed my ideas with her. She was the one who encouraged me to hire more help and take more time off. The key was hiring people that you trusted, and Miranda and Waylon had offered to manage the B&B so we could go on vacations.

Sam pressed play on the playlist on the sound system he'd installed outside, and couples started pairing off around us to dance. Mac's arms came around me as we swayed to the music.

I felt content as I looked up at him. "I hired a manager."

"You're kidding," he said, looking down at me. Despite the guests dancing around us, Mac only had eyes for me.

"She's moving into the owner's suite in two weeks. The bad part is, I don't have much time to find a new place." Then I waited to see what he'd say. I wanted him to invite us to stay with him, but I wasn't sure he was ready.

"I want us to be a family."

I closed my eyes. "I want that too."

"I'd love it if you moved in with me, but if you want to live on your own for a while, I'll understand."

I opened my eyes as they filled with tears. "We'd love that. I already asked Delaney, and she wants to live with you and Rocky."

Mac's lips twitched. "She wants to live with me, or is it just Rocky?"

"I promise it's both," I said as I kissed him softly.

"You moving in is the best present I could have asked for."

"There's more. But I'm not giving you your present until later." I had plans of going back to his house and seducing him after I revealed his real present.

"Can I see it now?"

I shook my head. "You'll spoil my plans."

Mac frowned. "I don't think I like surprises anymore."

"Who knew you were a big kid on your birthday?" I teased.

"That's me. A kid who's ecstatic he got exactly what he wanted this year: the woman of his dreams and a beautiful daughter."

I loved when he called Delaney his daughter.

Carter visited from time to time, always unannounced, expecting us to drop everything to see him. We never changed our plans and made sure to talk to Delaney about her feelings and be sensitive to what she wanted. We hadn't bothered to change any of the details in our original agreement because Carter hadn't asked for more time. At this point, she was starting to see Mac as a father figure.

Carter was back and forth with the girlfriend, moving from South Carolina to Texas and back again. I didn't get too entrenched in his life. I knew enough so I could protect Delaney.

"How do you feel about expanding your family?" I asked softly. I hadn't anticipated bringing this up at the party, but it just felt right.

He stilled, his expression surprised. "Are you—"

I nodded, pleased he'd guessed it.

His hand found mine, and he led the way to my apartment. Once we were inside, he asked, "You're pregnant?"

"Yes," I said.

Then he was kissing me, his hands cupping my jaw.

I touched his wrists when he pulled back. "Are you happy?"

His eyes were shining with unshed tears. "You're everything I've ever wanted. You're pregnant, and you're both moving in with me."

"Rocky isn't enough for you anymore?" I knew he'd sworn off commitment, but I was ecstatic he'd gone back on his word for us.

"He pales in comparison to you, but I have everything I've ever wanted. You. Love. A family."

I held a finger up. "I have one more thing."

"This is already the best birthday I've ever had," he said as I led him to my bedroom. On my dresser, I'd left an envelope. I handed it to him. "This is for you."

He looked from the blank envelope to me. "I don't need anything else."

"I know," I said softly. "But I want to give you this." It was hard to find the perfect gift. He was a man who could build anything he wanted for his house. He had a truck, a dog, and the perfect house. What could I get him that would be fun and exciting for all of us?

He opened the flap and pulled out the tickets. "Hawaii?"

"I thought we could go before the baby was born. I want to travel, and I want to see everything with you."

He pulled me in for a hug. "I'd love that."

"If you don't like the destination, we could change it for something else."

"This is perfect, and Delaney's been talking about it."

His forehead touched mine. "I want to make love to you."

"We can't. Your party." I wanted the same thing. I wanted to feel close to him in every way, but we had guests.

"They can wait," Mac said softly.

I shook my head as I led him back outside. "Nope. I planned all of this for you, and you're going to enjoy it. We have all night and the rest of our lives to make love."

"I'm holding you to that," he promised as he kissed me again.

We talked to our friends and family, danced, and ate. I saw more evenings like this in our future but at our house, Sam's, and his parents'. Maybe even Tyler's now that he was looking for property to build on.

I'd moved to Telluride for a fresh start, thinking I'd never get married again. It was almost as if he was meant for me all along. I couldn't escape his love. It was too pure and encompassing.

I was right where I was supposed to be with the love of my life.

* * *

Mac

THE NEXT MORNING, I got up early with Delaney to make her breakfast. When she was finished eating the tiny pancakes she insisted I make, I said, "I have something to show you."

Delaney's eyes lit up with excitement.

I ushered her to the couch where I got out the ring I'd bought for Natalie soon after we'd talked about our future. "I want to ask your mother to marry me, but I need to ask a more important question first."

"What?" Delaney's eyes were wide with anticipation.

I pulled out a second box. This one was a necklace with a diamond ring on it, smaller diamonds circling the band. "Will you be part of my family, Delaney? Because I love you and your mother. I'd never marry your mother without your okay."

"Yes," she said simply.

"Yes, what?" My heart was thumping wildly in my chest. I'd

talked to my mother and my brothers about the best way to approach Delaney about marrying her mother. They were all in agreement that it had to be something special. I'd come up with the necklace and decided to just ask her when we had a quiet moment, and after finding out about our baby last night, it was time to make Delaney and Natalie mine.

"I want to be in your family, and I want you to marry my mom," she said solemnly, as if she knew how important this moment was.

"I want that too." I clasped the necklace around her neck, and she threw her arms around mine. I squeezed my eyes shut, and when I opened them, Natalie stood in the doorway.

I cleared my throat as Delaney shifted to sit on my leg. I was still holding the velvet box that contained Natalie's ring. I couldn't think of a better moment to ask her. "I just asked Delaney if she'd be part of my family, and she said yes."

Natalie moved across the room to stand in front of us.

"But I have one more question," I said as Natalie's gaze met mine, and I shifted so Delaney was sitting on the couch. I urged Natalie to sit next to her, and then I dropped down on one knee. "I never thought I'd find what I wanted, love and a family, but I have everything with you. I know it's a forever kind of love, and I can't imagine a future without you in it. Natalie, will you marry me?"

Natalie's eyes filled with tears as she nodded. "Of course."

"The ring," Delaney prompted.

I didn't know how I would have done this without her. I popped open the lid, the diamond shining in the morning light. I couldn't have conjured up a more perfect morning than this.

I slid the ring onto her finger as Natalie kissed me. With Delaney next to us, I knew I was exactly where I was supposed to be. These girls were my life, and I couldn't imagine a future without them. They were finally mine.

BONUS EPILOGUE

MAC

I promised I'd take Delaney skiing after the first big snowfall. I bought skis and gear in anticipation of more adventurous weekends in our future.

The Saturday after the first snowfall, we took the gondola up the mountain. The land was covered in white, and the earth was quiet around us as Delaney kicked her feet between us.

As we rose up the mountain, the colored ski jackets of those at the Wilde Ski Resort came into view.

We told Delaney about the baby when Natalie passed the twelve-week mark. She'd been so excited to be a big sister, and I knew she was going to be a great one. Now, Natalie was in her second trimester and activities had gotten a little easier for her.

Delaney offered up names of kids in her class, books, and TV shows. But we'd decided to keep our names a secret along with the gender until the baby arrived.

It was driving Delaney and my family crazy, but it was fun. We were a unit now. We made decisions together. It was everything I thought it would be when I imagined a love in my future like my parents'. I had everything I'd ever wanted, and the fact that we were already growing as a family was just icing on the cake.

At the top of the mountain, we got off the lift and headed to the bunny hill where lessons were held. We had plans to drop off Delaney for her first lesson, and if Delaney felt comfortable, we'd take a few runs down the mountain too.

Xander hovered nearby as the instructor marked off names on the clipboard.

"You think she'll be okay?" Natalie asked me.

"She's got a good head on her shoulders." Over the last few months, she'd mentioned some mean-girl issues at school with other girls, but Natalie gave her great advice on being a good friend and avoiding being involved with all the girl drama. That stuff was foreign to me having brothers.

Xander tipped his head toward us. "You guys can go skiing if you want. I'll let you know if she needs you."

"Are you sure?" Natalie asked.

We'd cleared it with her doctor. If she felt dizzy or unbalanced, she was supposed to stop but otherwise it would be fine.

Xander dipped his chin. "Go. Have some fun."

We thanked him and headed to the line for the lift. Once we boarded, I said, "We didn't plan on getting pregnant before we got married." There'd never been a discussion about any of it. It just happened, and it was perfect. But it felt incomplete.

Natalie's gaze shot to mine. "Do you want to get married before the baby comes?"

"I would like you to be mine, but I understand if you want to wait until you're not pregnant. You deserve the perfect day." I was conflicted.

She chewed her lip. "What do you think about getting married at the courthouse by ourselves and then holding a ceremony after the baby is born?"

"That sounds perfect." I let out a breath. Marrying her before the baby was born would satisfy the caveman inside that needed to ensure she was mine in every sense before we brought a baby into the world. Yet I sensed she wanted a wedding with the dress and party.

"That was easy," Natalie said.

"This is how I always imagined it would be when I found the woman who was meant to be mine." I always imagined discussions before big decisions were made. We'd talk it out instead of arguing or holding grudges. I wasn't naïve enough to assume we'd never disagree, but I wanted to smooth over any issues before they got too big.

She rested her head on my shoulder. "Can we go to Hawaii before he gets here?"

I rubbed her arm. "We can do whatever you want. I can't believe we're having a boy." For some reason, I'd always imagined myself with three girls to my mom's three boys.

She grinned. "We can always try for another after this one."

"I'm happy with whatever you want." Although I secretly wanted multiple kids.

"What if I wanted more?" she asked me, her voice uncertain.

"I would love to have a big family with you." But I was flexible enough to change course if pregnancy or childbirth were difficult for her. Natalie's health and happiness were paramount.

She linked her arm with mine. "You always say the perfect thing."

"I just say whatever I'm thinking." I wasn't filtering anymore, worried that I'd lose her. I'd given her my whole heart and wasn't afraid to tell my truth anymore.

"How are you so great?" she asked, lifting her head.

"I think it's because I'm perfect for you." I kissed her softly.

When I pulled back, she said, "Mmm. So, we have a wedding to plan, a babymoon, and a baby."

"I think we should just do whatever feels good and let things fall where they may." I'd never felt so content, so happy before. I was confident we'd stand the test of time, and I wouldn't let doubts hold me back.

* * *

We got married at the courthouse with just Delaney and my family present. When we initially talked about it, I thought it would be just us, but then neither of us felt right about excluding my family. Not when they'd love to be at both ceremonies and wouldn't judge us for our plans.

Afterward, we flew to Hawaii for some relaxation in the sun before Natalie went into the third trimester. It was much-needed time to relax and unwind. We talked about having these getaways by ourselves in the future to strengthen our relationship and marriage.

When we returned, Natalie was a ball of energy, buying things for the baby and decorating the room. Alice said it was something to do with nesting, and it happened in the third trimester for most women.

I was happy to do whatever Natalie felt needed to be done before the baby was here, but it meant a lot of work for me. Not only was I helping her get the room and house ready for the baby, but I was also making a bassinet with Sam in his garage. It was difficult because I'd kept it a secret from Natalie. When it was finished, three weeks before the baby was due, Sam delivered it, and we carried it to the baby's room.

"What if she hates it?" I asked when we placed it in the center of the cornflower blue room.

Sam shook his head at me. "How could she possibly hate it?"

"Pregnant women can be unpredictable." I ended the sentence on a whisper in case Natalie came home early. She'd been more emotional the closer she got to her due date.

Sam hadn't spent much time around Felicia when she was pregnant. "I'll take your word for it." Then he clasped my shoulder. "Let me know how it goes. Maggie has her choral concert tonight. You still coming?"

"As long as this baby doesn't make an early appearance." Natalie wasn't a first-time mother, so she was relaxed about going into labor. I was not. I was uptight and stressed about the whole thing. The part that worried me the most was that she was the one who was going through childbirth, and I would just be standing nearby watching. I couldn't do anything to ease her pain. I hated that.

I walked Sam out just as Natalie pulled into the driveway. I loved that Natalie and Delaney lived with me here, that we were building a life together.

I opened her door and held a hand out to her to assist her out of the vehicle. I wasn't sure how she drove—her belly was so big—but I never mentioned those concerns to her. "I have something to show you."

"I was hoping to take a nap soon." I held her back as she walked slower than normal.

"Is everything okay?"

She offered a weak smile. "It's just some back pain. It's to be expected this far along."

"You don't think you're in labor, do you?" I asked, unable to keep my panic at bay.

She shook her head. "It's too early."

The doctor and the books warned that second babies come quicker, but I kept that tidbit to myself. She'd just laugh and say something about me being an overbearing first-time dad.

She grimaced slightly as we moved through the house. As usual, her legs and feet were swollen from being on her feet. I wanted to get her off them as soon as possible and let her rest.

At the baby's room, I paused, and Natalie gasped, "What is this?"

She entered the room to circle the bassinet, touching the wood lovingly with her hand.

We'd carved a moon and stars into the ends, not wanting to put a name since I hoped to have more children share the bassinet or even pass it along to Sam when he and Alice were ready for kids.

Natalie lifted her gaze to mine. "You made this?"

I shrugged. "Sam helped."

Her wide eyes met mine. "This is the most amazing thing anyone's ever made for me."

"I wanted to do more, but—" Natalie had very specific ideas for what she wanted in the nursery. She never mentioned a bassinet or a cradle, so I figured I could safely take care of it.

She winced. "I know I've been demanding the last few months."

"I wouldn't say that." I'd never tell her that, even if it was the truth. I'd read all about pregnancy ups and downs and liked to think I was prepared for anything at this point. Ice cream at eleven at night? I was on it. Chicken for breakfast? No problem. Her wish was my command. I couldn't carry the baby for her, so meeting her needs was the least I could do.

I drew her into my arms, adept at maneuvering around her stomach.

She rested her cheek on my chest. "Thank you for this. I'll always cherish it."

Suddenly, she cried out, leaning into me as I held her up. Water leaked onto the floor.

"Is that—" Had her water broken? My mind scrambled to catch up.

Natalie gasped as we watched the water accumulate on the carpet. "I think my water broke."

My mind raced with what I'd read about this scenario in the books. "We need to go to the hospital."

Natalie gripped my arm. "Call first. The doctor said to call."

I helped her to the bathroom while her water continued to leak. When she was settled, I grabbed her cell and dialed the doctor's emergency number. I left my number with the answering service and called Sam to have one of them come over to watch Delaney when she got home from school. When the doctor called a few minutes later, I explained what was going on, and she advised us to come to the hospital.

The moment felt surreal, the culmination of everything I'd always wanted in my life: a wife, a child, and our baby boy on his way. Yet, at the same time, I was scared.

We'd planned for this moment, but I hadn't accounted for the sheer adrenaline coursing through my body.

I carried Natalie to the car and settled her into the passenger seat. My brain was telling me we needed to get to the hospital fast, but my movements felt sluggish. The doctor had said something about labor being fast after the water broke, especially with a second child.

The car seat and the hospital bag were already in the back. When I moved to close the car's passenger side door, Natalie stopped me with a cool palm to my cheek.

The energy flowing off her was almost serene. "We're going to meet our baby boy."

Everything inside me settled and calmed. I leaned over to kiss her and murmured how beautiful she was, how much I loved her, and how I couldn't wait to meet our baby.

Everything would be all right because we had each other. We'd get through this together, and in a few hours, I'd get to hold my baby boy and later introduce him to his big sister, Delaney. My eyes stung with tears. I couldn't wait.

I hope you loved Natalie and Mac's story! Kylie and Tyler are next in *Forbidden Love*, a brother's best friend romance.

BOOKS BY LEA COLL

Mountain Haven Series

Infamous Love

Adventurous Love

Impulsive Love

Tempting Love

Inescapable Love

Forbidden Love

Ever After Series

Feel My Love

The Way You Are

Love Me Like You Do

Give Me a Reason

Somebody to Love

Everything About You

Second Chance Harbor Series

Fighting Chance

One More Chance

Lucky Chance

My Best Chance

Worth the Chance

A Chance at Forever

Annapolis Harbor Series

Only with You

Lost without You

Perfect for You

Crazy for You

Falling for You

Waiting for You

Hooked on You

All I Want Series

Choose Me

Be with Me

Burn for Me

Trust in Me

Stay with Me

Take a Chance on Me

Download a free novella, when you sign up for her newsletter.

To learn more about her books, please visit her website.

ABOUT THE AUTHOR

Lea Coll is a USA Today Bestselling Author of sweet and sexy happily ever afters. She worked as a trial attorney for over ten years. Now she stays home with her three children, plotting stories while fetching snacks and running them back and forth to activities. She enjoys the freedom of writing romance after years of legal writing.

She currently resides in Maryland with her family.

Get a free novella when you sign up for Lea's newsletter.

Check out Lea's books on her website.

Made in United States
Orlando, FL
21 July 2023